THE BUTTERFLY GARDEN

RACHEL BURTON

Boldwood

First published in Great Britain in 2024 by Boldwood Books Ltd.

Copyright © Rachel Burton, 2024

Cover Design by JD Smith Design Ltd

Cover Photography: Shutterstock

A CIP catalogue record for this book is available from the British Library.

Paperback ISBN 978-1-83533-795-0

Large Print ISBN 978-1-83533-791-2

Hardback ISBN 978-1-83533-790-5

Ebook ISBN 978-1-83533-788-2

Kindle ISBN 978-1-83533-789-9

Audio CD ISBN 978-1-83533-796-7

MP3 CD ISBN 978-1-83533-793-6

Digital audio download ISBN 978-1-83533-787-5

Boldwood Books Ltd
23 Bowerdean Street
London SW6 3TN
www.boldwoodbooks.com

This one is for me.

If you look the right way, you can see that the whole world is a garden.

— FRANCES HODGSON BURNETT
(THE SECRET GARDEN)

Take nothing on its looks; take everything on evidence. There's no better rule.

— CHARLES DICKENS (GREAT
EXPECTATIONS)

PROLOGUE

SATURDAY, 2 SEPTEMBER 1939

Clara Samuels picked the flowers herself, a small posy of anemones and dahlias, autumn crocus and daisies. The afternoon was warm, the sun beating down on the back of her neck as she stooped to collect her flowers, cutting them carefully with the little scissors Mrs Mackenzie had given to her. Clara was only nine, but she knew exactly which blooms she wanted, which ones looked right together. Afterwards, she would take them home to her mother, who would put them in water in a small glass jar on the mantle, just as she always did. Clara always hoped that the flowers would serve as some sort of peace offering, an exchange for the grass stains on her skirt and her dishevelled hair.

James stood and watched her, used to her delight every time she came into the garden, used to watching her collect flowers from the ever-changing beds that his mother tended so carefully. Even though he was only two months older than her, he always felt protective of her, like the older brother she'd never had. He knew, on an intuitive level – he wasn't sure he understood *how* he knew – that Clara was different from her family, especially her prim and proper older sister who, he also knew, would be cross with her for having muddy clothes and a sunburned nose. Esther did not approve of sunburn, or stains, or picking flowers or spending the unprecedentedly hot summer roaming the country lanes of the small Suffolk village in which they lived, hunting down butterflies and wildflowers. He also knew that her family did not approve of his, that he was somehow beneath Clara, not worthy of her friendship. But he didn't understand why.

James's father was the vicar of Carybrook, and the house he lived in and the garden his mother tended so lovingly belonged to the diocese. The Mackenzies had been there for two years now – they moved from a remote parish in Northumberland and, before that, one on the outskirts of London but James had no memory of that. He was only a baby when they left.

He preferred Suffolk to Northumberland – the

summers were warmer and drier, the winters shorter. He preferred the people here, the kind lady in the village shop, the churchwarden, the children at his school. He liked it in Carybrook and he especially liked his friendship with Clara Samuels. Her family might not like him, but he never got that feeling from Clara herself.

'I should go home,' Clara said, standing in front of him. She looked sadly down at her stained dress. 'I'll be in trouble.'

'You shouldn't listen to that sister of yours,' James replied. 'She's not your mother.'

Clara giggled, rolled her eyes. 'I wish I could stay here forever,' she said. 'It always feels more like home in the Butterfly Garden.'

They had started to call it the butterfly garden the previous summer because, back before it had become a vicarage, the house was called Butterfly Cottage – presumably because of the garden itself, home to more butterflies than either James or Clara had ever seen. His mother had told him it was the plants that grew there that attracted the insects – the lavender and marjoram, the ox-eye daisies and the buddleia, plants that had been here when they arrived but that his mother had coaxed back to life.

'But you'll come back tomorrow?' James asked,

even though he knew she would. This was their place, where they felt safe and comfortable. 'After church?'

'Of course I will.' She smiled before turning and running towards the back of the garden, disappearing through the gate in the wall, taking the shortcut through the allotments so she would be home in time for tea.

But Clara didn't come back the next day. She didn't even go to church. Instead, like so many people across the country, she sat with her parents listening as Neville Chamberlain announced that Britain was now at war with Germany.

And neither Clara nor James ever forgot the haunting tones of the prime minister's voice as it echoed from the wireless issuing words and instructions that would change both of their lives forever.

PART I

28 November 1963

My Darling

I should have written sooner. I should have had the courage to not lose touch completely.

No, that's not true. The truth is, I should never have left at all.

I suspect you know everything by now, I expect you've learned what happened and you will never know how sorry I am, how foolish I've been. I've destroyed everything, and for what?

I wasn't going to write at all. I was going to disappear, coward that I am, and let you get on with your life but then I read about President Kennedy's assassination and the first person I wanted to talk about it with was you. You and I, sitting in the Butterfly Garden, putting the world to rights just like we always did.

And then I had to write, although now I have put pen to paper I have no idea what to say.

There is nothing I can say.

There never will be.

I should never have left.

I hope one day I will find you again, spot you across a crowded room just like I did in

June. And I hope that if I do I will have the courage not to run away.

    Always,

    JM

1

LONDON, JUNE 2018

'But I don't have a great-aunt,' Meredith insisted. 'Not one that I know about, anyway. I've never heard of this person. Why would she leave me a house in Suffolk? I've never even *been* to Suffolk.' Truth be told, she wasn't completely sure where Suffolk even was.

'Miss Samuels's will is very specific,' the solicitor, Alexander Maddison, repeated. 'You have been left her house.' He looked bored, as though he'd rather be anywhere but here in this stuffy, airless room.

Why, Meredith wondered, did nobody open a window?

'How much is the house worth?' she asked suddenly, interrupting Mr Maddison as he droned on about this imaginary great-aunt that she had never known about before. Because if it was worth something it might just help her out of the mess she'd managed to get herself into.

The solicitor's eyebrows shot up, clearly not used to being interrupted. 'I have no idea,' he said, crossing and uncrossing his legs. 'Do I look like an estate agent?'

She slumped back into her chair, shaking her head. 'No, sorry,' she said, the wind well and truly knocked out of her sails. She had no idea what she was doing. She had never set foot in a solicitor's office before, let alone tried to negotiate an inheritance. And now, at the age of thirty-two, she was discovering that she had a great-aunt she had never known about. Perhaps she wasn't even the right Meredith Carling.

Mr Maddison sighed and seemed to soften, as though somebody had ironed him out. 'A local estate agent will be able to value the property for you,' he said. 'They will have more idea about that sort of thing than me and we will of course need the amount for inheritance tax purposes. Although...' He hesitated, his eyes flicking away.

'Although?' Meredith prompted him.

'Well, the property was empty for many years. You may find it somewhat...' He hesitated again and

Meredith wondered what he was hiding. 'Somewhat dated,' he finished.

Meredith shrugged. A developer wouldn't mind a property being dated, surely? They would be doing it up anyway. This could be the answer to everything. A new start, maybe even enough money left over for a flight to Spain to visit her mother.

It all sounded too good to be true.

Which, as her mother was always telling her, meant that it probably was.

'OK,' she said. 'So, what happens next?'

Mr Maddison produced a stack of papers as if from nowhere.

'I need you to sign these,' he said, explaining each one in detail. But Meredith had stopped listening. She was already planning what she could do with the money from the sale of the house. Paying off that debt, seeing her mum again and, most satisfying of all, telling Joe where he could shove his loan.

Until two weeks ago when Alexander Maddison first got in touch, the only family that Meredith was aware she had was her mother – married now to Lloyd Collins and happily living the dream in Alicante – her father, who she hadn't seen since her eighteenth birthday, and her father's mother who had died around the same time. Meredith's mother Bernice had no parents. Or none that she had spoken to for a very long time, anyway.

But now the family tree had begun to widen – even if it was too late to meet this mysterious great-aunt, the sister of her father's mother, the woman who was about to save Meredith's business – if by some miracle she *was* the correct Meredith Carling. It was hard to imagine that this wasn't some kind of hideous practical joke.

Why had nobody mentioned Clara Samuels before?

Meredith could remember her paternal grand-mother – a tired and angry-looking woman who lived in a large box-like bungalow just outside the centre of Stevenage. She would occasionally accompany her father, Dennis, on Sunday afternoons to visit her and she could remember being scared of Grandma Brad-shaw and her stuffy house and sour face. And then, when she was eleven and her father left, seemingly for good, she went a few times with her mother. Even-tually, both of them admitted how much they hated the ordeal and the visits had fizzled out. But in all that time nobody had ever mentioned Clara. Not then, not now. Not until Mr Maddison came along.

Meredith signed the forms without really thinking of their implications. She'd had the good fortune of being left a house. However bad the condition of it, it was a house. And houses were always in high demand.

'Are you sure you've got the right person?' she asked, as she handed the last piece of paper back to the solicitor. 'There are probably other Meredith Carlings in the world and...'

'Of course I'm sure,' Mr Maddison snapped, and then he sighed and softened again. His moods, Meredith thought, were like a spring.

He handed her a thick white envelope with a flourish. 'The keys to the house are inside,' he said.

'I...' Meredith hesitated.

'Yes?' Mr Maddison replied. He was tiring of her now, and of the whole situation, Meredith could tell.

'Well, I still don't know who this woman, this Clara Samuels is, and...'

'Then you must speak to your family,' he said, closing his file. 'I can't help you any further on that front.'

But then as she began to collect her things and leave Mr Maddison called her back.

'Miss Carling,' he said. She looked up at him.

'Yes.'

'Don't make too many plans until you've seen the house.'

Meredith sighed. All this unnecessary caution. 'I know, but—' she began.

'Prepare yourself for the unexpected,' he interrupted.

As though discovering she had previously unheard-of family wasn't unexpected enough.

'Like what?' she asked.

'Just prepare yourself.'

And that was when Meredith was sure that Alexander Maddison, LLB was hiding something.

* * *

'This must be something to do with your father,' Bernice said, her face far too close to the camera as usual and her features distorted on Meredith's laptop screen.

'I've already told you that Clara Samuels was his aunt,' Meredith replied. 'And you don't have to sit so close to the screen, Mum.'

Bernice backed away an inch or so. 'I know she's his aunt, but I meant all this secrecy. Why have we never been told she existed before?'

'It is really odd,' Meredith admitted. 'And it all feels a bit...' She paused. It felt unreal, like a strange dream.

'When you stop talking about a family member there's usually a reason,' Bernice went on authoritatively. She, after all, had never spoken about her own parents. 'A reason or a scandal.'

'A scandal? Do you think?'

'Well, I don't know, I'm just saying.' There had been no scandal between Bernice and her parents, there had just been no love lost.

We can't choose our families, Bernice would say.

'Dad would know I suppose?'

Bernice pulled a face as she always did when Dennis Bradshaw was mentioned.

It had been fifteen years since anyone had heard from Dennis. For all Meredith and Bernice knew he could be dead, although Bernice had always pointed out that if he were dead his debts would probably pass to Meredith so she'd know about it then. There was no love lost between Bernice and Dennis either. Meredith had always wanted to know more about her father, to not just parrot her mother as she had done when she was younger, into writing him off as a waste of space, but it was hard to do that when you didn't know where he was.

'It seems strange that this great-aunt of mine didn't leave Dad the cottage,' Meredith reflected. 'He would have been her closest relative, presuming she didn't have a family of her own. Closer than me, anyway.'

'I have no idea,' Bernice replied. 'Perhaps he annoyed this Clara as much as he annoyed me.'

'You've really got no idea where he might be, Mum?' she asked, just on the off chance.

'None whatsoever, and I'm as curious to know who this Clara Samuels is as you are, so I promise I'm not hiding his whereabouts from you.' Bernice smiled, softening just as the solicitor had done earlier that day. 'Why didn't you tell me about all this before, love? You've known about it for two weeks, you say?'

Meredith shrugged. 'I didn't want to bother you. It felt like it was a mistake – they'd got the wrong Meredith Carling, you know?' But there was more to it than that, not that she would ever admit it to her mother.

Meredith had been thirteen when her mother had married Lloyd Collins and it had felt as though she was finally part of a proper family. Lloyd had fitted into Meredith and Bernice's lives like the missing piece of a jigsaw puzzle, and for the first time Meredith had felt part of something special, something she'd only dreamed about before when she'd tried to imagine what life would have been like if her mother and father had married and lived happily together. It was a feeling that continued long after Meredith had left home, met her fiancé Joe and set up her hairdressing business. She still felt it now in a way, five years after Bernice and Lloyd had announced they were retiring and moving to Spain.

But Joe had let her down and the business was on its last legs and she felt as though her mother and Lloyd lived on the moon for all she could afford to go and visit them.

'I didn't want to get my hopes up about inheriting a house,' Meredith went on. 'Or yours, for that matter.'

'But it wasn't a mistake,' Bernice smiled. 'You've got a house all of your own. Lloyd and I will have to come and visit, you'll finally have a guest room.'

But it wasn't going to be like that at all, was it? She and Joe weren't going to move to the country and live some sort of idyllic life with guest rooms. There was a lot Meredith hadn't told her mother – she found the distance made it hard to talk about bad news – but she had to say something now before Bernice started planning the bedroom decor.

'You'd better visit quickly then,' she said. 'Because I'm going to have to put it on the market as soon as possible.'

Bernice looked thoughtful for a moment. 'I suppose it's quite rural out there in Suffolk. You and Joe could buy somewhere closer to London with the money – after all, you probably wouldn't want to be far away from the business.'

Bernice was so proud of Meredith's business venture – her own salon near Clapham Common. After school, Meredith had done her training and after years of hiring chairs in other people's salons, she had begun to want a space of her own. Just after her mum and stepdad had moved to Spain her dream had become a reality. It had taken a lot of blood, sweat and tears, a huge amount of saving and hard work – on both her and Joe's part – and a rather large bank loan, but she'd done it. She'd slowly expanded, renting chairs to other hairdressers and taking on a beauty therapist and nail technician. Everything had been going so well.

Until it wasn't any more.

'No, it's not that, it's...' Meredith paused. Where to even begin? 'Mum, there's a couple of things I haven't told you, important things, and I need you to listen.'

Bernice suddenly looked worried. 'What is it, love?'

'Joe and I... well...' she paused, took a breath. 'We're over,' she said.

Bernice's worried expression turned to one of

shock. 'But I thought you and Joe were the real deal, like me and Lloyd. I thought...'

'So did I, Mum, until the afternoon I came home early from work with a migraine and found him in bed with someone else.'

'That bastard,' Bernice exclaimed, and Meredith let her mother have a little rant while she collected her own thoughts. Talking about that afternoon, even thinking about it, was still too much. The image of Joe with someone else in their bed was burned onto her retinas and she didn't think it would ever go away.

'That's not all.' Meredith interrupted her mother's diatribe about the failings of all men – all men except Lloyd Collins, of course. 'He's moving in with her and he wants the money he invested in the business back.'

Joe had always been so supportive of Meredith's business dream and he'd invested some of his own savings in it.

'I know that you're going to make such a success of this,' he'd said on the night before it opened. 'So I see this as an investment in our future.' He'd kissed her gently then and it had finally felt as though things were going to be all right after weeks of worry about plumbing and burst pipes, decor and planning permissions.

'Well give him his bloody money back and tell him where to stick it,' Bernice said now.

'I can't, Mum, I don't have it.' She paused again. 'The thing is that the salon has been running at a loss for about a year now. I had to take out another line of credit with the bank to keep it going and I just don't have any way of paying him back. My only option, until I found out about Butterfly Cottage, would have been to sell the business as a going concern, but I don't know how much anybody will pay for that.'

Bernice nodded slowly, taking it all in in her usual non-judgemental way. 'Why didn't you tell me any of this, love?' she asked. 'We could have helped. Lloyd and I could have done something. Even if it was just to pay for a flight to Spain for you so you could have a break and a hug from your old mum.'

Meredith smiled despite herself. 'I just didn't want to bother you with it until I had a solution.'

'And you think Butterfly Cottage is the solution?'

'It feels too good to be true.'

'If it's anything to do with your father then it probably is,' Bernice muttered. 'Did this solicitor mention how much it was worth?'

Meredith shook her head. 'He was playing his cards very close to his chest, as though he was hiding something. He said the cottage would need a lot of modernisation but surely that wouldn't bother a developer. A house is a house – I'll make something from it.'

'Well that depends on things like inheritance tax and so on,' Bernice replied.

'Mr Maddison told me about that. I need to get the house valued and—'

'He should have sorted all that out himself,' Bernice interrupted. 'Are you sure he was a proper solicitor? What was his name, did you say?'

'Alexander Maddison,' Meredith replied.

'Spell it for me.'

Meredith did as she was told as her mother typed away on her laptop. 'Well, here he is on the SRA website, so he must be real.'

'The what?' Meredith asked.

'The Solicitors Regulation Authority,' Bernice replied.

'How do you know all this stuff, Mum?'

'I've learned to question everything over the years, love. You know that.'

'So you think the solicitor is legit but the inheritance tax might wipe me out?'

'The solicitor is legit,' Bernice replied. 'But it seems very odd that he didn't discuss tax and financial matters with you.'

'He gave me the key to the cottage and told me to visit and to expect the unexpected.'

Bernice frowned. 'There's definitely something peculiar about this,' she said. 'I think your best bet would be to take a day off and go and see the cottage, maybe speak to a local estate agent and take it from there.' She paused. 'I could fly over if you like, come with you.'

'No, Mum, it's fine. I can go to Suffolk on my own. You're right. I need to get to the bottom of this as soon as possible.'

'Well, call me as soon as you get there,' Bernice said. 'And if you need anything you only have to ask.'

'I know, Mum,' Meredith replied. 'I know.'

2

LONDON, APRIL 1963

Clara Samuels had been living in London for nearly twelve years now, since she'd graduated from Cambridge and trained to be a teacher. She visited her sister in Carybrook, the tiny village in Suffolk in which they'd both grown up, from time to time, but she rarely thought about it when she wasn't there.

Until recently.

Things were changing, Clara could feel it. Four young men from Liverpool had just released a record called *Please Please Me* and it seemed to be everywhere she looked. To Clara it had felt like a moment in time, an unravelling – although she wasn't sure what was being unravelled. Later, when she looked back on her life, she had known that was the point at which the

1960s had really begun and that she had had very little to do with any of it.

She'd listened to that Beatles record, of course. It seemed to have been on permanent rotation on the record player in the boarding house for the last month. She liked it and understood why the world was beginning to go crazy over it. But she also realised that it made her feel old, as though she belonged to a time that had been and gone. She had felt like this, on and off, for years and there was a part of her that could have lived in that September afternoon of 1939, just before war broke out, forever. She wondered, as she often did, where James was now. They had kept in touch for nine years, despite the war and the inconsistency of the postal service. They had kept in touch until she went to university and then his letters had stopped coming. She wondered if he had moved and not told her or if, more likely, her parents had stopped forwarding her post. They never had liked her friendship with the Mackenzies, they thought the family was common and beneath them.

James would have turned thirty-three last month and she would turn thirty-three next month. She was the oldest woman living at the boarding house by some years. The women who had been here when she first arrived from teacher training college, almost a decade before, had long gone – some to teach in other towns and cities, but most to be married and have families.

Clara remained behind, left on the shelf, old before her time. She wondered sometimes why she had never moved on. It scared her a little how stuck in a rut she had become. She loved her job – teaching was everything to her – but whenever she thought about moving from the boarding house it felt like so much effort, so much upheaval.

It had been a long, hard winter, colder than Clara had ever known. It had felt particularly bleak after an autumn spent wondering if the world was going to be melted away by the nuclear war that threatened from Cuba. The crisis had been ended by the handsome new American president at the eleventh hour. The world hadn't ended and life had gone on, but not quite as it had before. Clara felt older now, bleaker, lost in time and a little bit useless.

What had she achieved in her almost thirty-three years, after all?

The idea for Clara's overdue reinvention had come from her sister in one of their weekly phone calls. As spring finally started to make itself known in London, Clara had begun to feel homesick and nostalgic. She finally felt a longing for a fresh start as though the chill of the winter had pushed away that inertness Clara had been feeling for so long.

'Butterfly Cottage is up for sale,' Esther said. 'It went on the market just yesterday.'

'But I thought it was owned by the diocese for the vicar to live in?' Clara replied, a flicker of something fluttering in her stomach.

'Not any more. There's a brand-new vicarage now, much nearer to the church and so the diocese has put the cottage up for sale.'

Clara could still remember Butterfly Cottage, the warm welcome she always received from the Reverend and Mrs Mackenzie, the games she and James always played, and the garden – the beautiful garden with its multitude of flowerbeds. In her memories, it always seemed to be summer.

'Not a bad price either,' Esther went on. 'Or so Richard tells me. I wouldn't know at all.' Clara made the right noises as her sister started to tell her about all the new houses being built on the outskirts of Carybrook and how much they were according to Richard, but her mind was on Butterfly Cottage. She knew Esther would know a lot more about it than she was letting on. She pretended to defer to her husband, Richard, on all matters but Esther lived her own life and knew the cost of everything. It was Esther's money that had helped Richard secure the mortgage on the house that they lived in.

'Esther.' Clara interrupted her sister's flow of words very aware that, as usual, she was the one paying for the call. 'Butterfly Cottage...'

'What about it?'

'How much is it?'

'Three thousand two hundred pounds,' Esther replied without missing a beat. 'Minimum offer.'

Clara smiled to herself. Esther always knew everything.

* * *

The train from King's Cross to Ipswich had been one of the new high-speed diesels but the branch line to Carybrook still ran on steam. Clara settled back into her seat and listened to the soothing sound of the engine. She and Esther used to come on this line with their mother every year to go Christmas shopping in Ipswich. When Clara came back to Carybrook these days, twice a year – at Christmas and for a week in the school summer holidays – Richard usually picked her up from Ipswich in his car so it had been a long time since she'd taken the branch line. She was glad that her trip to Carybrook had been too short notice for him to collect her – she needed this time, and the memories that came with it, to gather her thoughts before she faced the questions her sister was bound to have.

When Clara and Esther's father died in 1951, two years after the death of their mother, he had left them, alongside the house they had grown up in, a surprising amount of money. Altogether it had amounted to over five thousand pounds each.

'All that scrimping and saving we had to do as children and it turns out there was all this money in the bank,' Clara hadn't been able to help saying when she'd found out.

'There was a war on for much of our childhoods, Clara,' Esther had replied, always the first to defend their distant, ungenerous parents. 'And rationing.'

'Even so...'

Esther had raised her eyebrows, a gesture of her own agreement, but would say no more.

Clara had just graduated from Cambridge when she'd inherited the money – held in trust by a solicitor until she was twenty-five. Esther was newly married by then, living in a small, rented house on the very outskirts of Carybrook while Richard completed his accountancy training. Her money went straight to him and helped them buy the beautiful Victorian home they had lived in for the last twelve years. But the children they had hoped to fill the bedrooms with had never come.

Sitting on the train now Clara felt sad for those two young women torn between the grief of losing their parents and the unexpected shock of having money for the first time in their lives. They had both, in very different ways, had so much hope and none of their dreams had really amounted to anything. Occasionally, when Clara was visiting her sister, they would walk together past their childhood home, which they had sold as soon as they were able for two thousand pounds, and Clara would think about the person she had been then, the hopes and dreams she'd had. She wondered what Esther thought as they looked at that old house. They never talked about it. Their childhood home was not far from Butterfly Cottage and Clara would have to get used to walking past it more regularly if she moved back again.

Clara had gone up to Cambridge in the autumn of 1948 on a scholarship and joined some of the first generations of women who were able to actually obtain a degree from Cambridge. Unlike Oxford, which had allowed female graduates in 1920, Cambridge had dragged its heels and suffered decades of protests and riots before becoming the last university in the country to award women degrees. Clara was one of those women, leaving Girton College three years after she'd arrived with a first-class degree in history and a place at Avery Hill Teacher Training College in south-east London.

She had such ambition then, so many hopes and dreams. She hadn't expected, ten years after leaving Avery Hill, to still be teaching in the same west London Junior School or still to be living in the same boarding house in Chelsea.

For Clara, much as it had for Esther, life had stood still for a very long time.

And that was why she was on her way back to Carybrook today. She had an appointment with an estate agent to view Butterfly Cottage.

* * *

Esther was waiting for her at the station.

'If you'd given us a bit more notice, Richard would have collected you,' she sniffed. 'He's at the cricket all day.' Clara could tell her sister was already put out over something and she could guess what. A single woman buying a property on her own wasn't really the done thing in rural Suffolk in 1963 – or anywhere, for that matter. Esther would undoubtedly disapprove.

Or at least *pretend* to disapprove. Esther, Clara had realised years ago when they were still children, liked to be seen to be doing the right thing and enjoyed the approval of her peers. But deep down she had a rebellious streak and these days, like so many women, she longed for change as much as Clara did.

'I don't mind,' Clara said, kissing her sister on her powdered cheek. 'It was lovely to catch the old steam train.'

'Well, make the most of it,' Esther replied. 'This is one of the branch lines the government have earmarked for closure.'

'Really?' Clara felt an overwhelming sense of disappointment even though she had been on the branch line precisely once since she'd gone up to Cambridge.

'Yes, soon enough nobody will be able to get anywhere without a car.'

'I can't even drive,' Clara said sadly.

'Richard is teaching me; perhaps he'll teach you too.'

Clara couldn't imagine herself driving. She could all too easily see Esther behind the wheel though.

'Anyway,' Esther continued, 'we'd better get on. Standing around talking about branch lines isn't going to bring them back. We've got an appointment to keep.'

'You're coming with me to Butterfly Cottage then?' Clara asked.

'Of course. If you're going to persist in this madness then you need a voice of reason to accompany you.'

'Do you really think it's madness, Esther?' Clara asked. This was the only thing she could think of that would help her escape being frozen in time in a Chelsea boarding house. Was it really nothing more than a ridiculous pipe dream? Having the money and being able to use it, as a woman, were two very different things.

'I'm not sure what I think, Clara,' Esther replied, her voice softening. 'But I do understand why you want to do this and I do want to support you.'

'Thank you,' Clara said, blinking back tears. She and Esther were close in some ways, but light years apart in others. It was nice that Esther had tried, at least, to see this from Clara's point of view.

'It's just a bit...' Esther paused as though searching for the right word. 'Unusual. And unusual things stand out a lot more in a little village like Carybrook than they do in London.'

Clara didn't respond to this but it was something she was well aware of. She needed to move on, to do something different but she knew, should she buy Butterfly Cottage, that she would be the subject of gossip for some time. It was a risk she was willing to take.

'You can leave your suitcase here,' Esther went on as she turned to start walking out of the station. 'The stationmaster will keep an eye on it until Richard picks it up when he's done with the cricket. We can walk up to the cottage.'

Clara nodded and let her sister take control. There was little point fighting it.

* * *

Butterfly Cottage was much as Clara remembered it. The pink climbing rose still grew around the green wooden door, the flowerbeds in front of the cottage were still perfectly kept, the front lawn was mowed and the paths were swept. Even the garden gate still creaked in exactly the same way as it had done when she was a child. As she pushed it open, the sound brought so many memories flooding back – happy memories, the times in her childhood when she was allowed to be herself.

The family home hadn't been a happy place, even before the war. Clara and Esther's parents were strict and distant, and Clara had constantly felt as though she didn't belong. Esther had always seemed to get on better with their parents – she stuck to the rules, dressed properly, never got grass stains on herself and always seemed to be on her parents' side whenever Clara was in trouble.

With the benefit of hindsight, Clara understood now that this was Esther's way of surviving in a house without love, it was her way of protecting herself. It had taken her years to realise this, to forgive her sister. When she first left for Cambridge – against her parents' wishes, of course – she and Esther hadn't spoken for nearly three years. It was Esther's marriage to Richard that had brought the two sisters close again. Richard was one of those people who thought family was important and believed that the sisters needed to talk through their differences, see if their relationship could be salvaged. It wasn't either of their faults that their parents had been the way they had and once they were both away from the confines of the family home, Clara and Esther were able to see each other in a new light. They would never see eye to eye over everything – Esther thought Clara's lifestyle wildly bohemian, and Clara felt that

Esther's was horribly claustrophobic – but they rubbed along, drawn together by the memory of their childhoods.

'It hasn't changed much, has it?' Esther said, standing behind her sister at the garden gate.

'It's exactly the same,' Clara whispered.

Butterfly Cottage and the Mackenzie family had been a refuge for Clara as a child. She'd longed to be part of their family from the moment she'd met them. Their cottage was always noisy with people coming in and out to see the Reverend Mackenzie and one room or other would always be in use for some church-related business or meeting. It was also, unlike Clara's childhood home, a house that looked lived in, where James was allowed to make a mess, to play with his toys and to laugh and chat with his friends. Mr and Mrs Samuels believed that children should be seen and not heard, and Esther and Clara tried their best not to be – although Esther was always more successful.

Standing now at the front door of Butterfly Cottage, all of these childhood memories washed over Clara like a wave. She could remember the smell of bread baking in Mrs Mackenzie's oven, the sound of Reverend Mackenzie's laugh, the scent of the honeysuckle in the back garden. And she could remember

James, his voice, his hand in hers, the way he always stuck up for her.

Even though they hadn't seen each other since they were nine years old, Clara still thought of James as the best friend she'd ever had. His letters, over the years, had strengthened that feeling until they stopped coming. They had both been eighteen by then and she had been hopeful of meeting him again – Cambridge wasn't so very far from London, after all.

The front door of Butterfly Cottage opened, snapping Clara out of these melancholy thoughts, and a man with thinning hair and a three-piece suit stepped out onto the threshold.

'Hello,' Esther said, pushing past Clara and extending her hand to the man. 'You must be Mr Molliner from Molliner Estates. I'm Mrs Bradshaw, I made the appointment.' She paused as Mr Molliner took her hand and then she turned to Clara. 'And this is my sister, Miss Samuels.'

Mr Molliner nodded in Clara's direction and she knew, instinctively, that he was the type of man who did not approve of women buying houses without the aid of a husband.

'Perhaps you'd better both come inside,' he said.

3

SUFFOLK, JUNE 2018

It was the most beautiful afternoon. The sun was shining, the birds were singing, and the hawthorn was in full bloom.

And Meredith was completely and hopelessly lost.

She had put the address and postcode of Butterfly Cottage into the maps app on her phone and it had directed her and her hire car out of London and towards Ipswich with no problem at all. But as she had driven around the east side of Ipswich she must have missed a direction somehow as she tried to drive on the narrow winding country lanes without slipping into a ditch or crashing into a car on the other side of the road, and she never quite found her bearings again. On top of that she appeared to be in a black spot where GPS signals went to die.

'I give up,' she said to herself, pulling the car into a small lay-by and willing herself not to cry.

The whole day had been a disaster. The whole week, in fact.

She had decided, after her conversation with her mother, that she would take a day or two off and go to see Butterfly Cottage for herself. She could spend a night there, maybe even talk to a local estate agent, and then get back to Alexander Maddison and see if he was more open to discussing inheritance tax. She couldn't just keep putting everything off. The salon debts were mounting as fast as her bank accounts were diminishing. She had taken over the rent on the flat that she used to share with Joe and she was barely managing. Almost every penny she had seemed to go on rent and ever-increasing bills. It was hard to make ends meet on your own.

She should never have taken on the salon. A voice in the back of her head had tried to tell her it was too much at the time, that people like Meredith, people who'd grown up in a one-bedroom flat at the top of a tower block in south London, did not end up owning their own hairdressing salons. Joe had told her that it was just her gremlins talking, her own self-doubt.

He'd told her to ignore it, that she was capable of anything she put her mind to. But where were Joe and his encouragement now?

The salon had been a daydream for years. Meredith had been planning it in her head even as she cut hair in other people's salons. She'd known exactly how she'd do things differently, exactly how she'd decorate. She'd known how important light and decor were. And she'd trawled around every shop and commercial space that was up for rent. None of them had ever been right, not until she'd found The One.

She still couldn't believe she'd done it and even now, sitting in the car parked in a lay-by somewhere to the east of Ipswich, she knew she would always be proud of how she'd carried out her only real dream, even if it hadn't ended up quite how she'd envisioned. She had allowed herself to dream too big, to imagine a string of salons across London. That was never going to happen now.

A tap on the window of the car nudged her from this rather depressing reverie. A man on a pushbike – a very ordinary-looking pushbike considering they were miles from anywhere – was signalling to her to wind down the window. She wondered where he'd come from. Usually, the only bikes you saw on roads like this were those expensive ones with drop handle-bars ridden by people dressed in Lycra.

'You're not really supposed to park here,' the man said as she opened the window. He was, she noticed, extremely handsome – dark eyes, dark hair, good teeth – and very sweaty. He rubbed his forearm over his face.

'I'm sorry—' she began.

'It's not a lay-by,' the man interrupted. 'It's a passing bay.'

Meredith must have looked confused because the man sighed irritably. 'The road—' he waved a hand at the thoroughfare as he spoke '—is sometimes too narrow for two cars at the same time, so these bays are important.'

'I'm sorry, I didn't know. I've never been here before and—' She stopped. The man did not need to know her whole backstory.

His expression was inscrutable. 'Are you lost?' he asked.

'Yes.' Meredith smiled as though it was no big deal.

'Where do you need to be?'

'A small village called Carybrook, but I can't quite find the right turning and I can't get a GPS signal.'

The man looked at her strangely then raised an

eyebrow in her direction. She expected him to say something, but he must have changed his mind and she saw him almost imperceptibly shake his head before turning his gaze back to the road.

'You've come too far,' he said. 'You should have come off at that last junction.' He pointed his thumb behind him. 'But you can't turn around here. There's a roundabout two miles up the road. Go all the way around it and then come back on yourself. Take that junction – the sign says Ipswich East, I think – and then follow the signs for Carybrook.'

Two miles, Meredith thought, looking at the petrol gauge, which was indicating almost empty. The hire company would expect the tank to be full again before she returned the car. Another expense she could ill afford.

'You can't miss it,' the man said.

'Thank you,' Meredith replied, admiring his confidence. She was pretty sure she could miss any junction, turning or sign. But she'd give it a go anyway.

'I'll let you go first,' the man went on. 'I'm cutting down the next bridleway anyway.'

Meredith pressed the button to close the window and pulled out into the road heading towards the roundabout.

As she drove her thoughts drifted back to Joe. She

had met up with him the previous evening, a stupid move as it turned out, but she'd hoped he would help her. For old times' sake if nothing else.

'You can't come here,' he'd said when she'd suggested meeting.

'I don't want to come there,' she'd replied. The thought of seeing the new house he was setting up with Jemma turned her stomach. It had all happened so fast it made Meredith's head spin. It was only two months ago that she'd had the migraine that had forced her to find a cover teacher and go home early, where she'd found them in bed together, and now Jemma and Joe (an alliteration too far in Meredith's mind) were a couple, living together in a small, rented house in Putney and talking of getting a mortgage. She didn't want to know how long it had been going on. She hadn't asked Joe, but she wasn't stupid. It was clear that Joe and Jemma had been a thing for a while.

'Well, let's meet at The Red Lion,' Joe had suggested. 'I can't be long though, I don't want to upset Jemma.' Meredith had smiled to herself at the thought of Jemma getting mad at Joe for seeing her, albeit briefly. It wasn't much but it was something.

When she had walked into the pub, Joe had already been there. He had a pint in front of him and was reading the paper – he still bought an actual hard copy paper every day. Everything about him was so familiar, his movements, his mannerisms and Meredith almost turned around. She still loved him, she knew that, even though she felt so angry and betrayed, and seeing him was torture. But she had to talk to him sometime.

He'd always been so supportive, her biggest cheerleader. He'd looked around all the unsuitable rental spaces in south London with her and he'd been there on the day that she found the perfect one – a large, airy space with a flexible landlord who was willing to let them make interior alterations. A friend of Lloyd's had done the building works – putting up partition walls, creating a kitchen area and customer bathrooms – but it had still gone over budget. What didn't? Even then Joe had been supportive, insisting on helping financially – a good investment, he'd said.

But now the investor wanted his money back because at some point when Meredith had been totally distracted by the increasingly dire finances at the salon, when she'd been completely embroiled in marketing and trying to fill empty chairs, Jemma had suddenly appeared.

At The Red Lion, Meredith had bought herself a glass of white wine and sat down opposite Joe who had taken a large draft of his beer before speaking.

'What's this about?' he'd asked without preamble.

'The money I owe you,' she'd replied.

'Got a cheque for me?' Joe had smirked over his beer glass.

'You know I haven't, Joe; you know I can't get my hands on all the money yet.'

'Then you need to sell the business as a going concern,' he'd replied. 'Pay off the debts, get a job and start paying me back. I'm not being unreasonable here, Meredith. Businesses fail, it's part of life. You did your best, nobody is denying that, but it's over. Accept it and move on. You and I can set up a repayment schedule. And I promise I'll be fair.'

Had Joe always been like this? So patronising and smug? Meredith never remembered seeing this side of him before he'd met Jemma.

'I think there might be another way,' she'd said, ignoring his attitude. 'Something's happened.'

She'd gone on then to tell him about Alexander Maddison and Butterfly Cottage and the great-aunt that she had never known about. And she'd explained how, if he could wait until all the legal formalities were out of the way, selling the cottage should be able to give her enough money to pay her debts, including the money she owed him, without having to sell her business.

Joe hadn't said anything for a moment when she'd finished.

'What do you think?' she'd asked.

'I think it sounds extremely unlikely that anything to do with your father or his family is legitimate.'

'You've never even met my father,' Meredith had bitten back. She was allowed to criticise him, as was Bernice, but when anyone else did, Meredith always became defensive. In a way, Meredith missed her dad and felt his abandonment was her fault. Was it her fault Joe had left too?

'Admittedly, no,' Joe had gone on. 'But from what you've told me about him I just feel that you should maybe lower your expectations. I'm in no hurry for the money and...'

'I'm going to Suffolk to see it tomorrow,' she'd continued, trying to ignore what he was saying. Did he really think she hadn't thought all of this herself? But she had to stay positive, she had to believe this would help her. 'I should have a lot more information then, the value of the place and so on.'

'OK. But I sense you want something from me. I can't go with you, Meredith. You know that.'

'I don't want you to come with me,' she had said, although she desperately wanted him to. Road trips with Joe had always been one of Meredith's favourite things. 'But I wondered if I could borrow your car, just for a couple of days.'

She'd looked at other ways of getting to Cary-brook. By train, she could get as far as Ipswich and after that it was an expensive taxi journey or a series of four buses. Even if she set out early, she wouldn't be at Butterfly Cottage until the evening. She hated asking but she was desperate.

Joe had sighed. 'You didn't think I might need more notice to lend you the car,' he'd said. 'This is so typical of you, Meredith – you don't think of anyone but yourself and your own problems, completely oblivious to everyone around you and the problems they might be having.'

Meredith wanted to ask him if he'd been thinking about her when he slept with Jemma in their bed but knew better than to get into a row in a public place.

'Anyway, Jemma needs the car tomorrow.'

'Can she not—' Meredith had begun.

'No, she can't,' Joe had snapped. 'She's got an appointment, a hospital appointment.' He'd stopped then and looked away from her, down towards the table, his finger tracing circles in a small puddle of beer. 'I may as well tell you as you'll find out eventually. Jemma's pregnant, about three months gone.'

Neither of them had commented that Joe and

Meredith had been living together in apparent domestic bliss just three months ago. Neither of them had needed to.

'Right, well...' Meredith had said, throwing back what was left of her wine and standing up. 'In that case, I'll go and—'

'Meredith,' Joe had said, catching her by the wrist. 'I am sorry, you know I—'

'Let go of me.'

He'd dropped his hand.

'I'll email you when I've got more news,' Meredith had said quietly, not looking at him. 'We can set up a payment plan or something.'

Joe hadn't said anything else until she was almost out of the door of The Red Lion. Then he'd called her name and she'd turned, instinctively.

'Good luck with the mythical cottage,' he'd called across the pub, the smirk firmly back on his face.

Meredith blinked back tears as she drove the hire car that she couldn't really afford towards the roundabout that the man on the pushbike had said would be there. As she navigated her way around it, she told herself that she wasn't going to let this get the better of her, that she wasn't going to let this be the end of something. She had inherited a cottage and had an appointment with an estate agent the next morning. She was putting wheels of change in motion.

This was a new beginning.

* * *

Half an hour later she pulled the car up outside Butterfly Cottage behind a dark-green van with the words 'Johnson's Gardening Services' emblazoned on the side in gold. It had been easy enough to find in the end, thanks to the man on the pushbike.

She turned to look at the house that was now hers. It was chocolate-box pretty, almost unbelievably so, and she immediately thought of Joe's parting comment. Her 'mythical cottage'.

But she was here, the cottage existed, and it was beautiful. Painted white on the outside, with a sage-green front door, and roses trailing around the front wall. It was almost exactly as she had imagined it to be.

She got out of the car, leaving her overnight bag to bring in later. She unlatched the white gate at the top of the garden path and listened to it creak as she closed it behind her. She felt suddenly sick, as though everything depended on the next few minutes.

Which, in a way, it did.

She took the key that Alexander Maddison had given her out of her handbag and felt its weight in the palm of her hand. Slowly she inserted it into the keyhole expecting something dreadful to happen like it wouldn't turn, or it would set off an alarm somewhere.

But the key turned easily, making a satisfactory click as she opened the door.

Meredith stepped into the hallway of Butterfly Cottage and thought about all the people who had done so before her, including Clara Samuels. Who was she? Why had Meredith never heard of her and why had she left a house to a great-niece she'd never met? Why hadn't she left it to her father, Clara's nephew? Did Dennis know that Clara existed?

She hoped some of these questions would be answered over the next few days.

Butterfly Cottage had the musty smell of buildings that have been shut up for a while, but as Meredith walked past the living room and dining room, she noticed fresh flowers had been put in vases in both rooms. Someone had been in here recently – maybe a cleaning service or a friend of Miss Samuels from the village, sprucing the place up for her. She would have to ask Mr Maddison. Or maybe the estate agent would know.

The cottage was clean and bright but, as the solicitor had warned her, despite recent redecoration it was in desperate need of modernisation – especially the kitchen, she noticed. She wondered if that would need to happen before a sale. Again, the estate agent would know.

She found herself being drawn through the kitchen, to the back of the house, toward the large French doors that led into the garden. She wondered if the same key opened these as had opened the front door but as she drew closer she realised that it was far too big.

Meredith looked around, wondering where the key to the French doors was. Not being immediately obvious she tried the handle anyway and was surprised when the door swung open easily. That was strange. How long had that been left unlocked?

She stepped out into the sunshine. The garden of Butterfly Cottage was beautiful, the grass relatively freshly mowed and the beds blooming with flowers and plants that she didn't know the names of. Butterflies and bees flittered around. It was positively bucolic and, to someone like Meredith who had spent a lot of her life in London flats with no outside space, it felt like a breath of fresh air. That new beginning she so desperately sought.

Not that she could afford to keep it.

The garden was long and she began to walk toward the other end where the lawn bent around in a dogleg to the left. As she turned the corner she saw a caravan parked up looking incongruous in the beautiful garden. She wondered where it had come from and how much that would cost to dispose of.

She was about to turn back towards the house when the door of the caravan opened and a man stepped out.

Not just any man. A shirtless man, with dark hair and a beard, damp as though fresh from the shower.

It was the man with the pushbike.

'Hello,' he said when he spotted her. 'It's you, from the passing bay. I wondered if it might be.'

Meredith was shocked at his seeming lack of surprise at seeing her.

'What the hell are you doing here?' she said.

'Well, I live here, of course,' he said, extending his hand to her in greeting. 'I'm Zach. Zach Johnson. And you must be Meredith Carling.'

4

SUFFOLK, JUNE 1963

By the time the two sisters returned to Esther and Richard's large Victorian house on the other side of the village, Richard was already home from the cricket and sitting in his favourite armchair with a copy of *The Times* and a large whiskey and soda.

'Look at this,' he said from behind the newspaper. 'All these bloody people swarming into London protesting against nuclear weapons like we don't have a right to protect our country against the bloody—'

'Richard, Clara's here,' Esther interrupted. Clara was used to Richard's disapproving rants and conspiracy theories but was grateful to her sister for silencing him. She had a lot to think about and couldn't quite bear to listen to Richard right now, especially as she was on the side of the protestors. Still, it was a little better than his usual spiel – who was and wasn't a KGB spy. Harold Wilson, the new leader of the Labour Party was, of course.

Richard flicked the newspaper aside and popped his head out to greet his sister-in-law.

'Hello, Clara old girl,' he said. 'How are you? How was Butterfly Cottage? I've left your bags up in your room if you want to freshen up.'

Clara nodded. It felt like a good idea to have a moment to herself. 'That would be lovely,' she said, turning to her sister. 'If you don't need my help in the kitchen.'

'No, no,' Esther said, waving her away. She never needed help anywhere. 'I made a shepherd's pie this morning, so I just have to pop it in the oven and cook the greens.'

'I'll have a gin and tonic ready for you when you come down,' Richard said, disappearing back behind his newspaper.

They had put Clara in the second-biggest bedroom at the back of the house – the blue room, they called it, as though they lived in a stately home. Her suitcase was already on the bed for her and a jug of water and a glass stood on the nightstand. Richard and Esther were nothing if not good hosts. She thought sadly again of the empty bedrooms and the future that her sister had hoped for when they'd first bought the house.

She unzipped her suitcase and took out her night-dress, placing it carefully on the pillow. Then she sat down at the dressing table and reapplied her face powder. As she did so she thought about Butterfly Cottage.

The estate agent, Mr Molliner, had spoken almost exclusively to Esther as though Clara, as an unmar-ried woman, didn't really exist. While it infuriated her – this ridiculous attitude always did – she rose above it as she saw more and more of the house.

There was no denying the fact that it was perfect, even more so than she remembered. There had been many changes – gone was the old tub and mangle in which Mrs Mackenzie had done the family laundry, replaced with a brand-new twin tub washing ma-chine. Gone also was the old oil-fired range, replaced with an electric oven and central heating.

'The diocese made a lot of changes over the years,' Mr Molliner had said to Esther.

'I can see,' Esther had replied.

'They needed to, apparently, to attract a good vicar, especially after the war. But in the end, it was more cost-effective to buy the new house near the church and make that the vicarage.'

Esther had nodded, admiring the oven. 'Almost as nice as mine,' she'd said to Clara with a smile.

The upstairs bathroom and toilet had also changed, and everywhere had been painted white so, according to Mr Molliner, the new owner could put their mark on it. Clara had been dreaming about putting her mark on Butterfly Cottage since she'd first heard it was for sale. She'd seen some wallpaper in Peter Jones that would be perfect for the front room and...

But she was getting ahead of herself. Butterfly Cottage wasn't hers and it looked very much as though Mr Molliner did not want to sell it to her. Not that it was his decision in the end, of course. But would the diocese approve of a woman on her own? Perhaps they would just want the highest offer available.

Despite all the changes to the cottage, the essence of the house remained – Clara could feel its spirit as she walked around, its warmth, its history.

She'd never wanted very much in her life, but she really wanted Butterfly Cottage.

When she returned downstairs, a sparkling gin and tonic awaited her next to her chair, ice cubes clinking on the sides of the glass. She sat down and took a fortifying sip. It had been a long day.

'So,' said Richard, flicking his newspaper aside once again. 'What did you think of Butterfly Cottage? Has it changed much or still the same? Esther tells me you spent a lot of time there as a child.'

'It's been modernised,' Clara replied. 'And very well, I think, although Esther says that the oven isn't as good as hers.'

'I'm not surprised, the price that oven set me back,' Richard grumbled.

'But in so many ways it's still the same, from the colour of the front door to the rose climbing over the house. The rear garden hasn't been as well maintained,' she went on, remembering Mrs Mackenzie's beautiful garden. 'But that could be fixed, I should think.'

'Do you remember the flowers you used to bring back from Mrs Mackenzie's garden?' Esther asked as she stepped into the living room.

'Gardens are all well and good,' Richard interrupted. 'But is the building structurally sound? It was built in 1882, you know.'

'And it hasn't fallen down yet,' Clara replied with a smile.

'If Clara decides to buy, of course she'll ask your

advice on such matters, Richard,' Esther said. 'Now I must check on the pie.' She disappeared back into the kitchen.

'Lucky for you, old girl,' Richard went on, pointing at Clara, 'I've been to see the house myself. I took Bill Nesbit with me – he's a surveyor, you know, plays golf at the club. Anyway, all seems to be in order.' He paused for a moment, looking intently at Clara. 'And Eric Molliner's at the club as well so if you want this house, and I think you probably do, then I can fix things for you. Now let's talk about money.'

Clara goggled at him. She had presumed he would be of the Mr Molliner school of thought and be set against her purchase of the cottage.

'You're surprised,' he said with a smile. 'Well, not all of us have views about women that have been dragged out of Noah's Ark, you know. I think it would probably be a good thing. And it would make Esther happy, so...' He shrugged.

Clara found her voice and explained that she did have the money to invest in Butterfly Cottage. 'And some left over for legal fees and decorating and so on. I still have all the money Father left; I haven't touched it. I've just left it with the solicitor who held it in trust and it's been gathering interest. I'd have to ask to find out exactly how much, but...' There was something about talking to Richard that always made her feel like a little girl, explaining something to her father. Richard reminded Clara of her father in many ways and she had never been completely sure if she liked him. It was clear that Esther loved him though and that he was very fond of Esther, so who was she to judge?

'Well, you don't need me to go guarantor on a mortgage then, that definitely makes things easier,' Richard said. 'Which brings me on to the next thing. What are you intending to do about work?'

Clara gulped down another mouthful of her gin and tonic because she hadn't thought much beyond leaving the west London school she was so tired of. She had secretarial skills as well as many years of teaching experience. She was bound to find some work somewhere. She just hadn't worked out what.

'Don't you worry about that,' Esther said, appearing suddenly in the doorway again. 'I've spoken to Miss Cheggers at the school – you remember her, Clara? Well, she's headmistress now and she'll see you tomorrow for an informal interview.'

'But tomorrow is Sunday,' Esther said with surprise.

'She'll see you after church. Now come along both of you, dinner is ready.'

Clara supposed she would have to get used to her sister organising her life again if she were to move back to Carybrook.

* * *

Miss Cheggers was waiting for Clara outside the church after the Sunday morning service. Clara hadn't seen her for years, not since she went up to Cambridge. Miss Cheggers had been the teacher of Class 1 at the village school when Clara had been there. She remembered the teacher as young and glamorous, wearing the most fashionable clothes of the time. She had always suspected that James had had a crush on Miss Cheggers back then. Her heart sank for a moment as she remembered James once more. She supposed she had better get used to inconvenient memories if she was to move to Carybrook.

The Miss Cheggers of 1963 was in her mid-fifties and still attractive and glamorous, although in a more subdued way. But something had changed about her. She looked like she carried the weight of the world on her shoulders now. A war and thirty years of teaching small children would do that to you, Clara thought. And Miss Cheggers had never married either. Clara wondered why as she saw her own future in Miss Cheggers' eyes.

'This is most irregular, of course,' the head-mistress said as she led Clara towards the village school. 'Usually, the vicar and the Board of Governors assist with staff interviews, but I owed Esther a favour so here we are.'

Clara wondered at the favour Esther was owed and Clara suspected that half the village owed her sister a favour. Esther was the sort of person that got stuff done. She had tried to talk to her the previous evening about this impromptu interview at the school but Esther had been very vague about it all.

'I just happened to mention that you were thinking of returning to Carybrook and would be looking for work,' she'd said. 'And by an amazing co-incidence, the school is rather desperate for a new teacher.'

Clara wasn't at all sure about this coincidence, but it did prove one thing at least: Esther was a lot more invested in Clara moving to Carybrook than she was letting on. She might sniff and disapprove but she'd been very encouraging at Butterfly Cottage the day before and now this chat with Miss Cheggers had been arranged. She wondered if her sister was lonely, despite seeming to be the heart and soul of the village.

She must spend a lot of time alone when Richard was at work or playing golf or cricket, and she didn't have the distraction of children like many of the other women in the village.

From the outside the school looked exactly as Clara remembered it but, much like Butterfly Cottage, once Miss Cheggers had opened the main door and led Clara inside it was clear that much modernisation had taken place.

'It is very good of you to see me on a Sunday morning,' Clara said.

'The thing is,' Miss Cheggers went on as she led Clara past the rows of tiny coat pegs and towards her own office, 'we have a situation here at the school, so when your sister told me that you were coming back to Carybrook I sped things along a little.'

The headmistress took out her keys again to unlock the office door.

'Please come in,' she said, removing a pile of papers from a chair. 'Take a seat.'

'Miss Cheggers...' Clara began.

'Oh, do call me Jean.'

Clara swallowed. It felt strange to be calling the woman who had taught her to read and write by her first name.

'Jean.' Clara tried the name on for size. 'I think my

sister may have jumped the gun a little. I'm really just toying with the idea of coming back. I had no idea you wanted to see me until last night.'

Miss Cheggers' face fell. 'But Esther said you were buying Butterfly Cottage.'

'Well, I did go to see it yesterday, but I haven't even put in an offer yet. In fact, I'm not sure that the estate agent, Mr Molliner, even approves of selling to a single woman so it may well go to someone else entirely.'

Miss Cheggers rolled her eyes. 'I'm afraid, Clara, that this village has not moved with the times as much as it should have done. It is stuck somewhere around the coronation. People like Mr Molliner make me want to—' She stopped herself and smiled tightly. Clara nodded gently to show she understood before the headmistress went on. 'Well, anyway, even if you don't get the cottage, there are other houses in Carybrook. They're building some lovely modern bungalows on the other side of the church, you know. Did Esther tell you?'

Clara suddenly felt as though moving back to the village was no longer her idea or her dream. She felt as though she was being press-ganged into it and that made her want to abandon all her plans and get on the first train back to London. This was exactly why she had left in the first place, exactly why she had pushed herself so hard to win that Cambridge scholarship. In Carybrook certain things had always been expected of her and she worried, if she allowed herself to be bossed around by her sister again, that it would all be the same.

But things were different now, weren't they? She was a grown woman, with her own money and, hopefully soon, her own house. She could stand up for herself and live the life she wanted to live. Besides, what was left for her in London? She was still in the same job and the same boarding house she had been in when she first qualified. She had worked hard and been promoted within the school but each promotion had brought more work and less time to look for an alternative, so she probably shouldn't look this current gift horse in the mouth.

'Shall we assume that I will be moving here,' Clara said with what she hoped was an encouraging and friendly smile.

Miss Cheggers – Clara simply could not think of her as Jean – visibly relaxed. 'Yes,' she said. 'So tell me what brings you back to Carybrook.'

'Well, I don't know if I will be coming back yet...'

'Clara, I thought we said that we would pretend as though you were.'

'Oh yes,' Clara grinned. 'Of course, I'm sorry.'

'You seem nervous,' Miss Cheggers said. 'You shouldn't be, this really is just a formality. The school is desperate for a new teacher.'

'Thanks,' Clara said. 'I think.'

Miss Cheggers laughed, a high-pitched sound that Clara was sure she had never heard in her seven years at Carybrook School. 'A back-handed compliment,' she said. 'My apologies, but your sister has sung your praises to me.'

'She has?' This seemed quite unlike Esther and Clara had that feeling of being manipulated once again.

'And in my mind, anyone who can work in one of those huge schools in inner London can manage the children of Carybrook,' Miss Cheggers went on. 'We'd be lucky to have you.'

Clara looked down at her lap, at her hands that were placed there, fingers entwined with each other. Was this really what she wanted? Did she really want to leave the hustle and bustle of London behind to return to Carybrook?

To return home?

She looked up at Miss Cheggers' eager face, at the playground that lay just the other side of the window. She imagined it full of children playing football or cricket or tag or whatever other playground games were fashionable in Carybrook at the moment. She imagined the school she had been at herself, the school that had first instilled a love of learning in her. She imagined standing at the front of the class and giving that gift to just one of the children here.

And then she imagined the school in London, the absences and the poverty, the abuse and the anger.

There was poverty in the country too of course, and abuse and anger. And Clara doubted very much that the school coffers received any more money than anywhere else.

So she thought about Butterfly Cottage and the boarding house in London.

'I would be lucky to work here at Carybrook School,' she said.

Miss Cheggers smiled knowingly. 'Just as I thought,' she said. 'And when can you start?'

5

SUFFOLK, JUNE 2018

'What do you mean, you live here?' Meredith asked, trying to keep the high-pitched panic out of her voice. 'This is *my* house.'

'I think you'll find,' Zach replied, still smiling inexplicably, 'that this is *our* house.'

Meredith stared at him and noticed he still had his hand extended in greeting. Rather pettily she shoved her hands into the pockets of her jacket to make it clear she had no intention of being companionable. Zach shrugged and dropped his hand, turning back towards his caravan.

'If you don't get yourself and your horrible van off my land in the next ten minutes I'll call the police,' she said.

He stopped for a moment and she briefly thought that she'd called his bluff. But then she noticed his shoulders shaking and when he turned back to her he was laughing.

'What is so funny?' Meredith asked. She was furious now and, if she was completely honest, a little bit scared. She wondered if any of the neighbours were in. If she shouted, would they hear her? Most places like Carybrook were dormitory villages these days – half empty during the week as the villagers commuted to work in bigger towns and cities.

Something must have shown on her face because Zach stopped laughing when he looked at her and when he spoke his voice was softer.

'You don't know, do you?' he said.

'Know what?'

'Look,' he said. 'Let me put a shirt on and we can talk. I can make you a cup of tea.'

'I don't want you in my house,' Meredith said, although her voice was less certain now and she kept thinking of that feeling she'd had as she left Alexander Maddison's office – that feeling that the solicitor hadn't been honest with her. What if this wasn't her house after all? She'd known it had been too good to be true and she thought of Joe in the pub last night.

Good luck with your mythical cottage.

Zach held up his hands. 'I hardly ever go in the house,' he said. 'Mostly I just live out here in the van.'

'But why, if the house is allegedly yours?' Meredith asked, her curiosity piquing.

Zach sighed and closed his eyes for a moment. 'I'm going to get dressed,' he said.

'Yes, please do. I'm going to phone my solicitor.'

She walked quickly back up the garden towards the house. She didn't look behind her. When she got inside and into the kitchen, she leaned against the counter and let out a breath. What was going on? Why was the man on the pushbike living in a caravan in the garden claiming that it was *their* house, not *her* house?

She didn't know whether to be angry or apprehensive. And if she was angry, who was she angry with? The man in the caravan or Alexander Maddison?

What had he said his name was? Zach. Zach Johnson. Why did that ring a bell?

And then she remembered the van that she had parked behind, the one that had said 'Johnson's Gardening Services' on the side. Perhaps he was here to deal with the garden; it did look beautifully well-tended, not like the garden of an abandoned cottage at all. And it explained the tidiness of the house, and the flowers in the vases.

She pulled her phone out of her bag and called Alexander Maddison's office, but his assistant told her that the solicitor was in a meeting.

'Do you know how long he'll be?' Meredith asked.

'I think it will be quite a long one. Can I help at all?'

'I'm not sure,' Meredith paused, trying to collect her thoughts. 'This is Meredith Carling. Do you know anything about Butterfly Cottage?'

There was a pause on the other end of the line, a pause that went on for just a little bit too long.

'I'm afraid not,' Mr Maddison's assistant said eventually. 'That's one Al is dealing with himself.'

Al. That's what his friends and colleagues called him? It didn't suit him at all, Meredith thought.

'Would you like me to take a message?' the assistant asked.

'I...' Meredith paused. 'No, can you just ask him to call me as soon as he's back?'

The next person Meredith called was her mother.

'I'm at Butterfly Cottage,' she said.

'Oooh, what's it like?' Bernice asked excitedly. 'It actually exists then? You should have Facetimed me and given me the guided tour.'

'It's not...' Meredith began. How did you even explain this? 'Yes, it's standing and it's in pretty good condition considering the amount of time it was supposedly empty.'

'But...' Bernice said, knowing that there had to be a catch somewhere.

'There's a man living in the garden.'

'What sort of man? Why is he living in the garden?'

'A man about my age with dark hair and beard and not very many clothes and...'

'Nice body?' Bernice asked.

'Mum! That is not the point!'

'I'm only asking. If he has got a nice body, it's less of a hardship to have him live in the garden, that's all.'

'Mum,' Meredith tried again, speaking slowly so her mother could grasp the gravity of the issue. She should know better than to distract Bernice with talk of semi-clothed men. 'There is a man, a complete stranger, living in a caravan at the bottom of the garden of Butterfly Cottage and he claims this is not my house.'

'Whose house is it?' Bernice asked, finally focussing on the important stuff.

'*Our* house apparently.'

'So he's claiming you both own the house.'

'I think so.'

'What do you mean, you think so? Have you not spoken to him about it? Asked him why he thinks he owns half of it?'

'No, I...' Meredith hesitated. 'I got quite angry at him and said I was going to call the police. I was scared, Mum, I was expecting the house to be empty.'

'Yes, I'm sorry,' Bernice replied. 'I can see it was probably quite a frightening situation.'

'He does seem OK, though. It was me who threatened him, now I think about it.'

'If this man with a beard does own half the house,' Bernice went on, 'why didn't Alexander what's-his-name tell you? What's he got to say for himself?'

'Mr Maddison is in a meeting,' Meredith said.

'It all sounds very strange,' Bernice said. 'And bloody typical. Anything to do with your father's side of the family is always a mess. I wish I knew where he was and then—'

'I think I'm just going to go back to London,' Meredith said, interrupting the incoming rant about her father. Sometimes she wasn't sure Dennis deserved it quite so often. He had grown up with Grandma Bradshaw, after all. 'I need to sort out the mess the salon is in and—'

'No,' Bernice interrupted. 'Don't do this, Meredith, you always do this. You give up too soon all the time.'

Meredith opened her mouth to try to explain that she wasn't giving up on the salon, she was just running out of options, but Bernice was in full flow.

'This solicitor chap has told you that Butterfly Cottage is yours, that it was left to you by a great-aunt you never knew you had. He gave you a key and that was pretty much it. I've already told you that there is a lot more to inheriting property than that – taxes, papers to sign, Land Registry formalities – you name it, there's a fee for it.'

Bernice had worked in a lot of clerical roles when Meredith was a child, before Lloyd came along, including in law firms. She must have picked all this up from then. Poor Bernice. She was smarter and cleverer and more curious than a lot of people Meredith had known, but she had never had a chance to shine.

'But despite all of that,' she went on, 'this solicitor just gives you a key and leaves you to it. Now you have a handsome, half-naked man in your garden who claims the house is half his.'

'I didn't say he was handsome.'

'Is he?'

'Yes, I suppose so.' Meredith had noticed how good-looking he was way back on the country road. It had been a long time since she'd noticed anything like that.

'Right,' Bernice continued. 'Now doesn't all that sound just a bit odd to you?'

'Yes, of course it's odd, but—'

'And don't you want to find out what's going on?'

'Yes, but I can do that from London.'

'And don't you have a meeting with an estate agent tomorrow?' Bernice asked.

'Yes...'

'Then meet with the estate agent, call Alexander whatsit, and sit tight in your property until this is all sorted. You don't want anyone swooping in and claiming living rights.'

Meredith shook her head and rubbed her eyes. Her mother was right in so many ways. She did have a tendency to run from things when they got too hard. Was she doing that with her business? She would certainly be doing that if she walked away from Butterfly Cottage right now.

'This could take days, weeks even, to clear up though,' she said. 'And the business needs me, now more than ever.'

'And on the other hand, the cottage could save the business. You've got a salon manager, haven't you? Could she run things for a little while?'

'Yes,' Meredith said simply, not saying that she didn't know how much longer she could afford to pay her.

'And could another hairdresser take over your appointments if you needed them to?'

Meredith reluctantly admitted that they could and would be glad of the work.

'So stay where you are for now,' Bernice said. 'In the meantime, I'll try to get a flight out as soon as I can.'

'You don't have to do that, Mum.'

'Yes, I do and I won't be told otherwise.'

Meredith sighed and rolled her eyes but didn't say anything. Truth be told it would be nice to have her mum there with her. Bernice always seemed to argue a case better than she did.

'Now try this solicitor again. It seems to me that he has a lot of explaining to do.'

As soon as Bernice had gone, Meredith tried Mr Maddison again but 'Al' was still in his meeting. Again she left no message.

She had no choice now, it seemed, other than to speak to the man at the bottom of the garden and see if he had an explanation.

* * *

As Meredith walked back down the garden she noticed that, while it was beautifully well-tended near the house – far too well-tended for a garden that had been left abandoned for such a long time – as she neared the other end the beds were empty and it was obvious that it was very much still a work in progress. She thought about the van outside the house again and took a breath. Zach Johnson was just here to finish up the garden. That must be what he meant. He didn't own the house, he had just promised Clara Samuels that he would finish the job.

You keep telling yourself that, a voice in Meredith's head whispered. She did, after all, have a propensity for burying her head in the sand until it was too late. But she couldn't think of the salon and its mountain of debt right now.

Zach was dressed when she got to his caravan.

'Hi,' he said softly.

'I'm sorry I was so rude before,' Meredith replied, feeling her cheeks burn with embarrassment. 'It was just a shock. I wasn't expecting anyone else to be here.'

'We should talk,' he said. 'I'll make some tea.'

Meredith nodded and walked closer to the caravan.

'I've got English Breakfast, Earl Grey, Peppermint,

Camomile...' Zach paused and looked at her. 'What would you like?'

'Earl Grey please, no milk or sugar.'

He stepped up into the van and came back out with a fold-up chair. 'Take a seat,' he said, unfolding it for her. 'This late-afternoon sun is my favourite time of day.'

She smiled and sat down, tilting her face up at the sun and wondering where her sunglasses were. It really was a beautiful day. She closed her eyes and listened to the sounds of the kettle boiling and mugs clinking from inside the van.

Zach reappeared a few minutes later with a tray. 'The blue-and-white mug is yours,' he said, holding it out to her. 'And help yourself to biscuits.'

She took two, suddenly realising how hungry she was. She hadn't eaten since breakfast.

'I'm guessing that you were Miss Samuels's gardener,' she said after a while when it was evident that Zach wasn't going to start what was clearly going to be a difficult conversation.

He nodded and took a mouthful of tea. He was sitting on the steps of the caravan – probably so he could escape inside if the conversation got too tricky.

'I was her gardener, yes, although you might have noticed that I didn't get a chance to finish everything.

I'd like to, though. Miss Samuels wanted a veg bed up this end of the garden, so that's what's going to go there.' He pointed at the empty beds that Meredith had noticed earlier. 'I just need to dig another load of manure into the soil and then I can start planting everything out.'

'Everything?' Meredith knew next to nothing about gardening and hadn't grown a vegetable since she grew cress on wet blotting paper at primary school.

'All the veggies are over in the potting shed and greenhouse.' He waved a hand to the other side of the caravan. Meredith hadn't noticed either of these things until then, she'd been too angry about the intruder in her garden – who was now seeming less and less like an intruder.

'OK,' she said slowly, placing her mug on the grass. 'And when you've finished up I guess you'll move on to your next job. I... Well, I suppose I should pay you and...' She hated talking about money; that was one of the reasons she'd got in such a mess with the salon.

'You don't need to pay me to dig my own garden,' Zach said, the frustration palpable in his voice. 'Did you phone the solicitor?'

'He was in a meeting.'

'So you still don't know?'

Meredith felt her stomach drop. She'd known really, deep down, that Zach wasn't just the gardener. Why would the gardener say that he owned half the house? What was going on and why hadn't Mr Maddison told her?

'Look,' Zach said. 'Miss Samuels, your great-aunt, left the house to both of us in equal shares. That's what it said in her will and what the solicitor told me when she died.'

'Mr Maddison?'

'Yes, Alexander Maddison.' Zach nodded. 'Miss Samuels told me she had a great-niece before she died. I asked about you but she never told me any more than your name.'

'She wouldn't have known anything about me,' Meredith said. 'We'd never met.'

'Never?'

'Until a few weeks ago I didn't even know I had a great-aunt.'

Meredith thought about her mum, about how she would be cursing Dennis's name over all this. Who else would have known about Clara Samuels but not told anyone? Who else would have told Clara she had a great-niece called Meredith Carling? And if it was

Dennis who had told Clara to leave the house to Meredith, why had he done it?

'You really didn't know?' Zach said incredulously. 'And Mr Maddison didn't tell you?'

'He told me about the inheritance, made me sign various documents and then gave me a key to Butterfly Cottage, and really that was all. He said he'd talk about everything else once I'd seen the house, because you see... Well, it doesn't matter.' She decided Zach did not need to know about the dire straits of her finances or Joe demanding his money back for the baby that was on the way. She couldn't begin to think about that. She hadn't even told her mother about that yet. 'But no, he never mentioned you or that you owned half the house and now I can't even get in touch with him so you can see why I'm a bit dubious.' That was the understatement of the year. She was suspicious as hell.

'Wait there,' Zach said, standing up and disappearing inside his caravan again.

Whilst he was gone Meredith wondered where her father was and how much he knew about Butterfly Cottage. Had he ever been here? Had Zach met him?

'This is a copy of Miss Samuels's will,' Zach said, flourishing some papers before handing them to

Meredith. 'She named me and Alexander Maddison as executors so that's why I have a copy. She didn't want to name you as an executor because she didn't know how busy you were. I had no idea you'd never met, that she didn't know you at all, I'm...' He trailed off as though he had no idea how to deal with this bizarre situation. Who would?

She scanned the papers Zach had given her – there were various small cash gifts to people she had never heard of and there, as clear as day, was the bequest of Butterfly Cottage:

> I leave Butterfly Cottage and all its contents to Zachary Anthony Johnson and Meredith Carling in equal shares.

There was no denying it.

She folded the papers back up and handed them to Zach.

'I don't understand how she knew I existed,' Meredith said. 'I don't understand how she knew my name to put in the will.'

'I wish I could help,' Zach said. 'But like I said, she never told me anything but your name, so she knew that from somewhere.'

'Did she ever mention anyone or have any visitors here?'

Zach shook his head. 'I never saw anyone visit her except other people who lived in the village the whole time I was working for her.'

'Which was how long?'

'Just under a year.'

'Did you not, well... Did you not wonder why she decided to leave you half the house? She must have had family. Why didn't she leave it to my father, for example?'

Zach shrugged and looked uncomfortable. 'To be honest, when she first mentioned it I thought she was joking. What would she be doing leaving me a house? She hardly knew me.'

'Exactly,' Meredith snapped, eyebrow raised.

'I didn't coerce her into it if that's what you're implying. I was as surprised as you when Mr Maddison told me and, to be honest, I wasn't very happy about it. Inheriting a house with a stranger wasn't exactly going to be easy. And now I've met the stranger...' He paused here and gave Meredith a very pointed look.

'I'm not over the moon about it myself.'

'No,' Zach said, the hint of a smile on his lips.

'Are you not curious as to why she left it to you, though?'

'Of course I am, but I figured that if she'd wanted to tell me she would have done when she was alive. She told me she had no other family, but that doesn't explain why she left it to me.'

'There's my dad,' Meredith said. 'But I don't know if he knew she existed either. Nobody ever mentioned her.'

'Really?'

'Never, not until Mr Maddison told me about the will.'

'Would your dad know more about it?' Zach asked.

'He might,' Meredith replied, looking away. 'But I haven't seen him for fourteen years, not since my eighteenth birthday party when... Well, never mind.' She still felt guilty whenever she thought about how she'd behaved.

'Oh... I... Well...' Zach stuttered.

Meredith thought of the day she turned eighteen, the party she had had in the local pub, paid for by Lloyd – good, kind, wonderful Lloyd. By that point she had thought of him as the only father she needed. She had been so happy.

And then Dennis had turned up. She'd recognised him instantly, standing by the bar arguing with Bernice. She hadn't seen him since he'd left her and her mother without warning or note one Monday morning when Meredith had been eleven.

'I just want to see her on her birthday,' he'd been saying when Meredith walked up to him.

'Well, here I am,' she'd said. 'You've seen me now. So you can leave again.'

'Happy birthday, sweetheart,' Dennis had said, his face breaking into a huge grin. 'Have you got a hug for your old dad?'

She'd stood for a moment, wondering. And then she'd said those words she'd always regretted.

'You're not my dad, you never have been. Lloyd is my dad now and he's all I need.'

She'd watched then as her father's face had crumpled. He'd held up his hands and walked away. Even Bernice had been shocked.

He'd left her a present, a delicately made gold watch, but Meredith didn't wear gold and she'd tossed it aside before going back to her friends and too many vodka and lemonades.

Meredith had never seen her father again, and the gold on the watch had started to flake away within a month. There was a metaphor in that, she'd always thought. But at the same time, she'd always wondered about that night. If she'd welcomed him instead of being horrible to him, if she'd drawn him into the party, introduced him to her friends, would he have stayed longer? Would he have stayed in touch? Should she have given him a second or third chance?

'It's mostly just been me and Mum,' Meredith said to Zach now. 'And then my stepdad Lloyd who's always been like a dad to me. But they live in Spain these days so mostly there's just me.' She smiled her best smile as though that was exactly how she planned her life. There was no need to mention Joe. She didn't want Zach Johnson to pity her. God forbid.

'I can tell you about Clara if you like,' Zach said. 'I might not be able to answer all the questions you must have, but I can try. We talked a lot in the few months I knew her. She used to insist I join her each morning for a cup of tea at the table on the patio over there.' He pointed in the direction of the house. 'Even on the coldest of mornings.'

'I'd love to know more about her,' Meredith said. She did want to know about Clara and she certainly wanted to know where Zach fitted into this whole puzzle. 'But I really need to sort things out in the house and get some food in. I haven't eaten since breakfast. Where's the best place to go?'

Zach pulled a face. 'The nearest supermarket is five miles away.'

'Is there not a shop in the village?' She'd imagined

herself going from shop to shop, basket in hand, buying fresh eggs and fruit and vegetables. She didn't own a basket, but still.

'Closed about half an hour ago,' he said.

'I'd best go to the supermarket then.'

'Look, I've got some bits I can let you have for breakfast – teabags, milk, bread and so on – and this evening why don't we go to the pub for dinner? I can tell you about Clara and introduce you to some people who knew her.' He smiled a half smile which, in anyone else and in any other situation, Meredith would have found very attractive.

'OK,' she said. She didn't know if she felt like meeting people right now and she wished suddenly, childishly, that her mum was here. 'I'll go and unpack and have a shower and meet you back here...' She hesitated with her next question. 'Why do you live here in the caravan and not in the house?'

'I guess it's what I'm used to,' he said. 'I lived here when I was working for Miss Samuels and then, afterwards...' His words hitched for a moment and Meredith remembered that Clara Samuels wasn't just some shadowy figure to Zach, she was someone he'd known and clearly liked. 'Well, afterwards I just carried on living here. I thought I'd wait and see what happened, and now you're here I'm happy to keep to my van.'

'OK.'

'How long were you thinking of staying?'

It was Meredith's turn to hesitate. 'Honestly, I'm not sure,' she said. 'I do need to go back to London next week and my mum wants to come over to see the cottage.'

'You can stay as long as you need, you know,' Zach smiled. 'It's your house.'

'Our house,' Meredith said, more pleasantly than she felt. 'Oh, and speaking of our house, I should have told you. I've got an estate agent coming over to-morrow to do a valuation and... Well, unless you've already got that under control?'

Zach looked away as though he was embarrassed. 'Meredith,' he said quietly. 'I'm not ready to sell yet.'

As Meredith walked back towards the house she thought how typical it was of her recent luck that she was stuck between one man who wanted her to pay him money and another who didn't want to sell her only source of money.

6

SUFFOLK, APRIL 1963

'Esther is so pleased, you know,' Richard said as he drove Clara into Ipswich that afternoon to catch her train back to London. There were no branch line trains on Sundays from Carybrook. Soon there would be no branch line trains at all. That made Clara sad and, like Esther, she may well have to ask Richard to teach her to drive.

'Why is she so pleased?' Clara asked. 'I mean, don't get me wrong, it's obviously a good thing to be near family but Esther and I, we...' She hesitated. 'We were never that close,' she finished diplomatically.

'I think she wants to make amends in a more permanent sort of way,' Richard said, keeping his eyes straight ahead on the road, his hands in their brown leather driving gloves sitting in the perfect ten and two position on the wheel. 'Make up for your childhoods. She wasn't very happy then either, you know. Despite what you might think, she never felt close to your parents either.'

It was the most Clara had ever heard Richard say that didn't involve ranting about the Labour Party or talking about golf.

'She got me that interview this morning,' Clara said. 'Well, she got me the job, to be fair. It was mine before I got to the school.'

Richard smiled beneath his moustache. 'I hope you don't feel too pushed into this?' he said.

'Maybe a little.'

'You know what Esther is like. As soon as she gauged your interest in the cottage, she had you moved in and working at the school, I'm afraid. She thought it was what you wanted. We both did.'

'It *is* what I want,' Clara clarified, remembering the happiness on her sister's face when she'd told her that Miss Cheggers had offered her the job, to start whenever the London school could let her go.

'Nothing to worry about, then. Her next goal will be to get you married!'

'I hope you're joking!' Clara exclaimed.

'Of course, of course,' Richard replied, although

Clara could imagine her sister lining up the eligible bachelors already, if there were any left in the Carybrook area who wanted to marry a thirty-three-year-old schoolteacher. 'Would it be such a bad thing though, old girl? Getting hitched?'

Clara looked at the Suffolk countryside as it passed by the car window. 'It's not bad,' she said. 'It's just not for me.' And then she closed her eyes to blink back tears that seemed to have come from nowhere as she thought, inexplicably, of James again. It was inevitable perhaps that returning to Carybrook would bring back memories, but she hadn't seen James since she was nine years old and hadn't heard from him since 1948. She didn't know anything about him any more – she didn't know what he did or where he lived or whether he was even still alive. She wondered again how they had lost touch so easily after nine years of almost obsessive letter writing.

She shook her head to try and push the memories away. She would have to get used to these flashes of nostalgia if she were to move back to Carybrook. Her being single had nothing whatsoever to do with James Mackenzie and everything to do with the fact she had put her studies and her career before anything else. Her tutor at Girton had warned her about the difficult choices that lay ahead of her. She had made those choices. She was happy with them.

Most of the time, anyway.

'Never say never, old girl,' Richard chuckled, taking one hand away from the steering wheel to pat her thigh in that way that he probably thought was affectionate but that always made Clara feel uncomfortable. She shifted slightly, away from him.

They were early for the train when they arrived at Ipswich and Richard turned off the car engine and cleared his throat as though he had an announcement to make.

'Now please don't take this as interfering,' he began. 'But have you actually put in an offer for the cottage?'

Clara nodded. 'I hinted to Mr Molliner that I was interested yesterday after we'd looked around.'

'I hope you didn't seem too eager,' Richard said.

'But I *am* eager.' Clara paused and looked at Richard, wondering how candid she could be, but he was already two steps ahead of her.

'I get the feeling,' he said, 'that if you didn't get the cottage you would change your plans and stay in London.'

Clara bit her bottom lip and thought of Carybrook

School and the boarding house in London. She started to make a list of pros and cons in her head.

'Not necessarily,' she said. 'I do feel ready to leave London but where else would I live if I didn't get the cottage?'

'Well, you could stay with us, of course, Esther would love that. They are building some lovely little bungalows on the edge of the village so you could apply for one of them, or...' Richard trailed off; he must have seen the look on Clara's face. She never had been very good at hiding her feelings.

A new bungalow on the edge of the village was not what she had in mind.

But then beggars, as her mother had often told her, could not be choosers.

'It's a possibility,' she said, conjuring up enthusiasm from somewhere.

'But you want the cottage.' It wasn't a question but Clara answered with a decisive nod anyway.

'Then let me speak to Molliner. I told you I play golf with him. I'll make sure he accepts your offer. I'll make sure he doesn't show anyone else the cottage.' Richard paused. 'I don't want to interfere like my wife but...' He held up his hands.

'You could do that?'

'I do the taxes for Molliner Estates,' Richard

replied cryptically. 'Trust me when I tell you that he'd listen to me.'

'I... Well... I...' Clara stuttered. She didn't know what to say. When she'd left Mr Molliner and Butterfly Cottage the day before, it had been quite clear that he hadn't been taking her interest seriously. 'Mr Molliner didn't seem keen on me buying the cottage,' she managed. 'I had the feeling he didn't approve of single women buying houses, or owning property.' She thought of her landlady back in London who owned the boarding house outright. Clara wondered if she had come up against this prejudice too, if that was what made her so sour-faced and always ready for a fight.

'Ernest Molliner is a bit of a chauvinist,' Richard said in such a way that implied he, Richard Bradshaw, was an enlightened and modern man, despite the leg patting. 'He has a lot of old-fashioned ideas that he's dragged out of the dark ages, but money speaks to him more than anything. So you leave him to me. You can afford the asking price?'

'I told you yesterday,' Clara said.

Richard nodded. 'And can you go higher than that? How high can you go without needing to borrow money?'

Clara told him the figure, the maximum she could

spend that left her enough over to decorate and make the cottage her own. She had no intention of borrowing money, of being indebted to anyone, especially Richard. She watched his eyes widen a little – although he must know that she was left the same amount as Esther had been.

'Oh, even Molliner will sell for less than that,' he said. 'Now let me help you with your suitcase.'

* * *

The next day, when Clara got home from work, her landlady was waiting for her in the communal sitting room. Her face was as sour as ever, as though she had been chewing on a bee.

'Miss Samuels,' the landlady's voice echoed across the room.

'Hello, Mrs Benyon,' Clara said. There had always been a lot of speculation and rumour about what had happened to Mr Benyon. Nobody in the neighbourhood ever remembered him existing which led Clara to believe that her landlady used the 'Mrs' prefix to make life a little easier. As she had discovered with Mr Molliner the day before, unmarried women were still looked down upon.

'I've a message for you,' Mrs Benyon said. 'From your sister.'

Mrs Benyon stopped talking but Clara wasn't quite sure what to say to fill the silence.

'I'm not a messenger pigeon, Miss Samuels,' the landlady said eventually. 'I'm not here to carry messages hither and yon and nor am I here to be answering a perpetually ringing telephone.'

What are *you here for, then?* Clara wondered to herself. Other than collecting the rent Mrs Benyon didn't seem to do very much at all. Clara looked pointedly at the thick layer of dust on the shelves above the fireplace. When she looked back the landlady was staring angrily at her.

'I'm very sorry to have inconvenienced you,' Clara said. It was easier to apologise for something that was in no way her fault than it was to have the wrath of Mrs Benyon brought down upon her. 'Could I trouble you for the message?'

Mrs Benyon sniffed. 'Your sister,' she said. Clara's stomach leapt; it would be news about the cottage. 'Says could you telephone her back.'

'Oh,' Clara said, looking towards the hall where the telephone was chained to the wall, as if anyone would make off with it. 'I'll go and...'

'She mentioned a cottage,' Mrs Benyon went on

and Clara looked back at the landlady. 'A cottage you're buying, apparently.'

A cottage I'm buying, Clara thought to herself. Did this mean Richard had woven his magic with Mr Molliner and her offer had been accepted? She was itching to get to the telephone.

'Well, I'd better...' she began.

'How does a teacher have the money to buy a cottage?' Mrs Benyon asked, crossing her arms across her formidable bosom as Clara's heart leapt with possibility once again. 'They must be paying teachers far too much if they can go around buying cottages if you ask me.'

'Well, I'd...' Clara tried to interrupt what she knew was about to become a tirade, but there was no escaping it once it had begun.

'Seems funny to me that you can suddenly afford a cottage. Why would you be living here if you had all that money?' the landlady asked, peering at Clara through her pebble glasses.

Clara found herself opening her mouth to explain that the money was an inheritance from her parents, that it had been sitting in a bank account for over a decade, but then she closed her mouth again and smiled her most benign smile. It was none of Mrs Benyon's business where her money came from; let her think Clara was turning tricks on a street corner in her spare time if she wanted.

Realising she wasn't going to get an answer, the landlady shook her head. 'A bloody funny business if you ask me,' she said. 'And I suppose this means you'll be leaving us?'

'Yes, Mrs Benyon,' Clara replied. 'I suppose it does.'

7

SUFFOLK, JUNE 2018

The pub was called The Queen's Head. It had a faded sign featuring the head of a very elderly-looking Queen Victoria above the door that swung gently in the breeze and it stood in the very middle of the village, right by the village green.

The hub of everything, Meredith thought. If she was going to find out about her mysterious great-aunt, this was surely a good starting point.

She leaned against the bar and looked around her. The outside of the pub betrayed the modern, airy rooms inside with white walls and a wood floor filled with long pine tables.

'Apparently, there was an outcry when it was first refurbished,' Zach had said as they'd walked in.

'That's why the outside has been left looking a bit shabby, for old times' sake or something. But as it still served all the same real ales it wasn't long before everyone came back anyway.'

It was hot and sticky in the pub tonight and Meredith longed to sit in the pretty garden that she could see through the back windows, but Zach seemed to know everyone and was embroiled in a series of greetings with a group of older men playing dominoes.

'They're in a league,' he told her as he turned back towards her. 'Tonight is their practice night and they take it very seriously so I won't introduce you.'

Meredith looked over at the group, their tiles clicking on the table in front of them. 'Do you think any of them would have known my great-aunt?'

'Most of the village knew who she was, but she never came to the pub. She never really left the cottage in the last few months she was back.'

'I meant...' She hesitated. 'Did they know her back in the 1960s when she lived here?'

Zach looked over at the men. 'Some of them will be the right age,' he said. 'But I honestly don't know. I've never really talked to anyone about Clara.'

'You haven't?'

He shook his head. 'She wanted to keep herself to

herself so I've respected that. But it's different for you; Miss Samuels was your family.'

Meredith didn't really know how to respond to this. It still felt odd that she had had this relative she had never known.

'The usual, Zach?' A tall man in his early sixties stood behind the bar with an empty pint glass in his hand.

'Thanks, Alf,' Zach replied. 'What would you like, Meredith?'

'Umm... Just a sparkling mineral water, please.'

'Ice and lemon in that?' the man whom Zach had called Alf asked.

'Please,' Meredith replied.

'This is Alf Turner,' Zach said. 'He's the landlord here.'

'The one that did the controversial refurb?' Meredith asked in a voice she hoped sounded friendly and light-hearted. She felt anxious and awkward tonight and had chosen mineral water over her usual dry white wine because she wanted to stay in complete control of her faculties. She felt that one false move, one inappropriate comment or question could ostracise her from the whole village and she was still hoping that Carybrook and Butterfly Cottage were the answer to all her problems, even though Zach claimed he didn't want to sell the cottage yet. There was hope in that word 'yet', wasn't there?

When he'd first told her that she'd been surprised as she'd presumed, clearly incorrectly, that he too would rather have the money. Half the value of the house was surely better than living in a caravan. Instead of saying anything to him then she'd smiled and told him she'd better go and get ready for dinner. She'd taken the teabags and milk and bread from him and walked back to the house, *their* house. By the time she'd showered and changed it felt as though too much time had passed to ask Zach why he didn't want to sell, why he wasn't ready. So instead they'd walked to the pub in awkward silence.

She had to ask him though, because she needed this to work out. She was running out of other options. She had wondered, briefly, when she'd been on the phone to her mother earlier, if Zach would be able to buy her out, but his 'I'm not ready to sell yet' had put paid to that.

'I am indeed responsible for the controversial refurbishment,' Alf replied with a smile. His accent was east London so he certainly wasn't a local and Meredith felt disappointed at that. She'd thought that the pub landlord would know everything and everyone, including the secrets of Clara Samuels.

She was going to need to ask a lot of people a lot of things if she wanted to find out what was going on.

'And you must be Meredith Carling,' Alf went on as he placed her mineral water on a cardboard coaster in front of her. He held out his hand and Meredith took it, feeling her fingers slightly crushed in his bear-like grip.

'How did you know...?' she began.

'Oh, we've been waiting for you,' Alf said with a wink.

Meredith swallowed the round ball of anxiety that had lodged in her throat and picked up her glass of mineral water just so she had something to do with her hands. She wished she'd ordered wine now. What did Alf mean, they'd been waiting for her?

'There's no need to scare her, Alf,' Zach said with a smile, turning back to her again. 'I'd told him about Miss Samuels's will, about how I would be sharing the house with her great-niece and... well... I know it sounds a bit creepy but we've all been intrigued by you. Who you are and where you come from. So I guess we've all just been waiting for you to come to the cottage.'

'And now here you are,' Alf said as he polished a pint glass. Luckily at that moment one of the dominoes players required a refill and Alf wandered off to the other end of the bar.

'How many people know?' Meredith asked quietly before taking a sip of her mineral water.

'Half the village, I should think. The owner of an abandoned house comes back after mysteriously disappearing decades before and leaves the house to her gardener and a great-niece. The whole situation has been pretty intriguing for them you've got to admit.'

Meredith looked up and saw the dominoes team staring at her and then back at Alf. The whole pub would know who she was long before closing time.

'Look,' Zach said. 'Why don't we pick something to eat and go sit outside? It's quieter out there and we can talk.'

Meredith looked at the menu that Zach handed to her and was surprised by it; lots of choices, even for vegetarians.

'I'll have the curry,' she said. 'And a glass of white wine.'

* * *

The pub garden was peaceful and warm and a gentle breeze cooled Meredith as she sat at the table opposite Zach. She took a sip of her wine. It was ice cold –

just as she liked it. There was nothing worse than warm white wine.

'So, tell me about yourself,' Zach said.

She looked at him for a moment. She hadn't been expecting him to ask that. She'd thought he'd go straight into talking about the cottage, about Clara.

He shrugged. 'Look, seeing as how we've inherited a house together, I figured getting to know each other was a good way to start. I can go first if you prefer.'

'I'm a hairdresser,' she began. It was the only thing she could think to say about herself.

'Useful,' he replied, running a hand through his shaggy hair. 'I could do with a cut.'

Meredith smiled. 'Always happy to have new clients,' she said.

'And you work in London?'

'I have a salon in Clapham.'

'And that's why you want to sell the cottage,' Zach said. 'Because you run a successful business in London and don't see yourself moving to a sleepy village like Carybrook any time soon?'

'Something like that.' She tried to smile like somebody who *did* run a successful business but recently she'd forgotten what that felt like.

Success slipped away much more easily than it could be caught so far as she could tell.

This would, of course, have been a perfect opportunity for her to ask why it was that he didn't want to sell but she didn't and then their meals arrived and the moment was gone again.

'One curry, one fish and chips,' the waitress announced as she put the plates in front of them. 'Do you want any sauces?' She looked at Meredith questioningly as though she already knew who she was.

'Ketchup, please,' Zach said.

After the condiments arrived Meredith found herself asking Zach how he'd become a gardener rather than why he didn't want to sell the cottage. Perhaps he was right. Perhaps getting to know each other a little better would help.

He told her about how his father had been a gardener. 'An odd-job man, really,' he said. 'No formal training or anything but he just had a knack for gardens, for flowers in particular. Mum died when I was very young so it was just the two of us, and I went to work with him a lot in the school holidays. When I was a kid I thought he was a magician the way he could make gardens grow. But he showed me that it wasn't magic, that it was something you could learn, so I went on to study horticulture after school and learned everything I could.'

'Where did you grow up?'

'All over,' Zach replied. 'Dad moved around a lot, but he always got work, wherever we were.'

'How did you end up in Carybrook?' Meredith asked. 'How did you end up working for my great-aunt?'

'I actually got lost on my way to the coast one day,' Zach said, turning back to his food. 'There's a caravan site just outside the village and I parked up there for a night or two and... Well, I guess I never left.'

Meredith stirred her fork through her curry, mixing the rice with the sauce. It was delicious, much better than she'd been expecting from a village pub, and had clearly been made from scratch.

'I arrived here last August, just as Miss Samuels was looking for a gardener,' Zach went on. 'She told me she'd been away for a while, that the garden needed a tidy up and could I help. I needed all the work I could get and so I said yes, but I hadn't quite bargained on how much tidying up Butterfly Cottage would need.'

'How long had she been away at that point?' Meredith asked.

'She told me she had been in Australia for over fifty years, but she never told me why she left.'

'Did she say where in Australia?' Meredith wondered if Australia was where her dad ended up too.

Not that even that explained why he hadn't been in touch.

'Hobart, in Tasmania.'

Meredith tried very hard not to let it show in her face that she wasn't really sure where Tasmania was other than one of those places they sent characters from Australian soap operas to when it was their time to leave.

'It's the little island at the bottom of Australia,' Zach said with a smile. 'I had to look it up.'

'Did she say what she'd been doing out there?' Meredith asked, moving on from her terrible geography. She bet Zach had known where Tasmania was and had just told her he needed to look it up to make her feel better.

'She'd been a schoolteacher but she didn't say where. She didn't tell me very much about herself at all, I'm afraid.'

'And she never mentioned my dad, Dennis.'

'I'm sorry, no.'

Meredith sighed. 'It's not much to go on, is it? Do you know why she came back?'

Zach's eyes flicked away for a moment. 'She'd been diagnosed with stomach cancer,' he said and Meredith could hear the sadness in his voice. 'It was slow-moving but untreatable. She just said she wanted to come home one last time, put her affairs in order.'

'Do you think she managed that?'

'Well, she clearly changed her will, didn't she?' Zach said with a smile.

'I guess so, but I still can't work out how she knew about me unless she'd heard it from my dad. Which means he could be in Australia.' Meredith voiced her earlier thoughts. She had always wanted to say sorry for what she had said to him all those years ago. Would she be able to find him now?

'When did Clara die?' she asked.

'In March, about eight or nine months after she arrived back in England. She didn't have quite as long as she'd thought.'

'Did she stay in the house the whole time?' Meredith wanted to know if her great-aunt had died in Butterfly Cottage but was trying to be tactful.

'Until the last couple of weeks. She died in hospital.'

'Did you visit her there?'

Zach nodded.

'Did anyone else visit her?'

She wanted to know if Dennis had ever been.

'I honestly don't know. We only talked about the garden. She wanted to talk about the things she was going to do in the garden when she got out of hospital – even though we both knew she wouldn't get out of hospital. But she loved that garden so much.' He looked so sad, as though he regretted more than just not finishing a job and that was when Meredith realised.

'That's why you don't want to sell, isn't it?' she asked.

Zach finished the last mouthful of his fish and chips and put his knife and fork carefully together.

'It's not that I don't ever want to sell the house,' he said. 'I know we'll need to do it eventually. I can't just own a house with a stranger and hope for the best. I just don't want to sell it yet. I hope you can understand. I want to finish the garden, make it exactly as Miss Samuels wanted it to be.'

Meredith had noticed the way that he still called her great-aunt 'Miss Samuels' as though she remained his employer, but it sounded as though they had become friends over the months he had worked for her. And she noticed the reverential way he talked about the garden, as though finishing it would help him with whatever other regrets he was holding on to.

I hope you can understand.

She found, surprisingly, that she could. Her own life was full of mistakes and miscommunications, regrets and stupid errors of judgement that had led her to be in the position she was in now. The salon was struggling because of her and none of it was Zach's fault. Things had changed since she first learned about the cottage and Mr Maddison should have told her about Zach when he first told her about her inheritance. But she would deal with him tomorrow. For now, she knew that if she had a chance to do something that would calm some of the doubts and regrets in her mind she would want to do it. Therefore she could let Zach finish the garden.

She looked up at him, at his dark hair and eyes, the way his smile wasn't quite straight. It might even be fun to help him.

'I understand that,' she said. 'Would you like me to cancel the estate agent?'

Zach shook his head. 'No, it'll be good to get some figures, see what we're looking at. Besides, Mr Maddison will need a valuation, won't he?'

She nodded and then thought of something else.

'Was there a funeral?' she asked. 'I know I'm bombarding you with questions and I'm really sorry, but I was just wondering...'

'There was a funeral,' Zach replied. 'At the crematorium in Ickbury. She asked for there to be no fuss or flowers. It was what she wanted, but it was still so sad that there was hardly anybody there.'

'But you went?'

Zach looked down at his hands. 'I went,' he confirmed, 'and Alf came with me.'

'Alf the landlord?'

'Yes. There were four or five other people but I didn't recognise them. Miss Samuels didn't have any family…' He trailed off, looking up. 'Well, other than you. I did wonder if you'd be at the funeral but there was nobody the right age. Of course, there's your father too but I didn't know about him at the time.'

Meredith wondered if one of those people at the funeral had been her father, but she didn't push Zach any more. He was clearly still finding it hard to talk about Clara's death and she'd probably asked enough questions about that. Besides, what good would it do? Even if one of those people was her father, it didn't bring her any nearer to finding out where he was now. So instead she asked about the team of old men in the pub.

'The dominoes team?'

'Yes. You don't think any of them knew Clara?'

'Before she moved to Australia, you mean?'

Meredith nodded, finishing up her food.

'We could ask them. Although...' He stopped as though he was thinking about something.

'Although what?' Meredith asked impatiently. She wanted answers and in her usual way, she wanted them now. 'Sorry,' she said. 'I didn't mean to snap.' She had to learn to wait for things. If she hadn't been in such a hurry to kit out the salon with all the latest, most up-to-date accessories, if she'd waited to save the money herself rather than letting Joe put his money into it, she might not be in the mess she was in.

'It's OK,' Zach replied. 'I was just thinking about the dominoes team, and most of the older people in Carybrook for that matter. Alf will be able to be more precise than me but, thinking about it, I'd say most of them would have moved here after Miss Samuels left. The village expanded a lot in the late 1960s, apparently. Lots of houses and bungalows were built towards the west of the village on the road out to Ickbury. They built the bypass out to Ipswich at the same time so Carybrook became quite a desirable place to live. You might have seen them on your drive in?'

'If I did, I'm afraid I didn't really notice,' Meredith said.

'Well, the point is that lots of the people who live in the village today moved here to live in the new houses, so everyone in their seventies and eighties who you might think were contemporaries of your great-aunt probably only moved here after she left.'

'Clara wasn't here for very long in the 1960s then?'

Zach shook his head. 'She bought Butterfly Cottage in the spring of 1963, that much our Mr Maddison told me because it's on the title deeds. I'm not exactly sure when she left but she told me she'd been gone for over fifty years so she can't have lived at Butterfly Cottage for very long, can she?'

'And she didn't talk about why she went?'

'She really didn't talk about anything to do with that time very much and I was just pleased that she let me park my caravan at the back of the garden and that she gave me so much work.'

'The garden must have been so overgrown after all those years.'

'It's been a lot of work, admittedly, but there were people in the village who popped into the garden to keep it tidy over the years. They all call it the Butterfly Garden.'

'The Butterfly Garden,' Meredith repeated. 'That sounds so lovely.'

Zach smiled. 'It does, doesn't it? And they are good folk who live in Carybrook. They gossip of course – you'll find that out as most of them have been waiting for you to arrive – but they always help each other out.'

Meredith tried to ignore the remark about everyone waiting for her. She expected everyone thought she would know more about the mysterious Clara Samuels who disappeared from Carybrook sometime in the sixties. 'The house must have been a bit of a state as well when Clara came back.'

'She'd had some things done to the house before I started working for her. I think she might have booked electricians and so on before she even left Australia. According to Mr Maddison, the house has been rewired and the plumbing sorted out. By the time I rolled up in the caravan, she was having things replastered and decorated.'

Meredith leaned her elbows on the table either side of her empty curry bowl. 'I wonder why my grandmother never mentioned she had a sister?'

'That is a bit odd,' Zach replied. 'So that would have been your dad's mother?'

'She died around the time my dad disappeared, actually. I wonder if those two events are connected. I'd never really thought about it before. I didn't know her very well and we didn't see her very often. She lived in Stevenage and she was very angry and bitter. I always felt as though she hated me but I've no idea why. I never met my grandfather, he died before I was born.'

'Miss Samuels never mentioned she had a sister, but I suppose if she had a great-niece that implies other family, even if she didn't talk about them.'

What had happened to Clara Samuels all those years ago? What had made her go to Australia? And why had nobody mentioned her since?

Alf came out to clear the plates.

'Everything all right?' he asked.

'Delicious,' Meredith replied.

'Now, you two,' he said, balancing the plates on his arm. 'I've thought of something. You want to know what happened to Clara Samuels and what brought her back to Carybrook, right?'

'Right,' Zach said.

'I never even knew I had a great-aunt until a couple of weeks ago,' Meredith explained. 'Nobody in my family has ever spoken about her, at least not to me. So yes, I am interested in anything anyone might know.'

'There's a lady my brother knows,' Alf went on. 'She lives in a bungalow on the road out to Ickbury. He delivers groceries to her.'

Meredith nodded eagerly. She wanted to meet anyone who knew anything.

'She used to teach at Carybrook school before it was closed down and I believe that's where your great-aunt used to teach, isn't it?'

Meredith had no idea but Zach seemed to.

'Yes,' he said. 'She told me she'd taught there briefly after she bought the cottage.'

'Well, pop in tomorrow when I'm not so busy and I'll give you her phone number. She's called Miss Cheggers.'

Later, as they walked back through the pub to leave, one of the dominoes men looked up at them.

'So you're the great-niece, then,' he said.

Meredith smiled, trying to put aside that disconcerting feeling of everybody waiting for her to arrive. 'That's me,' she said. 'Meredith Carling.'

The man carried on staring at her and nodded his head. 'Funny goings-on in that cottage over the years,' he said eventually.

'Like what?'

'Well, that's not my place to say,' the man said, clicking his dominoes together and going back to his game.

8

SUFFOLK, JUNE 1963

Clara flung open the French doors, allowing the sunlight to stream into the kitchen of Butterfly Cottage. She stood on the threshold of the house, half in and half out, breathing in the early morning air. It was a beautiful day, the sun already warm and with no hint of a breeze. 'Settled', as her mother would have said.

It was funny the things that Clara remembered about her parents. She had never been close to either her mother or father, and she'd certainly never felt as though she fitted into the family she grew up in, but every now and then snippets of memories would come to her as if from nowhere, leaving her feeling a little lost, a little nostalgic.

Every morning her mother would step out into the garden first thing and sniff the air before giving her one-word weather forecast for the day. 'Settled', she would say on a warm, still, sunny day like this, 'wet' for rain, 'blowy' for windy, 'unsettled' for wet *and* windy.

The day itself might be settled but Clara felt decidedly unsettled and she wasn't sure why.

Everything over the last few weeks had gone remarkably smoothly, despite Richard's constant puffing and blowing and warnings about delays and surveys and 'the bloody Land Registry'. The diocese that had owned Butterfly Cottage had accepted Clara's very generous offer via Mr Molliner (who had also spent a lot of time puffing and blowing about single women and the state of the nation, but who ultimately wanted to earn his very healthy commission), and Clara had handed in her notice at the school in Chelsea.

'I do need to leave as quickly as possible,' she'd said, remembering the promises she had made to Miss Cheggers about being able to start before the summer term ended.

Clara's London headmistress, Miss Higgs, had been reluctant to see her go. 'But I've been lucky to keep you for so long,' she'd said. 'So many of my best teachers leave too soon to marry and start a family.'

'Maybe one day,' Clara had said, 'there will be a way for women to forge a career *and* have children.'

Miss Higgs raised a sceptical eyebrow. 'Miracles may happen,' she'd said. 'But be careful what you wish for because if anyone is taken advantage of in that situation it will be the woman.' She'd paused then and looked at Clara over her reading glasses. 'I presume that's why you are moving away?' she'd asked. 'To marry.'

'Oh goodness, no!' Clara had replied, barely able to stop herself from laughing at the thought. She had never been able to imagine herself married. 'No, I'm just moving back to the village I grew up in, to live nearer to my sister. I have a job teaching in the village school.'

Miss Higgs had smiled. 'Well, good for you,' she'd said. It was no secret that Miss Higgs wholly disapproved of marriage almost as much as she disapproved of men. 'I'll write you a glowing reference if you don't mind waiting.'

Clara hadn't minded waiting and the reference had, indeed, been glowing. She had posted it immediately to Miss Cheggers at Carybrook School and had returned to her boarding house to start to pack up her things.

Richard had phoned regularly with updates on

the conveyancing process and Esther had called almost as often asking about sheets and towels, cutlery and crockery, all of which she, Esther, had in abundance and could pack up ready to move into the house with Clara on completion day. The regular phone calls sent Mrs Benyon into paroxysms of horror and endless muttering about messenger pigeons. Clara couldn't wait to see the back of her.

The sheets and towels, Clara had thought sadly, would take up more room than her own things which amounted to two large suitcases and a box of books. The rooms at the boarding house were small and she had never had much space for anything, really. Even her books, her most treasured possessions, had to be kept to a minimum. She was grateful for her sister's towels and forks, plates and sheets. It would be something to fill the cottage with. The cottage which, in comparison to the room she had lived in for the last decade, felt like a palace.

On the first Friday in June, Butterfly Cottage had become hers and a phone call from Mr Molliner himself – rather than a message via her brother-in-law – had confirmed everything. She had made sure to be at the boarding house all day so that Mrs Benyon didn't take the call and had ended up taking over ten messages for the other girls. She had started to see the landlady's point. But she was too happy to care and had bought some cheap fizzy wine to share with everybody when they returned from their respective jobs.

That evening, as the other women in the house had gone about their Friday night – dates and dinners, cinema trips and gossiping in cafes on the King's Road – and as Mrs Benyon had watched the television very loudly, Clara had packed up her last few belongings, got herself ready for bed and laid down under the scratchy boarding house sheets. As she'd drifted off to sleep she had been thinking of the sheets that Esther would give her, cotton-soft and a high thread count.

The next morning Richard had arrived in the Rover, put her meagre belongings in the boot and waited while Clara said goodbye in a flurry of tears and embraces and calls of 'we'll keep in touch' that nobody believed were true. Richard had grumbled about London traffic until they were way past the outer boundaries and then, before she had known it, they had arrived outside Butterfly Cottage to be greeted by Esther who had already made up the beds, filled the cupboards and had the kettle on. Clara had felt a warm fondness for her sister and a sense of homecoming that she had never felt before.

The feeling of warmness had lasted through Sunday lunch at Esther and Richard's, even though Richard had been very vocal about the recent goings-on of the government.

'Bloody disgrace,' he'd said, waving *The Sunday Times* in the air. 'John Profumo lying to the House about his affair with that Keeler girl. He should have owned up two years ago. This'll send Macmillan over the edge, you mark my words.'

Two years previously John Profumo, the Secretary of State for War in the Conservative government, had been rumoured to be having an affair with a young woman named Christine Keeler who was described variously, depending on the paper, as a call girl, a party girl, you name it. Clara suspected she was just a young woman looking for something more in her life. They'd met at a party organised by an osteopath called Stephen Ward. Clara wasn't at all sure she knew what an osteopath was but John Profumo had denied it all in the House of Commons in 1961. Now it seemed that he'd been lying. No surprise there, Clara thought.

'Richard, can we not talk about sex scandals at Sunday lunch please,' Esther had said as Clara had tried to hide her smile.

The problem with this particular sex scandal was that it seemed Keeler had also been having an affair with a Captain Ivanov who had something to do with the Soviet Embassy and may have been passing on state secrets which seemed, Clara thought, highly un- likely. It was typical that everyone blamed the woman rather than these powerful men who should know better. Clara was rather tired of the whole thing but suspected that the salacious stories had only just begun.

'Macmillan's done you see, old girl,' Richard had gone on, turning to his sister-in-law. 'Old and tired, been at this politics lark too long. But now...' He'd shaken his head and folded his paper up before tucking his serviette into the collar of his shirt. 'Well, the truth is now this just paves the way for that bloody KGB spy to become prime minister.'

'Harold Wilson, you mean,' Clara had replied. 'I've always quite liked him. He'd be a breath of fresh air.'

Richard, a lifelong Conservative, had made a grumbling sound in his throat.

'That's enough now,' Esther had said sharply as she dished up the roast potatoes.

Even Richard's opinions on the Profumo scandal – which continued long after his wife had tried to stop him – hadn't subdued Clara's warm mood.

And yet now, on Monday morning, as she stood on the threshold of her new home, looking out into the garden she had loved so much as a child, she couldn't shake this unsettled feeling.

So much had happened in such a short space of time. Just three months ago Clara had been living happily – well, living at least – in the boarding house she had been in since she left teacher training college. She had thought very little about her future, other than perhaps her next promotion within the school she taught in and one day maybe, if she was very lucky and kept her nose clean, becoming head like Miss Higgs. She had thought very little about anything except taking each day as it came and trying not to think too much about how it was possible to feel so lonely in such a big city.

And then Butterfly Cottage had gone up for sale, and everything had changed. Of course, she was feeling unsettled now the initial euphoria of owning her own home had fizzed out a little. And of course, she was worried about settling in, about people's questions, about whether she would be accepted.

When she was anxious she always found planning a to-do list helped. The inside of the cottage was almost complete thanks to the renovations paid for by the diocese in their attempt to sell the house and her sister's homemaking skills, but the garden was another story.

The last time she had been in this garden was the day before war was announced in September 1939. She'd spent so much of that summer in the garden with James and wandering the village lanes, foraging for elderflowers and blackberries, much to her mother's disapproval. She had thought that happiness would never end. She'd been nine years old and hadn't really understood at the time how much a war that was being fought so far away, in countries she had never been to, could disrupt her life. But within weeks everything had changed. Reverend Mackenzie had been called to the East End of London where younger vicars were desperately needed and the whole family had moved out of Butterfly Cottage.

'I'll write to you,' James had said. 'As soon as we're settled.' And he had – short letters at first about the boys at his new school and talk of evacuation, longer ones as he grew older, describing the arrival of the Luftwaffe, the air raid sirens and the nights spent in underground shelters. And then in 1942 he'd written that devastating letter that Clara had kept all of these years, about his mother and how she had died in a building collapse when she'd been helping others to escape.

I've always tried not to think about the war, he'd written. *Dad has always said that the Germans are just boys and men like us but now I feel differently. If this war is still going on when I'm eighteen I'm signing up on my birthday and joining the fight.*

Luckily the war had ended when Clara and James were fifteen and they wrote about happier things – plans for the future, plans to meet again, to count butterflies once they were old enough to make their own decisions – until the letters stopped altogether.

But however many letters Clara received, nothing made up for how much she missed both James and the garden which she had only been able to see by pressing her nose to the back fence.

She took a step now into that same garden almost unable to believe that she was here, that this was hers. She knew she had to get ready for her first day at school, she knew she couldn't be late, but she had time for just one slow walk down to the bottom of the garden and back – the Butterfly Garden as she and James had always called it.

As she walked she remembered how it had looked under Mrs Mackenzie's green fingers. She could almost smell the buddleia and the lavender, almost hear the buzz of the bees and the flick of the butterflies. And she knew what it was she had to do.

She had to bring the garden back to its former

glory. But to achieve that she would need to draft in some help.

* * *

The first few weeks at Carybrook School flew by. Despite being so different to the Chelsea school she'd taught at her whole working life, Clara settled in quickly and within a few days felt as though she had been there much longer. Having been a child at Carybrook School certainly helped as the layout hadn't really changed at all, so she knew her way around immediately. Not that there was much school to map out as it was so much smaller than the school in London and Clara soon felt at home.

The school had six classes, catering for children from five years old until they went to the nearby secondary modern or the grammar school in Ipswich when they were eleven. Clara was in charge of Junior Two, which was for children aged eight and nine. There were just thirteen children in her class, compared to over twenty-five in her previous school, and Clara could feel some of the stresses of teaching slide off her shoulders. She knew they would eventually be replaced by new stresses, different stresses – small classes and a more rural area did not mean the children and their families did not struggle with some of the same problems they did in London – but for now, she was just pleased to be getting on with her class. It certainly helped when they found out that she too had been a pupil at Carybrook School and they asked for stories about what the school was like back in 'the olden days' as they called it. Clara tried very hard not to feel extremely old.

The staff room buzzed with conversation during break time, mostly about the Profumo scandal, although the teachers had rather different opinions on the whole matter than Richard.

'Macmillan will have to resign eventually,' one teacher had said, 'and you know what that means?'

There were no mentions of KGB spies in the replies.

It certainly seemed to be the story of the moment and the whole village had an opinion on it all.

Settling into the school felt quite easy but settling into village life was going to be a lot harder. Visiting Carybrook once or twice a year was one thing; living here was quite another. It was a village stuck in time just as Miss Cheggers had warned her back in April. Some people welcomed her back, mostly people who were close to Esther – friends from the Women's Institute and, in particular, Mrs Churchill, who ran the local shop. Others were polite but slightly distant, even some of those who remembered her from when she was a child, and kept conversations strictly to Clara's job as a teacher. But then there were the handful who were quite hostile, clearly believing as Mr Molliner did that single women should not be owning houses that a family could live in.

Clara did her best to ignore the hostility and focus on the more friendly people in the village and she tried her best to fit in – she bought a bicycle to help her get to school in good time in the mornings, she always tried to remember to smile, and she wore her more subdued clothes. The outfits that she had spent far too much money on at Mary Quant's shop Bazaar on the King's Road would have to stay in a drawer for now. They would be too much for sleepy little Carybrook.

Despite the difficult people and the general sense of being unsettled, at no point during that first week did Clara feel as though she had made the wrong decision. She didn't miss the busyness of the London streets or the dark cloud of pollution that hung over them. She didn't even really miss the companionship of the women she had shared a boarding house with, most of whom had been younger than her and had often made her feel older than her years as they chatted constantly about make-up and played *Please Please Me* over and over again on the communal record player until Mrs Benyon turned it off in a rage.

She certainly didn't miss Mrs Benyon or having to live by someone else's rules.

For the first time in her thirty-three years, she felt free. And that was worth a little bit of hostility and being the centre of gossip.

The place where Clara knew she would make friends was the school staff room, even though there were far fewer staff to chat with than in her previous school. So when she wasn't on playground duty or involved elsewhere she made an effort, in her breaks, to join in conversations, to offer opinions, to make light-hearted remarks. She had always got on with the other teachers before and Carybrook was no different, even if it was all on a smaller scale.

'Great fun on Saturday, Clara,' Betty Edwards, who was a few years younger than Clara and in charge of Junior One, said to her. 'The school fete, the highlight of the year. You've arrived just in time.'

It was the organisation of the end-of-term activities – the fete, sports day, prize giving – that Clara had been asked to help with by starting in June rather than September and Junior Two was in charge of the jumble sale at the fete, so she was already well in the know about Saturday.

'I can't believe we're still raising money to fix the church roof,' Clara replied. 'We were always raising money for it when I was at this school over twenty years ago. The roof must be made of Swiss cheese.'

Betty laughed. 'It's all we ever raise money for. I once suggested a local charity but no, nothing but the church roof.'

'My class are very excited about the jumble sale,' Clara said. 'They are taking it extremely seriously and being rather ruthless about what can and can't be sold. I've tried to explain what a jumble sale is, but they seem to think they are running a specialist shop.'

'Well,' Betty said with a grin, 'even more exciting than your jumble is Friday night. You know about Friday night?'

Clara nodded. She'd already been told about the monthly dance in Ickbury. It seemed to be the highlight of the social calendar for the young and unmarried people of the area and several people had already insisted that she come and had offered her a lift.

'I don't think I'll come to the dance, Betty,' Clara said.

Betty's face fell in disappointment. 'Oh, but you must,' she replied. 'I know you must be used to much more exciting social events in London what with the Beatles being there and everything...'

'Not everyone in London has met the Beatles,' Clara smiled. 'And besides, didn't they play a concert in Ipswich earlier in the year?'

'Yes,' Betty's face fell. 'Not that any of us could get tickets. We're all probably a bit old anyway. But even so, London must be more exciting than Carybrook, which is why the dance is so important. It's all we have and it's only once a month. We go into Ickbury to go to the cinema quite often, but the dance is the place to be seen, Clara.'

'I'd certainly come along for a cinema trip,' Clara said. 'But I'm really not sure about the dance. I'm a bit...' She paused, looking for the right word. 'Past it, I suppose. I must be at least five or six years older than you.'

'Oh, who cares about that,' Betty said, waving a hand dismissively. 'Miss Cheggers comes sometimes, nobody minds how old you are. It's just a bit of fun. John's driving—' she pointed towards Mr Cragg who taught Junior Four '—and there's definitely room in the car for you. Say you'll come along.'

How could Clara possibly refuse? Maybe her Mary Quant dresses wouldn't have to sit in the drawer forever after all.

9

SUFFOLK, JUNE 2018

The estate agent arrived at eight thirty the next morning and Meredith was up and ready. In fact, she'd been up and ready for hours, giving up on sleep almost entirely at five thirty as the early morning sun streamed through the flimsy curtains. It had always taken a long time for her to settle into a new bed and this one was particularly lumpy.

By the time she and Zach had come back from the pub the night before, Meredith had been exhausted and turned down Zach's offer of a nightcap in favour of sleep, but that sleep had been elusive and she'd lain awake wondering what the man in the pub had meant by 'funny goings-on' in the cottage. She'd asked Zach about it as they'd walked home, when it had become clear that the dominoes men could not be drawn to comment further.

'I'd ignore it completely if I were you,' Zach had said. 'I think he's just winding you up.'

'So you don't know what he meant?'

'I mean, I haven't seen any ghosts or things that go bump in the night the whole time I've lived there.' Zach had smiled. 'Although I can't comment on what might be going on inside the house! But honestly, a house being left empty for fifty years is probably more than enough to count as "funny goings-on" around here.'

She'd tried to put it out of her mind, to dismiss the comment as Zach clearly had, but talk of things going bump in the night hadn't helped her sleep either and she had to stop herself yawning as she opened the door.

'Gary Molliner,' the estate agent introduced himself, holding out his hand when Meredith answered the door of Butterfly Cottage. 'Molliner Estates.'

'Meredith Carling,' she replied, taking his hand. 'Come in,' she went on, holding the door for him as he wiped his feet on the mat.

Gary looked to be a few years older than Meredith, his dark hair greying at the temples and his paunch hanging over the waist of his suit trousers.

There was a sheen of sweat on his top lip and fore-head. The day was warm already.

'Would you like a drink?' Meredith asked.

'Cup of tea would be lovely,' he replied. 'Milk and two sugars.' His eyes darted around the hallway and stairwell and he leaned forward a bit to see into the living and kitchen areas.

'I must say, this place looks to be more mod-ernised than I thought it would be. I was expecting it to need a lot more work than this.'

'I think it probably does need some work still,' Meredith said. 'The kitchen especially, but I know my great-aunt had the place rewired and the plumbing updated.' Zach would know more – he'd mentioned plumbers and electricians. She'd have to go and wake him. He had been happy enough to have the place valued when they'd spoken the previous night but he hadn't said anything about being there when the es-tate agent arrived. In fairness, Meredith couldn't re-member if she'd told him when the appointment was.

Gary looked at her and narrowed his eyes as though he was going to ask her something, probably about her not knowing anything about the work that had been done on the cottage, but he must have thought better of it and headed towards the stairs.

'I'll get started in the bedrooms,' he said.

'And I'll make the tea.'

Meredith walked into the kitchen and put the kettle on, putting three of the teabags that Zach had given her into three of the mugs she had found in the cupboard. Whilst the water was boiling she went to find Zach to see if he wanted to meet the estate agent. She felt he would be able to answer more of Gary's inevitable questions than she could.

But when she got to the caravan it was empty. She knocked half-heartedly on the door, but it was obvious that Zach was nowhere to be seen and his bicycle was gone from where he'd locked it to the back of the caravan the day before. He must have gone out early. Meredith wondered where he was and if he was deliberately avoiding the estate agent.

She went back to the kitchen and poured hot water over two of the teabags. She was just adding milk when Gary came back downstairs.

'I must say, the house has been done up beautifully,' he said.

'It's rather lovely, isn't it. My great-aunt had good taste!'

'That wallpaper in the front room is from the 1960s, if I'm not mistaken. That must have been put up when Miss Samuels first bought the house.'

Meredith handed him his cup of tea. She had

barely looked in the front room yet. She really needed to get more of a grip on the house that she now owned half of.

'Shall we sit down?' she asked as she placed the mugs down on the table in the sunroom, by the French doors.

Gary sat with a large exhale and looked at his notes. 'There's a few things you could do to make the cottage even better,' he said. 'I've obviously only had a cursory look so I don't know if you need any structural work but I am a chartered surveyor so I can do that for you if you want me to.'

Meredith nodded, signalling him to carry on.

'A downstairs cloakroom would be a bonus,' he said, taking a swig of his tea. The delicate china mug looked tiny in his enormous hand. 'Just a loo and a handbasin – you could fit it under the stairs, I think. Then in the main bathroom upstairs, you'll need a proper shower over the bath, not just the handheld thing. There's probably room for an en suite up there too, coming off the back bedroom.'

'Do people really need all these bathrooms?' Meredith asked. She'd never lived anywhere with more than one bathroom – even the house that she had lived in after her mother married Lloyd.

'It's a big selling point,' Gary replied. 'This is a

family home and parents like their children to have their own bathroom these days.'

Meredith raised her eyebrows but made no comment about the privilege that some people took for granted.

'Well, I'm not sure I can afford any more improvements,' she said. 'I'm keen to sell, although...'

It was Gary's turn to raise an eyebrow.

'I don't know how much you know about this house,' Meredith began. 'But my great-aunt didn't just leave it to me. She left it in a fifty-fifty share with someone else.'

'Your partner, perhaps?' Gary asked rather unsubtly.

'No, her gardener.'

'How very Lady Chatterley,' Gary chuckled to himself. 'And where is this gardener now?'

'I have no idea. He lives in a caravan at the bottom of the garden and...'

'My God!' Gary almost exploded with mirth. 'Forget about the bloody bathrooms, this story alone will sell the cottage.'

Meredith smiled tightly. She'd been told that Molliner's Estates were the best local agents, but she was beginning to wish she'd called someone else to do the valuation.

'The thing is that we're not really looking to put the house on the market immediately. I know Zach – he's the other owner – wants to finish the garden properly and, like you say, it would help to have some further work done in the cottage. I was just looking for an approximate value really, so I know what I'm working with.'

'And the man in the caravan at the bottom of the garden doesn't come with the house, I presume.'

Meredith laughed politely but found herself thinking of Mr Maddison who hadn't told her about Zach and *still* hadn't returned her call. She wouldn't hear from him until Monday now, she supposed.

When she looked at Gary again he was writing something on his clipboard.

'You want a figure?' he said looking up at her. 'Well, here you go – this is the amount you could sell for if you put the cottage on the market as it is today.' He turned his clipboard around and Meredith swallowed as she read the number.

'That much?' she said. It wasn't London prices, obviously, but it wasn't far off.

'Beautiful cottage with a 100-foot garden in sunny Suffolk,' Gary replied with a smirk. 'At least that much.'

Meredith took a breath. It was more than she'd

imagined, a lot more. Even with owning half the house and having to pay taxes, she would have enough to pay Joe, to pay the outstanding salon bills and still have some left over to invest.

Which would be easier said than done.

'Well, I'll have to talk it over with Zach,' she said to Gary. 'I guess we'll be in touch.'

Gary's expression softened then. 'There's no rush to sell, but when you are ready I do hope you put it on the market with Molliner's. You see, our agency has a bit of history with this house.'

'It does?'

Gary put down his clipboard and finished his tea. 'Molliner's Estates was set up by my grandfather in 1951,' he said, crossing his hands over his stomach. 'It was the first estate agency in the area, around the time people started to move around the country more than they had done before and, of course, then the village started to expand and he made quite a lot of money out of that. But I've been waiting for this cottage to come on the market for years and my father before that. It never did of course, as you know, until now.'

'Your father was an estate agent too?'

'Yes, he took over from my grandfather and then, after university, I started to work there too. Dad is mostly retired these days – prefers the golf course to work – but that just means I get to run the show and now, hopefully, put Butterfly Cottage on the market.'

'Why have you been waiting, though?' Meredith asked. 'Other than the obvious reasons that the whole village must be curious about the cottage and what happened here.'

'My grandfather sold it to your great-aunt in the first place,' Gary replied. 'Back in the spring of 1963. Then she disappeared and Grandpa was always hoping it would come back on the market. It never did and then last year your great-aunt returned and I had a feeling that she was finally getting it ready to sell.'

Meredith nodded but was only half-listening. There were people in this village who had known her great-aunt, who might be able to help her find out what happened all those years ago. First this Miss Cheggers that Alf mentioned in the pub and now the estate agent's family.

'You could contest that, you know,' Gary said.

'Contest what?' Meredith felt that she was losing track of the conversation.

'Your great-aunt's will. After all, she can't have known this gardener very long.'

'She never knew me at all, so I'd rather not start contesting anything.' Gary looked surprised at that but before he could question her about it, she asked how well his grandfather had known Clara Samuels.

'Not that well,' he replied. 'She bought the house in the spring, as I said. Everyone seems to remember that because it really wasn't the thing in 1963 for a woman to buy a house on her own. Legally she could, of course, if she didn't need a mortgage, but it really wasn't common.'

'How on earth did she afford it?' Meredith asked. She remembered something her mother had told her once about how women weren't allowed to take out mortgages until sometime in the 1970s. How had a schoolteacher been able to buy a house outright?

'No idea at all, I'm afraid, but that's what happened and Grandpa was the estate agent. She moved in around June 1963, but she was gone by the time Kennedy was assassinated in November. So nobody really knew her in that short amount of time and nobody knew where she'd gone.'

Meredith did a quick calculation in her head. 'So she was here less than five months? That's so weird. I wonder what happened?'

'We all wonder what happened,' Gary said.

'Your grandfather met her though; he must know something. Is it possible to speak to him?'

Gary shook his head sadly. 'He died about fifteen years ago, I'm afraid.'

'Oh,' Meredith said, realising the stupidity of the question. A successful estate agent in 1963 would be in his nineties by now. 'I'm so sorry.'

'And my father was only six in 1963 so he doesn't know much either.'

'So you don't know why she moved here, to Cary-brook, of all places?'

'Because she grew up here,' Gary said, looking at Meredith as though she must have known this. 'And she had family living here still. A sister and brother-in-law, name of Bradford or Bradley...' He paused for a moment, thinking. 'Something like that anyway.'

'Bradshaw,' Meredith said. 'Esther and Richard Bradshaw. They were my grandparents. I didn't know my grandfather at all and I barely remember my grandmother but I know they never once mentioned anyone called Clara. My mum remembers them better than me and she says the same.'

'This house has always been a mystery,' Gary said, standing up and tucking his clipboard under his arm. 'And you're just deepening it.'

'I wish I knew more,' Meredith said.

'I'd best be off, couple more valuations to do this morning.' He stopped and turned to Meredith. 'Do let me know when you decide to sell, won't you? I'll help you get the best price for Butterfly Cottage.'

'I'll have to speak to Zach, but I'll let you know.'

As Meredith watched Gary walk slowly down the garden path, hitching his suit trousers up, she wondered how much of this story Zach had known and how much he still wasn't telling her.

And then her phone rang.

'Meredith,' a voice she recognised said when she answered. 'Alexander Maddison here. I understand you've been trying to contact me.'

'Yes,' Meredith replied. 'I've been wondering why you didn't tell me about Zach Johnson.'

* * *

As soon as she said his name to Mr Maddison, Zach appeared at the French doors. Meredith gestured for him to come in, although she thought he didn't need to ask permission to come into his own house, and she whispered that she was on the phone to the solicitor.

'But I don't understand why you didn't tell me any of this,' she said to Mr Maddison. 'Why didn't you mention that my great-aunt had left the house to me and Zach?'

'Because my client asked me not to,' the solicitor

replied. 'She specifically said that when I found you and told you about the house I wasn't to mention Mr Johnson. She was concerned, I think, about your reaction.'

'Quite rightly,' Meredith said. 'A heads up would have been nice.'

'Perhaps, but Miss Samuels particularly stipulated this and I am obliged to abide by my client's wishes if they are lawful.'

Meredith sighed. 'I understand,' she said. 'And Clara didn't say anything else about why she didn't want me to know about Zach?' It was as though her great-aunt was playing a practical joke on her, one that she wouldn't be around to witness.

'It was a strange stipulation,' Mr Maddison admitted. 'But I don't know the full reason behind it.'

'Can you tell me what you do know?' Meredith asked.

'Of course.'

'Zach's here too now so I'm going to put you on speakerphone.'

'Clara Samuels first came to see me last winter,' Mr Maddison began, his voice echoing into the room. 'Not long before Christmas. She told me she was eighty-seven years old and it was time she made a will.'

'She hadn't had one before?' Zach asked.

'No, not so far as I know, certainly not in England. She told me that she'd been living in Australia for some time and she had come back to get her affairs in order. I didn't find out until later about her cancer diagnosis, but it made sense that she'd want to come back, I think. She told me she owned a small property in Australia that was being dealt with separately – that's all I know about that, I'm afraid – and that she had savings she wanted to be distributed as well.'

Meredith thought about the names in the will she had seen. She wondered who those people were.

'She also told me that she was having renovations done on Butterfly Cottage,' Mr Maddison went on.

'She had the place rewired, the plumbing and kitchen sorted, and she redecorated too,' Zach said.

Not the wallpaper in the living room, though, Meredith thought to herself, wondering if the wallpaper had meant something to her great-aunt.

'She wanted to make sure,' Mr Maddison went on, 'that Butterfly Cottage was left to the right people. Obviously, I asked who those people were and she told me her great-niece Meredith Carling and her friend Zach Johnson. It is not my job to ask for details about beneficiaries of wills. I had no idea she'd never met you, Meredith, and I had no idea who Zach was at all.

To be honest, when I wrote the will I'd presumed he was Miss Samuels's partner and that you, Meredith, already knew him.'

It was a fair enough assumption, Meredith supposed. Who on earth would have guessed that they had never met each other before?

'The next time I saw Miss Samuels was in the January when she came into my office to check and sign the will. She was of sound mind, she knew exactly what she wanted and was happy with the will as drawn. I do remember thinking that she hadn't looked well and I'd asked her if she was all right. That's when she told me about the cancer, about how she didn't have long to live.' Mr Maddison paused. 'That was also when she explained who Zach was and that she didn't want you to know about him until you had seen the house. I should have dealt with that better though and...'

'What happened then?' Meredith asked. It was too late to wonder if things should have been done differently and she was too intrigued by her great-aunt to dwell on it.

'We put the will into safekeeping,' he replied. 'I remember asking her if she wanted a copy to take with her but she said she didn't. My assistant put the will in the strong room here at the office and there it stayed until Mr Johnson called me to tell me that Miss Samuels had passed away.'

'I knew I was an executor,' Zach said. 'She'd asked me to do that for her and I didn't mind. It meant I had the details for her solicitor when the time came.'

'But you didn't know she'd left you half the house?' Meredith asked.

'Not until after she died, no.'

'Do either of you know why she didn't use a local solicitor, why she went to London?'

'I wondered if it was perhaps for privacy reasons,' Mr Maddison said. 'She did tell me she used to live in London after the war so perhaps she was taking a trip down memory lane. I'm afraid I really don't know.'

'And when you told Zach about the house,' Meredith went on, directing her statement to the phone on the table, 'she said it was OK to tell Zach about me but not the other way around?'

'Yes.'

'And that's everything you know, is it?' Zach asked. 'Miss Samuels didn't tell you anything else about why she came back to England or what she'd been doing in Australia?'

'She told me she was a retired schoolteacher,' the solicitor replied, 'so I assume she taught in Australia, but that is all I know.'

'OK,' Meredith said, rather weakly.

'Now there are still a few things to go over,' Mr Maddison said. 'And if you're going to sell the house we'll need to talk about taxes and—'

'Can we get back to you on that in a week or so?' Zach interrupted. 'It's good of you to call on a Saturday but we probably all want to get back to our weekends.'

'Of course, of course.' And with a series of salutations, Alexander Maddison was gone.

'You looked like you'd probably had enough,' Zach smiled. 'I had wondered why Miss Samuels went all the way to London for him. A local solicitor would have been half the price.' He looked at Meredith again. 'Are you OK?'

'I guess. Nobody seems to know very much about Clara, do they? The estate agent was here this morning too.'

'How did it go? I'm sorry I wasn't here. I didn't know he was coming so early.'

Meredith told him about Mr Molliner and Mr Molliner's grandfather who had known her own grandparents.

'Everybody seems to know a little bit of information about Miss Samuels and the cottage, but nothing useful,' Zach said.

'Did you know that Clara had lived in Carybrook as a child?'

'Yes,' Zach said. 'Yes, she did mention it.' His brow furrowed. 'I think she said that Butterfly Cottage used to be a vicarage or something. I'm sorry I can't remember and I'm sorry if I didn't tell you. Most of this didn't seem that important when she told me, you know.'

'I know,' Meredith replied. 'And it's hard to understand which pieces of information are important and which aren't. Did Clara ever mention my grandparents?'

'She never mentioned any family other than you. And she certainly never told me that she had a sister who lived here in the 1960s too. I wonder when your grandparents moved away? Where did you say they lived?'

'Stevenage,' Meredith replied. 'I don't know when they moved there, though. Mum might know more.'

'So, what's the verdict?' Zach asked.

'What verdict?'

'The value of the house, of course!'

'Oh, well, very good news on that score,' Meredith said, telling him the figure that Gary had given her.

Zach's eyebrows shot up. 'Over half a million?' he said. 'I mean, I was expecting a good price – Cary-

brook is one of those sought-after areas these days –
but that's ridiculous.'

'He says we could get even more if we modernise
the kitchen and get the bathrooms sorted out.'

'In what way do we sort out the bathrooms?'

'He says we could put in a downstairs bathroom
under the stairs and an en suite in the master
bedroom.'

'How many bathrooms do people need?' Zach
asked. 'Did you tell him about the outside
bathroom?'

'There's a bathroom outside?'

Zach laughed. 'There's an outhouse by the shed.
It's nothing special.'

'Is that where you—' Meredith stopped herself
and looked away.

'Yes,' he replied matter-of-factly. 'But I have a
shower in the caravan. I fill the water tank from the
outside tap.'

Meredith remembered him the day before, shirtless and damp from the shower.

'This is your house too,' she said, not looking at
him. 'You can shower in here. You can even sleep in
here.'

'I'm fine where I am, but thank you.'

'The estate agent wanted to know about the work

that Clara had done to the house last year,' Meredith said. 'Can you help him?'

'All the paperwork is in the desk in the front room,' he replied. 'I wonder what else might be in there?'

'You mean like letters or diaries or something, letting us know more about Clara?'

'You never know.'

'That's too easy,' Meredith laughed. 'This isn't a movie.'

'No. More's the pity. Although I did go out hunting for clues this morning.'

'On your bike?'

'Yes, hunting for clues on my bike like a character from an Enid Blyton book.'

'And what did you discover?'

'I went to talk to Alf about this Miss Cheggers he told us about last night. She was the head teacher at Carybrook school back in the eighties and nineties.'

'But that's years after Clara would have taught there.'

'It is, and unfortunately before that she'd taught in a school in Ipswich but apparently her aunt – also called Miss Cheggers, just to confuse you – was the head teacher in 1963 when Miss Samuels was teaching there.'

'She couldn't have taught there for very long though,' Meredith said. 'According to Gary Molliner, she moved here in the early summer and she was gone by the time Kennedy was assassinated, which Gary says was in November.'

'22 November.'

'How do you know that?'

'There's a Stephen King book about it, but never mind, go on.'

'That's pretty much it, Gary was as full of missing information as Mr Maddison. But this Miss Cheggers must know something. Did you see her or speak to her?'

'No, but Alf gave me her phone number for you so why don't you call her? She's expecting to hear from you.'

Meredith hesitated. She needed to get back to London, she needed to get the hire car back by Sunday evening, but she also needed to find out what had happened to Clara Samuels. Why had she left Carybrook? Why had she gone to Australia? She took the piece of paper that Zach was holding out to her.

'I'll call her now.'

10

SUFFOLK, JUNE 1963

They met outside the school at 6 o'clock on Friday evening. Clara was surprised to see that several of the schoolchildren were also there, mostly still dressed in their uniforms.

'They aren't coming to the dance too, are they?' Clara laughed.

'No, they always come along when they know we're off to Ickbury for the evening,' Betty replied. 'I think they like to see what we look like in the wild when we're not teaching them and, by the way, you look amazing!'

Clara was wearing a dress she'd bought from Bazaar back in the spring, before she'd known about

Butterfly Cottage being put up for sale, and this was the first chance she'd had to wear it. Mary Quant's shop had opened in the mid-fifties and was an instant hit with the young women of post-war London. She sold clingy dresses in stretchy comfortable materials and thick, colourful tights. Alterations were done in-store which meant women could have the dresses cut as short or as long as they wanted – Clara went a little longer than the younger women she'd lived with in London.

Things change very quickly, Clara had thought to herself as she'd got ready to go out. It was almost impossible to believe that it was the middle of June and she had been in Carybrook for nearly three weeks. It was even harder to believe that three weeks ago she had been packing up her belongings and getting ready to move from the boarding house she had called home for nearly a decade. She had imagined that would be her life forever until Butterfly Cottage, the house that had been sitting in the back of her mind for most of her life, had been handed to her on a plate.

'Thank you,' she said to Betty.

'It looks so like a Mary Quant.'

'I'll let you into a little secret,' Clara said. 'It *is* a Mary Quant!'

'Oh, my goodness.'

'I know, I don't make a habit of it – I only have this and one other, the other clothes I bought in London are very good fakes, but I used to teach in Chelsea and lived in a boarding house just off the King's Road. I walked past Bazaar nearly every day and I saved like crazy to get the two dresses I bought.'

'I think Mary Quant is amazing,' Betty said. 'Proper comfortable clothes that look good – no more girdles and hard zips.' She was wearing a rather Quantesque mini dress herself, made up of blocks of white, grey and black jersey that clung to her in all the right places. 'I made this one based on one of her designs,' she said.

'Goodness, how talented you are!'

Betty blushed a little but didn't reply as John's Morris Minor pulled up next to them.

'Come on then, get in,' he shouted through the open window and Clara and Betty joined another woman in the back of the car. The man in the passenger seat turned around and held out his hand.

'Billy Cragg,' he said. 'John's little brother and this is my girl, Wendy.' He introduced the other woman. Soon the car was full of chat and laughter as they made their way towards Ickbury.

It was a Suffolk market town and much bigger

than Carybrook. As a child, their mother had taken Clara and Esther into Ickbury twice a year for school uniforms and new shoes and, on one very memorable occasion in 1940, to the small cinema there to watch *The Wizard of Oz* in all its technicolour glory. Clara's father had recently gone away on military training and her mother, Clara suspected with the benefit of hindsight, wanted to take her mind off the horror of war that surrounded them.

John parked in front of the Ickbury Royal and it felt slightly strange to Clara to be revisiting these places of her childhood that she had all but forgotten. Not that she had forgotten the Ickbury Royal – who could forget the first time they saw *The Wizard of Oz*, after all? Clara had been so enthralled and could remember writing to James about it in some detail which couldn't have been very interesting for him considering he hadn't seen it. As the others in the car began a tuneless rendition of 'Please Please Me', she found herself wondering, yet again, what James was doing now.

Ickbury in general hadn't changed at all and, after John had parked, they all tumbled out of the car and walked along the street to the hall where the dance was taking place. When they arrived the place was busy with a queue at the bar and the band already playing on stage. The singer was a local woman, Betty had told her, and some of the crowd from Carybrook knew her quite well.

'They'll play some of their own songs first,' Betty said as they walked across the dance floor towards the bar. 'And then later lots of hits you'll recognise.'

Clara had been to many similar dances in London, on a much larger scale of course, and had danced to all sorts of music with all sorts of people. Not that any of the men she had danced with had ever become anything more than friends. Clara had always put her career first. She didn't see much chance of that changing now that she'd moved to Suffolk. She still wanted to be a head teacher one day, even if it was of a small school like Carybrook.

'I'll get John to get us a couple of Babychams,' Betty said, her eyes bright with excitement. 'Then we'll find someone to dance with us. There's a bunch of people from Carybrook here that I'll introduce you to – some of them ever so handsome!'

Clara smiled and nodded, not wanting to ask for the Vermouth that she and her friends had often drunk in London, mostly because she suspected that a small hall in Ickbury probably didn't have Vermouth.

'Here you go, ladies,' John said, appearing from the crowd with two glasses of Babycham. 'Cheers!'

They clinked their champagne coupes with his pint glass and joined him in the salutation. 'Now,' John went on. 'Who's going to dance with me first?'

'Well, Betty I think,' Clara said. 'I know she's keen for a dance.'

Betty nudged Clara playfully and linked her arm through John's. Clara already knew, even though Betty hadn't told her, that she and John were an item. Everyone in Carybrook knew. Everyone in Carybrook always knew everything.

'Are you sure you'll be all right?' Betty asked. 'There's a group from the school over there.' She pointed and waved and, as John led her off to dance, Clara moved towards the group of other teachers who all immediately started to ask her about her dress and what dances in London were like.

During a natural lull in the conversation, Clara took the last mouthful of Babycham, trying not to wince at the warm, overly sweet, pear wine. She turned around to put her glass down when a man standing behind her caught her attention. He was tall and dark, his hair fell onto his shirt collar, and he had the complexion of somebody who spent a lot of time outside. He leaned against the bar with his shirt-sleeves rolled up and his hands in his pockets and, when he caught her eye, he smiled at her.

Clara smiled back; what was the harm after all, and it would be nice to dance with somebody.

It wasn't until he started to walk towards her that she realised who he was.

* * *

He looked at her left hand before he spoke. It was quick and subtle, but she noticed the smile on his face when he saw the lack of a ring.

'Clara Samuels,' he said, just loud enough to be heard over the band. 'It is you, isn't it?'

Clara nodded, dumbstruck. How could this be? It was as though she'd brought him to life, conjured him up, just by thinking about him.

James Mackenzie was standing in front of her, smiling down at her.

Of course, he was a very different James Mackenzie to the one she'd known. He was a lot taller for a start, at least six feet if not more, and his face was thinner, his jaw sharper and he seemed sadder somehow. She stood staring at him like a fool for a moment, unable to move or speak. Then she dropped her eyes, embarrassed, and noticed his forearms – strong and tanned – which was the moment her stomach turned over and she felt suddenly hot. Not only was

James standing in front of her but he was also one of the most handsome men she'd seen outside the cover of a magazine.

'Are you all right?' she heard him say. She hadn't spoken for too long. She was making a mess of this.

She took a breath and stood up straighter, looking him in the eye. 'I'm fine,' she said. 'Just a bit...'

'Shocked?' he asked, still smiling. 'Sorry, I should have given you a bit of warning. I'd already worked out it was you. I'd been looking at you for a while from...' He stopped and ran a hand over his face. 'Sorry, that sounds so creepy. I...' He hesitated, looked away. 'Sorry.'

'Shall we start again?' Clara asked.

'That would be great, but first, let me get you a drink. Babycham, was it?'

'Oh, please no,' Clara said. 'I only had that because my friend bought it for me.' She looked around for Betty and John but couldn't see them. 'It's disgusting.'

James laughed then, and in that moment Clara remembered the boy he used to be, the garden they used to play in, the butterflies they used to try to identify. She remembered everything. 'What do you usually drink?' he asked.

'Vermouth,' she said.

He pulled a face. 'Don't think you're going to get that tonight, but how about a gin?'

'That would be lovely.'

'Don't go anywhere,' he said, reaching out to touch her arm for just a moment as though he wanted to check she was real. 'Please.'

She wasn't going anywhere.

'You all right there?' one of the men from the group she'd been talking to asked her. 'Not giving you any trouble, is he?'

Clara laughed. 'No, not at all – he's an old friend. Haven't seen him for years.'

'Friend from London?' the man asked.

'Sort of,' she said.

'I was about to ask you to dance,' the man said, sounding a little put out as though James's miracle appearance had scuppered his plans.

'I'd better wait for my friend.'

The man nodded. Clara knew she'd been introduced to him but she couldn't remember his name. He didn't teach at the school but he was the friend or sibling of someone who did. 'Well, we'll catch up with you later, no doubt.'

James came back, glancing briefly at the man before handing Clara her drink. 'It's not very cold, I'm afraid,' he said. 'They've run out of ice – they always do on dance nights. The whole bar is improvised, really.'

She took a sip of the gin which was warm and strong against her throat. 'It is better than warm Baby-cham though,' she said.

'Who's the fellow?' James asked, nodding towards the retreating back of the man as he and the rest of the group headed towards the dance floor.

'I can't remember his name,' Clara replied. 'Although I'm sure I was told. He lives in my village, I think, but doesn't teach at the school.'

'So, you're a schoolteacher then?' James took a long drink from his beer.

'I am,' she stopped. 'Guess where I teach?'

'No idea.'

'Our old school!'

'In Carybrook? Do you live there too?'

She nodded.

'I've only recently come back though,' she said. 'I had to get away for quite a long time from everything – my parents, my sister...' She paused. He'd have known this if he'd kept in touch. Had he received all her letters? Why had he never replied?

'Where did you go?' he asked, although he must know she'd gone to Cambridge – he'd replied to the letter in which she'd told him she'd won her scholarship. Was he deliberately avoiding the subject of the letters?

'Cambridge first, for university, then London. I've been teaching in London since I graduated and then, three weeks ago, I came back.'

He didn't ask her why, for which she was glad as she didn't think it could all be explained in such a crowded, noisy place. It wasn't the place to bring up the sudden way they'd lost touch either, however much she wanted to ask. They were practically shouting at each other over the music.

'And you?' she asked when he didn't say anything. 'Are you back in the area permanently?' The conversation felt stilted and unnatural, as though they were two strangers. It was nothing like Clara had imagined it would be if they ever met again.

And then she realised that they hadn't seen each other for nearly twenty-five years. They *were* two strangers.

'Ickbury,' he said. 'I'm working up at the Manor.' He paused to drain his glass. 'I work as a gardener up there.'

Ickbury Manor was a huge stately home on the edge of the town. It had a long history dating back to Tudor times and there was a rumour that Elizabeth I had stayed there but no real evidence.

Before Clara could say any more the band launched into a cover version of the Beatles' 'I Saw Her Standing There', and James reached over, taking her glass off her.

'Let's dance,' he said. 'Show me those London moves.'

* * *

They danced for song after song. The band played all the recent hits that Clara knew including 'Da Doo Ron Ron' by the Crystals.

'Oh, I love this song,' she said into James's ear and he grinned at her, as he had done every few minutes since they'd stepped onto the dance floor, as though, like her, he couldn't quite believe what was happening.

Dancing had been a good idea of his, a way to break the ice. They couldn't really talk much over the band and their own breathlessness, but they could be together, learn to feel comfortable in each other's presence again.

After a while the band changed gear to a slower song and Clara felt suddenly embarrassed. Did she want to dance a slow song with James Mackenzie? Did he want to dance a slow song with her?

He didn't take his eyes off her but he could obviously sense her discomfort at the change in rhythm.

'Let's give those London moves, which are impressive by the way, a break,' he said. 'I could do with some air.'

She nodded her consent and she felt his fingers touch hers as he led her through the crowd.

'I can't be long,' she said as they got to the door. 'My friends are driving me home later.'

'Don't worry,' he replied. 'I'll get you back safely.' And she didn't know if he meant to her friends or back to Carybrook. Either way, she didn't mind. In that moment she wanted to be with him, to talk to him, to tell him everything and ask him all the questions that had been bubbling up in her head while they were dancing. She needed to start with what had happened, where he'd gone, why the letters stopped.

He led her over to a bench and let go of her hand as they sat down together, not quite touching. He took a packet of cigarettes out of his pocket and lit one, passing it to her. She shook her head.

'I don't,' she said. He took it back and inhaled.

'Only person in Suffolk who doesn't,' he said, blowing smoke into the air.

'Only person in Britain.' Everyone seemed to smoke. Even Esther had a packet secreted away from

Richard's prying eyes, and Richard himself was rarely far from his pipe. Clara had tried, but she'd never got the hang of it. It was easier not to bother.

It was a warm, balmy evening and the sky was perfectly clear.

'You can never see the stars in London,' Clara said, looking up at the sky overhead. 'It's always too polluted.'

'Tell me about it.' James smiled as he too looked up at the stars. 'I couldn't get my head around it when I first got there. And it got much worse of course, after the war.'

'Why did you stop writing?' Clara asked. She had to know.

James didn't say anything for a moment. He looked up at the sky and exhaled a line of smoke. 'I didn't,' he said eventually. 'But something obviously happened because I never heard from you after the summer of 1948.'

Clara sat up and turned to him. 'I wrote every week,' she said. 'From Cambridge. I thought that maybe we could meet up, that I could get the train to London and...'

'So you never knew that we'd moved?'

'No, I was still writing to your address in London. When did you move?'

'1948, at the end of that summer!' James sat back in the seat and pushed his hair back with his hand. 'You never knew! Well, that explains why I didn't hear from you.'

'Where did you go? What happened?'

'Dad was transferred to a parish in Lincolnshire. He was never really the same after Mum died – neither of us were – but he was so busy during the war and then helping with rehoming and rebuilding projects afterwards that I suppose he thought he could push through. He couldn't, of course, none of us can...' James stopped, looked away. He ground his cigarette out underneath the sole of his boot.

'James, I'm so sorry, I...'

'Plenty of people lost someone, Clara. It's just life.' He was trying to sound stoic but his hand found hers and he squeezed it gently. 'Dad wrote to the bishop, asked for a transfer to a quieter parish and we packed up what few belongings we had and went to Lincolnshire.'

'And I never knew.'

'This is no conversation for a night like this,' he said. 'A night of renewal, of finding you again.'

'Finding me? Have you been looking?' Maybe she should have been looking too instead of thinking about him all the time since the letters stopped. It wouldn't have been that hard to find a vicar's son and she wondered why she had never thought of it. Because, she supposed, he might not live up to the dream version she had created of him.

But here he was next to her, real and solid. And from what she could tell he was living up to a lot of dreams right now.

He laughed softly. 'This sounds stupid,' he said, 'but I've often thought of you over the years, wondered where you were, what you were doing. It's one of the reasons I took the job at Ickbury Manor. Just in case you were still here.'

'Really?' she asked, amazed that he'd been thinking of her too.

'You think I'm a fool, don't you? We were nine years old the last time we met. Perhaps I am a fool.'

'No more than me,' Clara confessed to the night sky. 'I've often thought of you too.'

He turned to her then, looking into her eyes. 'Have you, Clara?' he asked and she nodded. 'My dad always told me I was a dreamer,' he went on. 'And he's right, of course, I always have been. But here you are sitting next to me, so not all dreams are a waste of time.'

She laughed then, clear and loud into the darkness, his words so similar to her own thoughts. 'This is unbelievable,' she said. 'Us sitting here together after all this time.'

'Maybe, or maybe it's fate.'

'I've never known if I believe in fate.'

'I'm a vicar's son, I'm supposed to believe this is all pre-ordained.' He waved his hand up at the sky above.

'Do you?' Clara asked. 'Do you still believe in God?'

'After the war, it was hard to believe in anything,' he replied, turning to her again. He took a breath and furrowed his brow. 'All of this explains why your letters never got to me, but what about my letters? I kept writing to you at your parents' address for months before I gave up. What happened to those letters?'

'I suspect,' Clara said, 'that after I left home my parents simply put your letters in with the rubbish. I suspect they saw it as a good opportunity to sever a connection they never approved of.'

'They never did like me, did they?' James asked but when Clara looked at him she saw he was smiling as though he simply didn't give a fig for who liked him and who didn't.

'You were the boy who always got me in trouble. I was always coming home with muddy shoes and a dirty dress. I think they hoped we'd just lose touch when you moved.'

'And when we didn't they decided to interfere.'

Clara nodded. 'I can't think of any other reason your letters never got to me, can you?'

'How long did you say you'd been back?' James asked, lighting another cigarette.

'Three weeks.'

'And your parents, are they still here?'

'No,' Clara said. 'They both died whilst I was at university.'

'I'm sorry.'

'It's OK. Like you say, a lot of people lost somebody in the war. I was lucky I didn't.'

'Was your dad called up?'

'He was an engineer so he was much sought after, or so he said. He was gone for over three years but I don't know what he did. He never talked about it.'

'Nobody does though, do they? It's understandable if you think about it.' James paused again and turned to her. 'So this is your first Ickbury dance?' he asked, changing the conversation to something lighter.

'I almost didn't come,' she said. 'But I'm glad I did.'

She told him then about Cambridge, and about training to be a teacher and the school in Chelsea that she'd worked at for so long. She told him about Mrs Benyon and the other girls at the boarding house and she told him about her parents, how they'd been so much richer than either she or Esther had imagined, and the money they had left behind. And she told him that Esther had never left Carybrook, lived there still with her husband.

'Esther told me about a house that was for sale in the village and it felt that it was time to do something with the money our parents had left, something for me.' She didn't tell him that she'd bought his childhood home; it felt strange and awkward to do so.

'You and Esther get on better than you used to, I take it?'

'Yes, though we're still very different. Her husband is an accountant called Richard who plays golf and drives a Rover but it's easier to put those differences aside when you've grown up. It got easier after our parents died, to be honest.' She paused, realising what she had said. 'Oh God James, I'm so sorry – I didn't mean that parents dying was easy, I just...'

She felt the comforting squeeze of his hand again. 'I know,' he said. 'And you didn't marry anyone?'

'Not yet,' she smiled. 'So what about you? How did you come to be a gardener?'

'I fell into it, really,' he replied. 'It was the first apprenticeship I could get and I threw myself into it after we moved to Lincolnshire. I needed to do something

with myself. The fellow I apprenticed for had travelled all over the country with his work and that
sounded great to me – so many opportunities. And I
did it for Mum, too. She loved gardening, do you remember? She hated that we didn't have a garden in
London.'

Neither of them spoke for a moment, each quietly
remembering Mrs Mackenzie.

'So, have you travelled all over the country then?'

'Here and there. I worked in Kent for quite a long
time, helping them rebuild the parks after the war
and then up to Essex.'

'You never felt like settling down yourself?'

'The opportunity never arose,' he replied. 'So I
just kept going until I ended up back here. And then
nine months later you were standing there, just like
the Beatles song. Opportunity is never where you expect it to be.'

He held her gaze then and, for a moment, she
thought he was going to kiss her. She wanted him to,
more than anything, but she had to tell him something first.

'James,' she said. 'The house I bought.'

'Yes, what about it?'

'Well,' she hesitated. 'I... I bought Butterfly
Cottage.'

She watched as his eyes lit up and his face broke into a grin. She felt relief. She'd been worried about what he would say.

'You did? I thought it was owned by the diocese for the vicar.'

'The diocese sold it. They built a new vicarage.'

'And what's it like?'

'Oh James, it's exactly the same. Well, almost of course, they've redecorated, installed a washing machine, that kind of thing but otherwise the same.' She paused. 'Although...'

'Yes?'

'Well, the garden is a bit neglected.'

'I think I could help you with that!'

Just as he said it Clara could hear somebody calling her name across the town square.

'Betty.' Clara waved at the figure. 'Over here.'

'There you are, Clara, I've been looking all over for you.'

'Sorry, I bumped into an old friend.'

She introduced the two of them and they shook hands.

'Listen, Clara,' Betty said. 'Sorry to interrupt, it's just John and I both have to be up early for the fete tomorrow and we're going to head back. Do you want to come with us or will you get a lift back with the others? Wendy and Billy are going home in Doug's car. Do you know Doug?'

Clara did not know Doug and didn't particularly want to get a lift home in his car.

'Go,' James said softly. 'I know where you are, I'll come and find you.'

11

SUFFOLK, JUNE 2018

'Have you explored the house at all?' Meredith asked Zach. 'Looked through the drawers and cupboards for any clues as to why Clara had been away so long?'

Zach shook his head. 'I've not really been inside the house much, other than to keep it clean and put fresh flowers in the vases,' he said. 'I've just sort of carried on living as though she were still here, working in the garden, doing the job she hired me for.' He looked away, but Meredith had already noticed the sadness in his eyes.

'I'm sorry,' she said. 'This is all so different for you than it is for me. I never knew her, but for you, well, you lost a friend.'

'I know she left me half the house and I know that

means half of what's inside too, but it didn't feel right to come in here and use her things.' He paused for a moment, collecting himself. 'But I know that eventually we will have to sell the house, I know you want to and I can't afford to buy you out. What would I do with a huge house like this anyway? So I know we have to start sorting things out.'

'I thought I'd start today,' Meredith said. 'For want of anything else to do.'

She had phoned Miss Cheggers earlier that morning.

'Call me Delia,' she'd said on the phone as Meredith had explained why she was calling and where she had got the telephone number.

'So you're Meredith Carling, the great-niece,' Delia Cheggers had gone on to say. Everyone seemed to know about Meredith and had been anticipating her arrival in Carybrook. It was quite unnerving.

They'd arranged to meet at Miss Cheggers's house after church the next day. 'It'll be nice to see you,' she'd said. 'I don't get many visitors these days.'

And so, seeing as she was in Carybrook until at least the next afternoon, Meredith decided to take the advice her mother had given her and spend the day doing a bit of investigating.

'I've looked through the bedrooms,' she said to

Zach. 'And apart from a few clothes and toiletries and a bottle of aspirin that expired in 1965, there really isn't much.'

'She didn't bring much with her,' Zach said. 'I don't even know if she had much – I hadn't known that she had a house in Australia until Mr Maddison told us this morning. The more I think about it the more I realise that she didn't tell me very much about her life at all.'

Meredith wondered what had happened to the Australian house Mr Maddison had mentioned, what he meant about it being 'dealt with'.

'Are you all right?' Zach asked.

'Other than the whole shock inheritance, mysterious great-aunt extravaganza?' Meredith replied with a smile.

'Other than that, yes,' Zach smiled back. 'You seem a bit... well, on edge.'

Meredith ran a hand through her hair and turned from Zach, ignoring how that smile had made her feel. 'Oh, ignore me, I'm sorry. I'm just a bit worried about work, that's all.'

'Saturday must be your busiest day.'

'It is, but I'm sure they're all coping without me. I guess I'm a bit of a workaholic.'

'You can give me a haircut,' Zach said with a grin

whilst pulling on the ends of his overlong hair. 'I'd pay you.'

'Lovely as that would be,' Meredith said, thinking how lovely it would be to run her hands through Zach's hair, 'I don't have my scissors and us hair-dressers are very precious about our scissors.'

'That's a shame. I suppose I don't have any excuses left not to help you clear out some of the house.'

'No, I suppose you don't.'

'We should start in the living room,' Zach went on. 'I do know that she kept her important documents like her passport in the desk in the front room. That's where the paperwork about the plumbing and rewiring will be. The estate agent will need all that before we put the house on the market.'

'Seems as good a place as any to start.'

They moved into the living room which sat at the front of the house and Meredith homed in on the desk, starting with the drawers which were disap-pointingly empty – just some old writing paper and envelopes and a dried-up fountain pen.

'Are you looking for anything specific?' Zach asked as he started to look through a cabinet that seemed to be full of wine glasses.

'I don't know, really.' Meredith opened the main part of the desk which was full of all sorts of papers

and looked much more promising. 'I suppose anything that might hint as to why she left – letters, old
newspapers, a diary, that sort of thing.' As she said the
words she knew it sounded ridiculous. This wasn't an
adventure novel where all the clues were placed in the
right order for the main character to find.

'It's unlikely you'll find a diary that tells you everything you need to know,' Zach laughed, echoing her
own thoughts.

The only person who was likely to know anything,
Meredith thought, was her father. And who even
knew where to begin looking for him?

Twenty minutes later it was clear that there wasn't
anything interesting in the desk. Of all the papers re-
lating to the house, only a few were relevant like the
plumber's and electrician's certificates. Everything
else was wildly out of date. She found an envelope of
old receipts and invoices from 1963 when Clara had
first bought the house, but none shed any light on
what had happened later that year.

'Oh, look,' she said, unfolding one of the invoices.

'What?' Zach said, springing up from his mountain of wine glasses. What did anyone need so
many for?

'Sorry, nothing exciting,' she said, noticing that
underneath his grief it was clear Zach wanted to find

out what had happened in 1963 as much as she did. 'It's just the invoice for the wallpaper.'

'The wallpaper?'

'On the walls in here.' Meredith indicated the blue and white stripes. 'This morning when he was looking around the estate agent said that the wallpaper was vintage, dating from the sixties.'

'Really?' Zach rubbed the back of his head. 'But Miss Samuels had the place redecorated when she first arrived.'

'Not in here she didn't,' Meredith said, showing Zach the invoice. 'And she bought the wallpaper from Peter Jones on the King's Road.'

'Where?'

'It's a big department store in Chelsea. John Lewis owns it now.'

'I wonder why she kept it?' Zach asked.

'It must have meant something to her, I suppose, if she left it up after the redecoration.'

'Well, we're not going to sort out the mystery by staring at four walls,' Zach said after a moment. 'So I'm going to make lunch and then get on with the garden. Do you want anything?'

'No,' Meredith replied, disappointed that she hadn't found the answer to the mystery yet.

'You need to be more patient,' Zach said with a

grin. 'Wait and see what this Miss Cheggers has to say. Maybe try to find your father?'

'Maybe.'

It wasn't that she didn't want to find her father – she'd thought about trying to find him for years simply so she could apologise for what she'd said at her eighteenth birthday party – she just didn't know where to start.

Her phone started ringing and she pulled it out of her jeans pocket. 'It's Mum,' she said. 'I'd better take it.'.

'I'll see you later then,' Zach said as he walked back towards the garden, clearly the only place he felt comfortable.

'Mum,' Meredith said into her phone. 'How are you?'

'Solved the mystery yet?' Her mother got straight down to business.

'I think it's got even more complicated than we thought, but I have heard from Alexander Maddison and he's confirmed that Clara Samuels left the house to both me and Zach.'

'And Zach is your handsome man in the caravan?' Bernice asked for clarification.

'I never said he was handsome, that was all you,' Meredith replied. 'And it wasn't Mr Maddison's idea to not tell me about Zach inheriting half the house. Great-aunt Clara had requested that I wasn't told, that I should go to the cottage and find out for myself.'

'What a very weird request.'

'That's what I thought.'

'Have you talked to Zach about it?'

'Yes, he's actually really nice and...'

'Oh, yes!' Bernice teased.

'And I've just got out of a very serious relationship and need to put my own problems in order before I think about anything else,' Meredith said clearly before her mother got any ideas. 'But Zach and I have talked. He doesn't know why Clara didn't want me to know about him but he did explain that he'd been her gardener, and also her friend. It seemed that he was her only friend at the end. He was with her when she died and he still clearly misses her.'

'Isn't it odd that he knew this woman that neither you nor I realised existed,' Bernice mused. 'It just seemed like we should have known something. This is so typical of your father.'

Meredith wasn't at all sure that the secrecy around great-aunt Clara came from her father at all. What if it came from Clara herself? What if she was the one who didn't want to be found? She was the one who had run away, after all. She was the one who had come back to England and not got in touch with any-body. She was the one who had asked Mr Maddison not to tell Meredith about Zach. And if she hadn't wanted to be found for all those years, perhaps her secrets needed to die with her. Should they really be digging into all this?

But on the other hand, when somebody you didn't know existed left you half a house in very odd cir-cumstances, it was impossible not to want to know why.

Before her mother could launch into another chorus on her father's shortcomings, Meredith told her about what she and Zach had discussed in the pub the night before, about Alf, Delia Cheggers, Gary Molliner and his grandfather and the price they may be able to get for the house.

'So, this Delia Cheggers might know something?' Bernice asked.

'She might, but I don't know how much. She didn't start teaching at the local school until after Clara had left, but her aunt was the head teacher in 1963 so she might know something.'

'I keep thinking about your father,' Bernice said. 'I try not to, but I can't help wondering...' she trailed off.

'I keep thinking about him too. I'd like to find him. I wondered if he was maybe in Australia. He must have known about Clara, mustn't he? Otherwise how else would she have known about me?'

'Good point, but Australia is a big place to start looking for a man who is very good at not being found.'

'I also can't stop thinking about Clara and why she didn't get in touch when she knew where I was,' Meredith said quietly. 'If she was in England for nearly a year before she died, why didn't she contact me?'

'Would she have known where to find you?'

'She must have done because otherwise how would Mr Maddison have known how to get in touch?'

'Another good point. Did he write to you at home?'

'No, at the salon, which I thought was a bit strange at the time.'

'He probably got the address off Companies House, then.'

'So Clara wouldn't have known where I lived?'

'No, and I'm not sure your dad does these days either. I wanted to tell him when we moved to Spain just so he had a way of keeping in touch with you if he wanted, but I had no way of letting him know.'

'Dad might know about Butterfly Cottage though,' Meredith said.

'And that leaves us relying on him turning up, doesn't it?'

Meredith had no idea what she could do. She felt strangely envious of Zach's obvious grief. She wished she too had known Clara Samuels.

'Anyway,' Bernice said, putting on her jolliest voice. 'There was a reason for this phone call that was more than just guessing at a mystery. I've booked a flight and it lands at Stansted on Monday night. Do you think you'll be back in London by then?'

Meredith felt a warm sense of relief as though all of this would be easier if her mum was there with her.

'That's great news, Mum,' she said. 'And I'll definitely be back. I'm intending to leave after I've spoken to Miss Cheggers tomorrow. I need to get the car back before they start charging for extra days.'

'We'll get to the bottom of this, love – two heads are better than one.'

After Meredith had finished speaking to her mother she found herself looking at the old desk in the living room again. There must be something in it, she thought, something of Clara's that would shed some light on why she had left so suddenly.

Why was it so important to her to find out what had happened to this woman she had never known? It felt like something she needed to do but, like finding her father, she had no idea where to start.

She opened the desk again and that's when she saw it – the small drawer hidden towards the back, the sort of place you would keep valuables. Maybe...

Even as Meredith pulled it open she tried not to get her hopes up. Surely anything valuable or necessary, like keys, would have been left with Mr Maddison.

So when she saw the locket nestled in the bottom of the drawer she thought she was imagining it.

* * *

She practically ran down the garden looking for Zach, clutching the locket to her chest.

'What on earth...' Zach said, standing up.

'Look what I found in the desk,' she replied, pressing the locket into his hand.

It was a small, round, silver locket on a matching chain and it looked old, although not particularly valuable. It was inscribed on both sides with depictions of tangled ivy.

'Have you opened it?'

Meredith nodded, taking the locket from him again and opening it to show him what she'd found.

Inside was a black and white passport photo that looked like it had been taken in one of those photo booths that had always been in Woolworths when Meredith was young. She and her friends had taken all sorts of ridiculous photos in them. The one inside the locket had been cut into a circle to fit inside properly and was of a young couple who seemed to be messing about almost as much as she and her friends had done. The woman was laughing and her eyes were almost closed with mirth, and the man was pulling a face that distorted his features in an admittedly amusing way.

Zach peered at the photograph. 'You know, I think that's Miss Samuels,' he said.

'I assumed it was, but obviously I have no idea. Do you have any photographs of her?'

Zach shook his head. 'No, but there's something about the way she's laughing. I'm sure it's her.' He looked up at Meredith. 'You look like her, you know,' he said.

Meredith had seen a vague family resemblance when she'd first looked at the photograph, but what had really struck her was how happy Clara looked. Meredith couldn't remember the last time she'd felt that happy, that carefree. She knew appearances, and photographs, could be deceptive, but there was something so genuine about this candid shot and she wondered what had made her great-aunt so happy. Was it the man she was with? Or was it Carybrook itself?

'And what about the man?' Meredith asked, trying not to dwell on her own life too much.

'No idea, I'm afraid.'

'There's something familiar about him,' Meredith said as she closed the locket and put it in her pocket. 'But I can't quite put my finger on what it is.'

* * *

The next morning Meredith was already waiting in Miss Cheggers' front garden when the older lady returned from church.

'I'm Meredith Carling,' she said. 'I'm so sorry to be early like this.'

Miss Cheggers smiled at her. She was a small, neat woman, who looked to be in her late sixties although from what Alf had told her Meredith knew that she was older than that and more likely to be in her late seventies or even early eighties – just a few years younger than Clara would have been. Everyone seemed rather hale and hearty in Carybrook, and whatever it was they were putting in the water Meredith could do with some.

'That's quite all right, my dear,' the older lady said, taking her hand and shaking it vigorously. 'It's lovely to see you. I don't get many visitors these days.'

She passed in front of Meredith, unlocked the bright blue front door and led the way into her small house.

'It's not much,' she said apologetically. 'But I don't need much.'

'It's so good of you to see me, Miss Cheggers,' Meredith said. 'I hope I'm not bothering you in any way. Alf at The Queen's Head said you might be able to help me.'

'No bother at all.' Miss Cheggers led the way towards her kitchen and gestured for Meredith to sit down at the large pine table. 'Although I'm not sure how much help I will be as I never really knew your great-aunt.'

'But you taught at the same school here in Carybrook, didn't you?' Meredith asked.

'I did indeed. I started there in 1964 after teaching in Ipswich for many years. My aunt was the headmistress of the school at the time, but obviously your great-aunt had left by then.' She paused and started to take things out of a cupboard. 'Now,' she went on, 'let's have a cup of tea before we continue, shall we? Talking always makes me thirsty.'

Meredith had a thousand questions that she wanted to ask but accepted the tea and the digestive biscuits that were offered to her on a small green plate.

'Thank you, Miss Cheggers,' she said. 'You don't need to go to any trouble.'

'No trouble at all. And do please call me Delia, will you?'

Meredith nodded and took a sip of her too-hot tea, waiting for Miss Cheggers – Delia – to sit down.

'Now,' she said as she settled herself at the table opposite Meredith. 'As I said, I started at Carybrook School at the beginning of the summer term of 1964. I can't remember the date now, but it would have been April, I should think. I'd grown up in Ickbury and had been thinking of coming back to the area for some time. My aunt – also Miss Cheggers, but her name was Jean – asked me if I wanted the job as she'd been terribly short-staffed since your great-aunt left. Apparently, two of the other teachers had moved away to be married not long afterwards so she was in dire straits.'

'And you swooped in to help?' Meredith asked.

Delia chuckled. 'Yes, I suppose I did.'

'Did you work there until you retired?'

Delia nodded and took a sip of her tea. 'Yes, I worked my way up to headmistress and fought off closure until the inevitable happened in 2003 when the school was closed for good. I retired then and the local authority announced they were shutting it down almost straight away. The children of Carybrook take a bus into Ickbury every day for school now.'

Meredith thought for a moment of her own primary school at the end of the road. Looking back she didn't think it had been very good. If the children were all still alive at the end of the day that seemed to be a win in the teachers' eyes, but she had been able to walk there with her mother every day. She hadn't had to get on a school bus, which she would have hated.

'Anyway, you're not here to listen to my memories of being a schoolteacher, you're here to find out about your great-aunt.'

'I know absolutely nothing about her,' Meredith said. 'Until the solicitor told me about the house, I didn't even know she existed.'

'Frederick – that's Alf's brother who delivers the fruit and veg – told me after church. The whole village is talking about you, I'm afraid – one of the downsides of living in such a small place.'

'It's inevitable, I suppose,' Meredith replied, thinking of the old men playing dominoes in the pub on Friday night.

'It's an unusual situation, bound to get tongues wagging – much like Clara Samuels's disappearance fifty-five years ago.'

'So, she did just disappear then? She didn't tell anyone where she was going?'

'Not as far as I know – at least, if she did nobody said anything. She probably told her sister and brother-in-law, but they moved away from Carybrook around the same time.'

'Yes, the estate agent I saw yesterday was telling me about that.'

'Gary Molliner?'

Meredith nodded.

'I knew his grandfather, he was an estate agent too and sold the house to your great-aunt. I think the Molliners have been waiting for it to go back on the market ever since. Anyway, did you know your aunt's sister, Esther?'

'She was my father's mother.' Meredith paused. How to explain this complicated relationship? 'I don't see very much of my father though,' she said diplomatically. 'My grandmother, Esther, died around the time I was eighteen but I hadn't seen her since I was about twelve. Truth is I never really liked her. My grandfather – my father's father – died before I was born.'

'More tea?' Delia asked, pouring herself another cup. Meredith shook her head. 'Well, I'll tell you everything I know, which isn't much. Your aunt Clara started at the school in June 1963 – my aunt Jean always remembered the date because it was the same week that it all started to come out about John Profumo and Christine Keeler...' She trailed off. 'But of course, you're too young to know about that.'

'I've seen the film,' Meredith replied. 'I've got some idea.'

'Anyway, it was a strange time to start at a school, mid-term like that, but apparently Jean was very short-staffed – that seems to have been a continuing theme at Carybrook School over the years! So she started then and by the first week of November she was gone.'

This all added up to what she knew so far from Alf, Zach and Gary Molliner.

'Was there any hint that something was wrong? Something that might have made her leave?'

'Nothing, or at least not so far as my aunt was aware. Clara had been seeing a young man over the summer, a gardener I think he was, up at Ickbury Manor. Do you know it?'

Meredith shook her head but felt a small tingle of excitement in her spine. Could Ickbury Manor hold a clue? She touched the locket which she had in her pocket. Was this the man who was in the photograph?

'It's a big manor house just the other side of Ick-bury. It's owned by the National Trust now and is open to the public, but it was privately owned in the sixties – although they opened on certain days in the year. Bank holidays and so forth. There was a huge team of gardeners back then and he was one of them.'

'Do you know his name?'

'I'm afraid not,' Delia said. 'Or if I ever did, it is long forgotten. All I remember is that my aunt told me Clara had been seeing this young man and had brought him to some of the Carybrook village events that summer. I have a feeling I was told that he was someone your great-aunt had known years ago when she was a child growing up in the village, but please don't quote me on that. My memory is not what it was.'

'Can I show you something?' Meredith asked, pulling the locket out of her pocket.

'Of course you can, dear.'

She opened the locket and passed it to Delia who peered at it like Zach had. 'Do you recognise either of those people?' It seemed unlikely that she would, con-sidering what she had said, but it was worth a try.

'That's Clara Samuels,' Delia said. 'But I've no idea

who the man is. I suppose it could be the fellow from Ickbury Manor.' She looked at the photograph again. 'I never met Clara, of course, but there was a photograph of her that hung in the assembly hall of the school when I first started there. She and her class had been in the newspaper – something to do with a jumble sale that had raised some money, I think – and my aunt had put the photograph up on the wall along with other school and village-related pictures. It disappeared eventually and I don't know where it went, but I can tell you that is Clara.' She closed the locket and passed it back to Meredith.

'I was just wondering about what you said about the man who worked at Ickbury Manor. Did he leave the area at the same time as my aunt, do you think?'

'I don't know, but I wonder if perhaps the Manor kept records. You might be able to find out.'

Meredith brightened at that. It was something to take back to Zach.

'And there is one other thing too.'

'Yes?'

'There was a lot of gossip after Clara Samuels disappeared, as you can probably imagine, but everyone in the village was very fond of her and the cottage. I don't know if you know this, but various people helped look after the garden after she'd gone.'

'Gary Molliner mentioned that,' Meredith said. 'And on Friday night, in the pub...' She stopped, not wanting to sound ridiculous, but Miss Cheggers – sharp as a tack – was a step ahead of her.

'That dominoes team,' she said, rolling her eyes. 'Always spreading some tall tale or other. Honestly, they sit there all day comparing conspiracy theories.'

'They said there had been "funny goings-on" at the cottage,' Meredith said, smiling as she realised how stupid it sounded.

'As I said, there was a lot of gossip when your great-aunt left, but I should tell you that there was a rumour that persisted so much that I've always thought it must be true.'

Meredith leaned forward in her chair, her elbows on the table. 'What was it?' she asked.

'After your great-aunt left, letters started to arrive at Butterfly Cottage. About one a month for several months after she disappeared.'

'Who were they from?'

'Nobody knew and the postman, who was obviously quizzed a lot, only said that the postmark was sometimes from Essex and sometimes from Lincolnshire, that's all he knew. But those letters must have still been in the house when your great-aunt returned last year, and my guess is they are still in the house somewhere now. Find those letters and you might find out what happened.'

* * *

Meredith walked slowly back through the village to Butterfly Cottage. As she passed The Queen's Head she saw Alf standing outside talking to one of the dominoes men. He had a tea towel draped over his shoulder and as he saw her he raised a hand in greeting. She waved back but didn't go over. He'd want to know what Miss Cheggers had told her and she wasn't sure what to say. Had she learned anything new? Anything certain?

Mostly Miss Cheggers had just confirmed things that Meredith and Zach already knew, but there was this story about the letters, although it did seem more like rumour than truth. Meredith wondered if it was worth asking around to see if anyone else remembered it or had any proof. If the letters were delivered, Delia Cheggers was right in that they could have still been there, sitting on the doormat, over fifty years later when Clara returned. Had she read them when she got back? Had she hidden them somewhere in Butterfly Cottage? Or had they simply faded to dust from the sunlight that shone through the glass in the front door every morning?

Meredith shook her head in frustration. She'd learned nothing and she really needed to get back to London, back to the salon, back to sorting out this financial mess she was in and getting ready for her mother's arrival tomorrow, but all she felt like doing was slowing her pace and enjoying the walk through a beautiful village on a warm summer's day. She had often read the cliché about the English countryside in the summer, how there was nowhere as beautiful, but as a born-and-bred city girl she had never paid much attention to it. As she looked around her this afternoon, she knew it was true – the chocolate box cottages, the roses in full bloom, the sound of church bells in the distance as, according to Miss Cheggers, the bell ringers began their practice.

And as she walked she realised something else. Her shoulders were no longer wrapped up around her ears with worry, her back didn't ache in that way it had done for years, pretty much since she started cutting hair, and she hadn't thought about Joe all day. Her troubles hadn't disappeared – nothing was sorted out yet and wouldn't be until they could put the cottage on the market – but she discovered that when she was in Carybrook, all of those things stopped being front and centre of her mind, just for a while.

If Alf was already waving at her from outside the pub after she had only been here two days, Meredith could only imagine what it would be like to live here, and she didn't hate the idea as much as she thought she would.

She let herself into Butterfly Cottage via the back gate, which led into the bottom of the garden, near to where Zach's caravan was parked. The man himself was busy digging into what Meredith presumed was a vegetable bed, wearing nothing but a pair of cargo shorts and boots. He hadn't noticed her arrival and she watched him for a moment and thought about that other gardener from fifty-five years before who may or may not have been dating her great-aunt.

'Hi,' she called, realising she had been staring at Zach for a little too long.

He turned and smiled at her, and she noticed her stomach flip as he did. Now, that was a feeling that would cause nothing but inconvenience.

'Hello,' he said. 'So what's the news from Miss Cheggers?'

Meredith was surprised to feel a little disappointed at this – as though he had only been smiling at her return because she might have news about the mystery of Butterfly Cottage.

'I don't know,' she replied. 'I'm not sure I've learned anything new – but she did say that the woman in the photograph inside the locket was definitely Clara.'

'I could do with a break,' Zach said. 'I've got some beers in the fridge, would you like one?'

'I would but I've got to drive back to London this afternoon.'

'Cup of tea then? Or lemonade?'

'Lemonade sounds good.'

'I should make some lunch too – just bread and cheese, but I'm happy to share.'

'Thank you,' she said.

He disappeared into his van and she sat down on one of the chairs outside watching the garden. She could see why the house was called Butterfly Cottage – the nearby flowerbed was full of butterflies, swarming all over various purple-coloured flowers. Of course, she had no idea what they were.

She smiled at how bucolic it was – bread and cheese and beer on a warm summer's afternoon. Had Clara Samuels shared bread and cheese with her gardener here in the garden of Butterfly Cottage all those years ago? Was that who the man in the photograph was? Finding the locket and speaking to Miss Cheggers hadn't really thrown any light on her great-aunt but it had certainly made her more determined to find out who Clara was and what had driven her away.

Meredith had grown up without any family except her mother and she had always envied her friends with many siblings and cousins. She'd always wondered what it would have been like to have a big family and although one great-aunt did not make a particularly large family, the idea of Clara – who she was and what motivated her – made Meredith long to find out more.

Zach returned after a while, fully clothed now and holding a large plate of bread and cheese in one hand and two bottles in the other. He put the plate down on the table and passed her the bottle of old-fashioned lemonade before taking a swig of his beer.

'That's better,' he said, sitting down.

'What are these plants here?' Meredith asked. 'The ones covered in butterflies.'

'The taller flowers are lavender and the others are marjoram.'

'They smell amazing. Is that what attracts the butterflies?'

'Sort of,' Zach replied. 'Although you should see the number of butterflies on the buddleia when it flowers in July.' He pointed to a larger bush on the other side of the garden. 'Miss Samuels wanted to attract bees and butterflies to the garden.'

'I know nothing about plants and flowers,' Meredith said. 'Or nature, really.'

'Anyone can learn, it's pretty easy.' He paused, looked at her. 'Now tell me what Miss Cheggers told you.'

Meredith helped herself to crusty bread and chunks of cheddar and stilton as she began to tell Zach everything she'd learned that morning – the dates that Clara taught at the school, the man that she may have been seeing over the summer, the way that her grandparents had left Carybrook at the same time as Clara and, of course, the letters that had supposedly been delivered to an empty cottage.

'Well,' Zach said after a moment, 'there's a lot of conjecture and rumour there. Much of which is what I presume the dominoes team were talking about on Friday.'

'Miss Cheggers did admit that she didn't know anything concrete.'

'But amongst all that there are bound to be little bits of truth – like the man Miss Samuels was meant to be seeing. Do you know his name?'

Meredith shook her head. 'No. I thought that there

may be employment records at Ickbury Manor and we could look to see if he left that autumn too, but without a name that would make it difficult.'

'Or if we found that one of the gardeners had left in November 1963, we might have our man.'

'Do you think it's the man in the locket?' Meredith asked.

'Perhaps,' Zach said. 'Can I see it again?'

She pulled it out of her pocket and passed it over.

'He's pulling that face so it's hard to tell what he looks like,' he said. 'But he clearly made Miss Samuels happy.'

'She never mentioned any of this to you, did she?' Meredith asked.

'She never really talked about the past at all, although I would have thought coming back here would have brought up memories. But then I was just an employee, she wouldn't have talked to me about it.'

'It sounds to me as though you meant a lot more to Clara than that. But I wonder if you reminded her of another gardener who might have spent time here.'

Zach raised his eyebrows and Meredith laughed.

'I don't mean in a weird *May to December* kind of way, I just mean you might have reminded her of her youth, of what used to be.' She stopped. 'Oh, I don't know, I'm probably being overly romantic about it all.'

'We could definitely go to Ickbury Manor and find out about employment records,' Zach said. 'That might help. And I'll ask around about the letters, see if anyone knows about them or has heard that rumour before.'

'And I guess I should start thinking about going back to London,' Meredith said reluctantly. She had never wanted to do anything less in her life. Whenever she went to Spain to see her mother and Lloyd she was always sad to leave, and at the same time excited to get back to her own life, but today felt different, as though returning to London was a step back into something she no longer wanted.

Which was ridiculous. She'd been in Carybrook for all of forty-eight hours. It couldn't possibly feel like home, could it? She thought of Alf waving to her from the pub again. She thought of the smell of honeysuckle in the lane behind Butterfly Cottage. She thought of the sunny bedroom that she'd slept in, the one with the lumpy mattress that Gary Molliner thought needed an en suite, and she thought of Clara Samuels and the mystery that surrounded her life.

'When will you be back?' Zach asked as though reading her thoughts.

'I'm not sure. My mum is coming over from Spain

tomorrow and I suspect she'll want to see the cottage, so maybe next week sometime?'

'It's the church fete next Saturday,' Zach said. 'I know that probably sounds terribly parochial to you but it's a lot of fun. We're raising funds for the church roof. It'll be a fun day if you fancy it, and you might get to meet some more people from the village.'

Meredith nodded. 'Well, we couldn't possibly miss something like that!' She made it sound like a joke but she was already excited to come back and participate in village events, to feel part of something that she didn't owe money to.

'I'll see you next week then,' Zach said. 'And you've got my number if you need anything in the meantime.'

Meredith held out her hand as though to shake his but instead, he pulled her towards him and into a hug. It was unexpected but not unwanted. It felt good to have him near her, to know he didn't resent her presence in this little world he'd created with Clara.

'We'll work all this out,' he said when he let her go. 'I promise.'

12

SUFFOLK, JUNE 1963

The first thing that Clara thought about when she opened her eyes the next morning was James Mackenzie. She thought of the swoop of his cheekbone and the way he blew smoke rings out into the night sky. She thought about his eyes, deep and brown that hadn't changed since he was a boy, and she thought about the press of his body against hers as they'd danced.

Had it really been him? It was almost impossible to imagine that the friend she had always regretted losing touch with should turn up like that, suddenly, out of the blue, when she moved back to the village she grew up in.

But was it really that strange? Many people have a

yearning, at some point in their lives, to return to the places of their childhood. It wasn't that surprising that he'd returned to the Carybrook area, and the dance at Ickbury was the only place for young people to go without travelling all the way to Ipswich. Not that either she or James were particularly young any more. But for whatever reason James had been there. It felt serendipitous...

Oh, for heaven's sake, Clara, she chastised herself as she got out of bed and headed to the bathroom to run herself a bath. *You're thirty-three years old. Don't be so ridiculous.*

But by the time she'd had her breakfast, sitting at the beautiful pine table that had come with the cottage, she found she was still thinking of James Mackenzie. She wished she hadn't rushed away like that the night before, she wished she could have asked Betty to just hold on for five minutes while she and James made arrangements to meet again.

I know where you are now, I'll come and find you.

But what if he didn't? What if he disappeared like his letters had done in the summer of 1948? What if she never saw him again?

She was catastrophising – a side effect of spending too much time alone. She needed to get on with her day. She had some shopping to do and she needed to find someone to help her in the garden, someone who could bring the Butterfly Garden back to the splendour that James's mother had created all those years ago.

She'd already planned out on a piece of paper how she wanted the garden to look. She'd sketched the flower beds running down either side of the lawn and listed the plants she wanted to grow there – lavender, hydrangea, buddleia, anemones, peonies – lots to attract the bees and butterflies. She wanted to plant a lilac and bring the old apple tree back to life. At the bottom of the garden, she wanted a vegetable bed or two for peas and beans, marrows and cauliflower. Was all of that possible? She had no real idea and made a note to visit the library in Ickbury, become a member and take out as many books on gardening as she could.

As she wrote her list of things to do before she had to start getting ready for the fete this afternoon, there was a knock on the front door. Clara wondered if it was the postman finally bringing her longed-for wallpaper. On her very last day in London, she had gone into Peter Jones and purchased the wallpaper she had been dreaming of for the living room walls. Despite pestering the postman almost daily, it had still not arrived. Maybe today was her lucky day.

And it was, in more ways than one.

Because it was her wallpaper, packaged up in a brown box with 'Peter Jones' printed on the side, but it wasn't the postman holding it.

It was James Mackenzie.

For a moment Clara didn't know what to say. She had been thinking about James for most of the morning, and now he was standing there on her doorstep, those thoughts made her blush.

'Good morning,' he said, breaking the silence. His voice was soft and did nothing to stop the feelings of anxiety and desire fighting for dominance in Clara's stomach. He looked even more handsome in the morning light and as he smiled at Clara she couldn't believe that he was real, that he was here, that he had indeed come and found her.

'These are for you, I believe,' he said, holding out the box of wallpaper and a copy of *The Times*. She took them from him as though in a dream and it was then that she realised she hadn't spoken yet. Her mouth felt dry, as though it wouldn't form words.

'Clara, are you all right?' he asked. 'I'm sorry, perhaps I shouldn't have come unannounced like this, I just...'

'It's lovely to see you,' she managed, stepping back into the house. When he had said he would come and find her she hadn't expected it to be so soon, so suddenly. Part of her hadn't expected it at all. 'Would you like to come in?'

He stepped into the hallway and stood on the doormat as he took off his cap. He looked uncomfortable. 'Would you like me to take my boots off?' he asked.

'Don't be silly,' Clara said, using the sing-song voice she used on her pupils to encourage them that always seemed to come out when she was nervous.

'Sorry,' he said. 'It's been a while since I've been in a house.'

'Where do you live?' she asked, realising he hadn't told her the night before.

'At Ickbury Manor. The gardeners live in a bothy on the estate. It's all good fun but it's a bit, well, uncivilised, I suppose. One day I'll make it to head gardener somewhere and get a house of my own.' As children, Clara hadn't noticed the differences between her and James. She'd known her parents weren't keen on their friendship, thinking the Mackenzies beneath them somehow, even though they went to Reverend Mackenzie's church services every week. Those differences that her parents had seen but she hadn't were more evident now. But she wasn't her mother, or her sister, or Richard. She didn't care about any of that.

James Mackenzie was standing in her house, just touching distance away from her. She'd dreamed of this moment for years.

She looked at him and could almost see the thickness of the air between them. It had all felt so easy the night before when they had been talking on the bench, but now everything felt horribly awkward. Clara hadn't expected to be so attracted to James when she saw him again.

'How did you come to have these?' she asked, indicating the parcel and newspaper in her hands.

'Your postman stopped me as I was coming up the path and, while I was talking to him, your paperboy shoved *The Times* into my hands. Although—' he looked at his watch '—isn't it a bit late for the morning paper?'

'The paperboy is the vicar's son,' Clara replied, raising an eyebrow at him.

'Well, vicar's sons have always been a tardy, unreliable lot.'

They both laughed as though letting go of something and a feeling of relief washed over Clara.

'This is just some wallpaper I ordered.' Clara placed the box down by the front door. 'And the news can definitely wait until later.' She glanced at the headline. 'More Profumo scandal, when will it end?'

When she looked at James he looked uncomfort-able again. Stories of sex and orgies in the morning papers were causing salacious gossip all over the vil-lage and she'd noticed how men sort of clammed up whenever a woman talked about it. 'Don't worry,' she said. 'I've lived in London long enough to not be of-fended by the stories of what powerful men get up to in their spare time. Come and have a cup of tea. I was just about to make another pot.'

He smiled and followed her into the kitchen, looking around him as he did.

'It's the same but different,' he said.

'I know, that's what I thought when I first came to see it in April.' She poured hot water into the teapot. 'The diocese did a lot of the work – decorating, re-doing the kitchen and that sort of thing – but I still need to put my mark on it. Hence the wallpaper.'

'What about the garden?' he asked, looking to-wards the French doors. Of course he was going to ask about the garden.

'Go and have a look,' Clara replied. 'I'll bring the tea out in a moment. But a word of warning – the years of vicars living here have taken their toll on the garden and the diocese didn't go so far as to do any-thing about it when they put the cottage up for sale.'

He stepped out into the garden, putting his cap

back on his head as he went. She watched as he gradually looked more comfortable now he was outside again and she wondered what he was thinking, what he was feeling, what he was remembering. He had only lived here for a couple of years but the garden must remind him of his mother.

She set a tea tray and put a few biscuits on a plate, taking it out onto the patio where there was an old wrought iron table and chairs. He came to sit next to her, not quite close enough to touch, just as he had the previous night. She wondered if he would take her hand again and her palm tingled at the memory of his touch.

'It needs some work,' he said as Clara poured the tea. 'But the bones of the garden are still there.'

'That's what I thought too,' she replied. 'Look, let me show you something.' She pulled out the sketches she had made of the garden and what she hoped to do with it. She had brought them out with the tea tray, hoping to be able to show him that she hadn't forgotten how beautiful this garden used to be and how beautiful it could be again. She showed James how she had thought it could be brought back to life, the flowers and shrubs she hoped to plant, the vegetables she hoped to grow.

He looked at her plans and nodded. 'All this is

great, Clara,' he said. 'But it's a lot of work to do on your own.'

She laughed. She had sensed his 'but' before it came, worried that it would be disappointment or criticism. 'I wasn't intending to do it on my own,' she said. 'Honestly, I wouldn't know where to start. I was going to try to find somebody to help me. I might put a card up in the post office and...'

'Try to find a gardener you mean?' he asked.

'Well, yes...'

'Because I might be able to help with that.' And there it was again, that slightly crooked smile, the dimple on the left side, the smile she had remembered her whole life.

But the way that smile made her feel was very different now.

'You must be so busy up at the Manor though, James,' she said. 'I don't like to ask you to help.'

'Would you like me to, though?'

'Yes,' she said. 'Yes, please! Absolutely, if you don't mind. I'd love someone to help me return the garden to its former glory, someone who knows what they're doing. I'll pay you, of course, but do you have time?'

'I'll make time,' he said. 'I get to restore my mother's old garden and spend time with you. Who wouldn't make time for that?' He leaned across the table and took her hand, just for a moment. 'And of course you don't have to pay me; getting to know you again is all I need.'

Clara felt herself go hot again and, knowing she must be blushing, she ducked her head to fiddle with the teapot.

'So tell me, Clara Samuels,' he said. 'What made you leave an exciting life in London to buy Butterfly Cottage?'

'Well, firstly, let's be clear – my life in London was far from exciting.' He already knew about the school she taught in and the boarding house she lived in. 'Sometimes,' she said, 'late at night when I couldn't sleep, I would think my fate would be like Mrs Benyon's – who may or may not have made up her husband – running a boarding house for women who were living out the dreams I never managed to make come to fruition.'

'That's not your fate, Clara,' James said softly.

'Maybe not, but it's how it felt. Everyone thinks that London is exciting, and it is in some ways. But it's also dirty and polluted and, when you don't have a huge amount of money, it's quite a struggle. You must know that.'

He nodded, looking down the garden. 'It's why my father wanted a countryside parish again and why, I think, I enjoy my work so much – it keeps me out of London.'

'Then you understand,' she said.

'I understand.'

'And then my sister told me about Butterfly Cottage.'

James smiled to himself. 'Esther wasn't my biggest fan if I recall.'

'Oh, it was my parents who weren't your biggest fans, James. Esther just found that siding with them made her life easier.'

'Rather than rebelling against them every day like you?'

'Yes, well, that didn't stop. They didn't want me to go to Cambridge, they said it would make me unmarriable.' She paused. 'Perhaps they were right. Anyway,' she went on before she read too much into that, 'when Esther told me about the cottage, I knew I had to try to buy it.'

'Brave step to buy a house as a single woman in a tiny, gossiping village,' James said. From any other man, it would have sounded patronising and insincere – as though it wasn't a brave step at all but a scandalous one. But from him, it sounded supportive, as though he knew the trouble it would have caused and he knew how ridiculous that trouble was.

'I was lucky that because of the money my parents left I was able to. Many women don't get that sort of chance. And my brother-in-law Richard helped a lot.'

'So Esther married a forward-thinking man?'

'Well, no, not exactly. He's quite conservative – in both senses of the word. But he is also very fond of my sister and so he agreed to help without too much complaint or lecturing.'

Clara realised then that she had told James more about London and her family than she had told anyone before. She was so comfortable talking to him, trusting him implicitly that what she said wouldn't go any further. It was exactly as it had been when they were children. He was the only person she'd ever told about how out of place she felt in her family, how different she was, as though she were a changeling from a fairy story.

She could sit here all day and talk to him, but then she realised the time.

'Oh no,' she said. 'It's only an hour and ten minutes until the fete begins and I haven't organised myself or had any lunch.'

James stood up, taking his cap off again. 'I should go,' he said. 'I shouldn't have come like this, surprising you, taking up your time, I...'

'Stay,' Clara said, aware of the desperation in her

tone, but she didn't care. She didn't want him to leave, not yet. 'I'll rustle us up some lunch and then you can come to the church fete. Miss Cheggers will be beside herself to see you after all these years.'

'Miss Cheggers,' James said. 'She's still here?'

'She's my boss, the headmistress of Carybrook School.'

'Well,' he said slowly. 'In that case, I'd love to come.'

'Good, you can help me with the jumble sale.'

* * *

By the time they arrived at the village green that afternoon, it felt to Clara as if the years between their last letter and now had disappeared. It felt as though she and James had never lost touch.

They'd talked over lunch about their childhoods, their very different memories of the war and James spoke about his life as a journeyman gardener – the places he'd travelled, the gardens he'd seen.

'I just wanted a job at first,' he'd said. 'But honestly, it's become a sort of calling. Helping to bring gardens back to life and seeing the results of our hard work, well...' he'd trailed off. 'It's made me the happiest I've been in a long time, probably since my family had to move away from Carybrook if I'm honest.'

'So when you heard about the job at Ickbury Manor I suppose you felt you had to come back,' Clara had said.

'It seemed like a sign.'

'That's exactly what I thought when I heard about Butterfly Cottage.'

They had both agreed that Carybrook had a way of drawing you back when you least expected.

At the village green, the children were already setting up the jumble sale when Clara and James arrived. Or rather the girls from Clara's class were setting things up. The boys were playing some sort of complicated fighting game which involved many of them rolling around on the grass.

'Come along now everybody, stand up!' Clara called in her most authoritative teaching voice. Everyone stood up straight. Even James seemed to roll his shoulders back. 'We've got work to do and we don't want to be seen by everybody covered in grass stains, do we?'

'No, Miss Samuels,' the boys chorused.

'Now, this is my friend Mr Mackenzie and he is here to help us with the jumble sale.'

James raised an eyebrow as though wondering how he'd ended up roped into this on his day off.

Clara examined the table that was to be the jumble sale. 'Hmm,' she said. 'The problem is that everything is a little too neat.' The girls had set everything out in tidy rows on the tabletop. 'The point of a jumble sale,' she went on, 'is that everything is a jumble. People want to have a good rummage about and hope to find a bargain. And remember, just because you wouldn't want to buy it doesn't mean that somebody else doesn't.' She directed this comment towards two of the more particular girls in her class who had spent most of the last few days trying to ferret out and dispose of everything that they deemed not worth selling.

'But Miss...' one of the girls started to say.

'Come along, Amelia,' Clara interrupted. 'Let's get everything on display and remember, it doesn't have to be neat.'

The boys had become interested when they had finally realised that the point of the jumble sale was to jumble everything together and were already hard at work doing just that. With James's help, they were soon throwing piles of clothes and toys onto the table, their work accompanied by hoots of laughter. Clara smiled to herself as she watched James throw himself into things.

Amelia stood at the edge of the table looking very annoyed at proceedings, so Clara asked her to help put the signs out.

'How will people know how much to pay for things when they are all jumbled up like that?' she asked.

'They will make an offer and you'll accept it. Nothing is worth more than a few pennies, but every penny counts when it comes to the church roof,' Clara replied, trying to sound enthusiastic about a roof she didn't think would ever be fixed.

'How's everything going here?' a voice asked from behind them, and Clara turned around to see Miss Cheggers. 'Just checking that everyone is all right and has enough help, but I can see everything is well underway here.'

'We're all ready to go,' Clara said. Amelia still didn't look convinced.

'And such a beautiful day for it,' Miss Cheggers replied.

'There's somebody I'd like you to meet,' Clara said to the headmistress before calling James over, distracting him from a struggle with an old sheet.

'Hello, Miss Cheggers,' James said, grinning. 'Clara told me you were the headmistress these days.'

Miss Cheggers stared at James for a moment, as though trying to place him. Clara was about to introduce him, realising that the headmistress must have seen hundreds of children over the years and probably didn't remember one who had left the village well over two decades before, when Miss Cheggers broke into a smile.

'James Mackenzie,' she said.

'You remember me?' James looked surprised.

'I remember everyone who passes through this school,' Miss Cheggers said, although Clara couldn't possibly see how. 'And what brings you back to Carybrook after all these years? Have you two kept in touch all along?'

'No,' Clara replied. 'It was sheer coincidence that we bumped into each other at the dance in Ickbury last night.'

'It's the first time we've seen each other since before the war,' James said, explaining to Miss Cheggers about his work and the job at Ickbury Manor.

'I always say that Carybrook draws everyone back in the end,' Miss Cheggers said, echoing what James and Clara had discussed over lunch. 'Now, I hope to catch up with you later, Mr Mackenzie,' she went on, 'but I must check on the other stalls.'

James tipped his cap at her as she went on her way.

'She's not changed a bit,' he said. 'Nothing has, really.'

'Carybrook is a village preserved in time,' Clara laughed.

'With a church roof that will never be mended.'

The afternoon flew by and the jumble sold surprisingly well. The children watched in awe as their little pot of pennies grew and grew.

'Look how much we've raised, Miss,' Amelia crowed, her previous doubts about jumble sales seemingly forgotten.

'Can we sneak off yet?' James asked quietly. 'Take a look around?'

Clara was torn, but only for a moment. Her responsibility had to be with her class.

'I can't,' she replied. 'I have to stay with the children, but why don't you have a wander around and meet me back here in half an hour. The parents should have all been along to collect their darlings by then and I'll be all yours.'

James smiled. 'Well, there's an offer I can't refuse,'

he said and, as he walked away from her, he winked and she felt herself melt.

When she'd moved back to Carybrook she hadn't expected any of this, but she certainly wasn't complaining.

'Ah, there you are, old girl.' A voice penetrated her thoughts and she looked over to see Richard giving the jumble sale a cursory glance. She knew he would have already made a generous donation to the church and would have no desire to buy anything second-hand.

'Hello, Richard,' Clara said. 'Are you having a nice afternoon?'

'Not bad, not bad. Very good cream teas in the tea tent this year. Have you had a chance to try one?'

'Not yet, I've been manning the stall.'

'Good, good.' Richard looked awkwardly at the children.

'Where's Esther?' Clara asked, but as soon as the words came out of her mouth her sister was there in front of her.

'You will never believe who I've just seen,' Esther said.

'Who?' Clara asked, knowing full well who Esther would have seen. Damn, she'd been hoping to introduce James to Esther gently and a little further down the line when she knew what, if anything, was happening with their very tentative and new friendship.

As Esther was about to open her mouth some of the parents arrived to pick up their children.

'Hold on, Esther,' Clara said. 'I just have to deal with this.' She started to line the children up, making sure they had all their belongings and the shoes and clothes they arrived in.

All the parents seemed to arrive at once and there was the usual gentle chaos that reminded Clara of school pick-up time. Everybody walked in Carybrook, so parents often found themselves loaded down with all sorts of items that the children found important.

Once the madness had subsided, Clara turned back to Esther and Richard.

'Sorry about that,' she said. 'I wasn't expecting to see you both down here today.'

'Oh, Richard wanted a cream tea,' Esther said, a note of irritation in her voice. Richard pretended to be very interested in the jumble sale table.

'So what was it you wanted to tell me?' Clara asked, still scanning the crowd.

'James Mackenzie,' Esther said.

'Oh?' Clara replied, desperately trying to think of something to say.

'Yes, and he's standing right behind you!'

Clara turned and there James was. He took off his cap and stepped towards Esther, hand extended. 'Hello, Esther,' he said. 'How lovely to see you after all these years.'

Esther sniffed and took his hand tentatively. 'Not so many years,' she said. She hated to be reminded about how fast time was ticking away.

'And this is my brother-in-law, Richard,' Clara said. 'Richard, this is James Mackenzie. Esther and I were at school here in Carybrook with him years ago. He left with his family just before the war.'

'Good to meet you,' Richard said, giving James a much more friendly handshake than Esther had. 'Have you tried the cream teas? They are very good.'

'For goodness' sake, Richard,' Esther muttered.

'So what brings you back to Carybrook then?' Richard asked.

Before James could say anything, Esther interrupted. 'You don't seem very surprised to see him, Clara,' she said.

'Well, no,' Clara replied. 'We met last night at the dance in Ickbury, quite by chance. James has been kindly helping with the jumble sale today and he's going to help me with the garden at Butterfly Cottage.'

'Is he?' Esther asked, eyebrows raised.

'Well, I am a gardener by trade these days,' James

said, explaining about his work and the job at Ickbury Manor.

'I thought you were going to be a vicar like your father,' Esther said.

'Unfortunately not. The calling never came.'

Esther sniffed again. 'Well, we can't stand around here chatting all day,' she said. 'Richard and I have a dinner at the golf club tonight. We'll see you for lunch tomorrow, Clara. We'll talk then.' And with that, Esther and Richard were gone.

'That sounded ominous,' James said.

'I'm sorry, she wasn't very friendly.'

'I did tell you she didn't like me much. I wasn't expecting her to roll out the red carpet. I wouldn't mind one of those cream teas, though, and then I'll walk you home, if you'll let me.'

Together they finished packing up the tables and returning everything to the school and then they headed for the tea tent to see if there was anything left. They were in luck and were soon enjoying the last two scones in the tent. Miss Cheggers found them there and came over to say goodbye.

'Another wonderful fete,' she said. 'And more money raised for the church roof. One day perhaps it will be fixed.'

Afterwards, James walked Clara back to Butterfly

Cottage, the long way round so they could spend a little more time with each other. When they arrived they stood nervously at the door.

'Would you like to come in?' Clara asked.

'I can't really stop but I will step in for a moment.'

She unlocked the door and they both stepped inside. James closed the door behind him but made no move to come further into the cottage. He took Clara's hand, drawing her towards him. She felt her stomach flip again. 'Before I go...' He paused and looked into her eyes, ducking his head for a moment and letting his lips brush hers.

'I've been wanting to do that since I first saw you last night, Clara Samuels,' he said.

13

LONDON AND SUFFOLK, JUNE 2018

Meredith stood on the concourse at Liverpool Street station waiting for the train from the airport to arrive, one hand wrapped around the locket that she wore around her neck. She had found that she didn't want to be parted from it as though if she stared at it for long enough, it would answer all her questions.

She was early, of course; she was nearly always early for everything. Everything except returning the hire car the evening before. She'd procrastinated for so long at Butterfly Cottage – lingering in the dappled shade of the garden, sitting in the bedroom that may once have been her great-aunt's – that the hire car office had been closed when she'd got back to London.

She had posted the keys through the letterbox and hoped that they wouldn't charge her for another day.

What had made her so reluctant to leave Carybrook and come back to London? She loved London, had lived there all her life and had never been able to imagine herself anywhere else.

But Carybrook hadn't felt like that at all, not after the initial shock of it had settled over her. When she'd first arrived and met Zach, she'd wanted to hotfoot it straight back to the city, to run from a situation she hadn't been expecting. But once she'd spoken to Zach, eaten in the pub, and met some of the people who had known of her great-aunt (nobody other than Zach, it seemed, had actually known her), she'd begun to feel oddly at home. And as she'd walked back from Delia Cheggers' house the afternoon before, she had felt as though she had been in Carybrook for months, not days, and as though she never wanted to leave.

Driving back on Sunday evening, she had felt more and more anxious the closer she'd got to London. Everything had started to feel heavy again as the buildings grew closer together, the road signs became more familiar and she drove past shops and tube stations that she knew. It hadn't felt like coming home at all.

'Perhaps it's just the novelty of it all,' her mother had said when she'd phoned this morning before setting off for the airport. 'The newness of the countryside, a home of your own – well, half of one anyway – and an escape from the drudgery. Because you know daily life can be a drudge sometimes.'

Bernice had managed to escape her drudgery to Spain – or at least that was always the impression she gave – and so Meredith had agreed with her, even though she'd known there was more to it than novelty. More to it even than solving the mystery of Clara Samuels, and certainly a lot more to it than Zach's smile and the way he had hugged her. She shivered slightly at the memory of it.

Someone was calling her name and waving madly at her. Bernice's grinning head appeared from the crowd followed by the rest of her, dragging two huge pink suitcases. How long did she intend to stay? Meredith tucked the locket inside her top to avoid questions before she was ready.

'Darling girl!' Bernice called across the concourse as Meredith walked towards her.

As soon as they were within hugging distance, Bernice's arms were around her and suddenly, much to the surprise of both Bernice and herself, Meredith burst into tears.

***

She told her mother everything that evening as they sat in the flat she used to live in with Joe. They'd discussed it briefly when they'd talked the previous week, but it was time to confess the truth about the level of debt she was in and how she wasn't coping at all since Joe left. She told Bernice how Joe had insisted on giving her money when she was first opening up, knowing how much she wanted her own salon, and how he was demanding it back.

'And then the night before I left for Suffolk I met up with him. I wanted to borrow his car rather than hire one, but of course he said no because Jemma needs the car because Jemma is...' The words stuck in her throat for a moment.

'Jemma is what, love?' Bernice asked.

'Jemma is pregnant.'

'Oh.'

'And quite evidently became pregnant before Joe and I split up.'

'Oh,' Bernice said again.

'And now he wants the money back for Jemma and the baby. Which I understand, of course I do, but I don't have it.'

'You don't have to be sympathetic with Joe's

plight,' Bernice sniffed. 'Men can be such bloody bastards, screwing around, having babies all over the place and then making you feel guilty because they can't afford the product of their own loins. Honestly, if—'

'Mum, that's sort of disgusting and I beg you not to go on.'

'Well,' Bernice sniffed again. 'Let's just agree that we are not going to sit around "understanding" what Joe is going through. He gave you that money because he believed in you and wanted to help you but he knows as well as any of us that no business is guaranteed to be a roaring success.'

'And mine is quite the opposite of a roaring success,' Meredith admitted. 'We're busy and we charge a good rate, but the overheads are so expensive and...' She paused.

'And?' Bernice said.

'There's a bank loan as well,' she said, unable to look at her mother whose mantra had always been 'neither a borrower nor a lender be.'

'Well, what's done is done and now we have to move forward. Let's start with the money you owe Joe. How much is that?'

'Five thousand pounds, plus interest. I'd have to work it out exactly.'

'Well, he can forget about the interest for a start,' Bernice said. 'Did he ever mention it was a loan with interest when he gave it to you?'

'No, but—'

'But nothing. Now, Lloyd and I talked as he drove me to the airport this morning. We agreed that we would help you out.'

'Mum, no. This is my mess and I need to fix it. I just need everyone to wait until Zach is ready to sell the cottage and then...'

'Darling girl,' Bernice said, leaning back in her chair. 'If we wait for a man to do something we'll be waiting forever.' Bernice really didn't like men very much, which was understandable after years with the disappearing Dennis. Meredith had always been surprised when she'd settled down so happily with Lloyd. But then they both knew that he was a very special person and it gave Meredith faith that there were still special people in the world. 'I think we have to put a pin in the cottage for the moment. When and if you do sell it that will be a lovely nest egg for you. But you've explained why Zach doesn't want to sell yet and it seems to me that if money is owed it should be paid back, so we'll start with Joe. Lloyd and I will pay him back that five thousand and no more, and then you can start the messy business of getting over him. You can't start that if you owe him money.'

'But then I'll owe you and Lloyd money and...'

'No, you won't, because this is a gift. Think of it as me making up for all the times we had to do without when you were younger.'

'Mum, I can't...'

'Meredith Carling, this is non-negotiable.'

Meredith wrapped her arms around her mother. 'Thank you, Mum,' she said. 'I'll call Lloyd tomorrow and thank him too.'

'The next thing you need to do is move out of this flat. You can't possibly afford the rent on your own. When can you move out? Is it a long-term lease?'

Meredith felt sick at the thought of having to move out of her flat and the idea of having to find somewhere new. But she also knew her mother was right, she couldn't keep floating along throwing good money after bad and she couldn't wait for Butterfly Cottage to sell either. She'd been a fool to think all her problems were immediately over when Mr Maddison had given her the news. Even if the problem of Zach hadn't existed, a house doesn't sell overnight. There were weeks and weeks of finding a buyer and of the buyer finding a mortgage and then the entire legal process of the sale. She knew about that from friends and from the research she and Joe had done, hoping that one day they could afford the house they dreamed of.

'I'm on a two-month rolling contract,' she said. 'If I hand in my notice tomorrow I'll have to leave by the middle of August.'

Bernice nodded. 'And then we'll have to find you somewhere to go. You could come back to Spain with me. You'd be very welcome, you know, and you'll easily find a job in a salon. I can talk to my hair-dresser. Everyone speaks English round there and—'

'Mum, just because Joe and I have split up doesn't mean I can just drop everything and come to Spain.'

'Well, you have a house of your own now of course. Or at least half a house.'

'To be honest, it's a whole house in terms of living,' Meredith said. 'Zach lives in a caravan at the bottom of the garden.'

'He doesn't come into the house at all?'

'Not really.'

'How does he wash and so forth?'

'Mum, for goodness' sake!'

'It's a reasonable question,' Bernice said, clearly horrified at the thought of anyone living in a caravan when they had other options.

'There is a shower in his van, he has it hooked up

to the water. And electricity somehow and he uses the outside loo.'

'How peculiar. This whole business is very peculiar, you know.'

Meredith explained how sad Zach seemed whenever he talked about Clara. And about Alf and his brother and the old men in the pub and what Delia Cheggers had told her about the letters.

'And I found this too,' she said, looping the locket from around her neck. 'In Clara's old desk in the cottage.' She passed it to her mother who opened it and looked inside. 'I have it on good authority that the woman in the photo is Clara but we have no idea who the man is.'

'No, but I know who *this* man is,' Bernice said, turning the locket around. She had managed to prise out the picture of Clara and her mystery man and underneath was another photograph. This was of a severe-looking man, no funny faces here, in army uniform with a thick moustache.

'You probably don't remember,' Bernice went on, 'but Grandma Bradshaw had this photograph on her mantlepiece.'

'I don't remember. Who is it?'

'That is your great-grandfather, Esther and Clara's father.'

'Was he in the army?'

'No, but he joined up in the Second World War – I've no idea what he did or where he was stationed though. It does look like this locket had been in Clara's family. It's likely to have been her mother's, judging by this photograph of her father.'

'And she covered it up with a picture of her and this other man.'

Bernice nodded. 'Nobody knows who this chap is then?'

'Well, neither Zach nor Miss Cheggers did, but somebody might.'

'It's hard to know what he looked like pulling that face, isn't it?'

Meredith nodded but didn't mention the strange feeling of recognition she'd had from the locket.

'Getting back to the state of my life,' Meredith said, changing the subject. 'The problem with moving to either Spain or Carybrook is that I won't be in London to see my clients and run my salon, and if I want any hope of getting out of this mess I need to work.'

'How long have you been trying to get out of this mess?' Bernice asked. 'Tell me the truth now.'

Meredith sighed. Admitting this to her mother felt

overwhelming and embarrassing. Bernice and Lloyd had been so supportive, so proud, and now she'd messed it all up and let everyone down. 'Over six months,' she admitted. 'Nothing seems to be working. I'm so sorry.'

'You have nothing to be sorry about. Businesses succeed and fail all the time. You've given it your best and that's all that matters.'

'I have no idea what to do.' It was the first time Meredith had admitted not only what a mess she'd got herself into but also how at the end of her tether she was, how she genuinely didn't know how to get the salon back on its feet, or even if she wanted to.

'Perhaps it's time,' Bernice said slowly, 'to think about moving on.'

* * *

They talked into the night and then, after a few hours' sleep, into the next day – making lists and going through the finances and the long lease on the salon to see what the options were for getting out of it. Meredith didn't want to give up on the salon, she didn't want to move on. What was there to move on to, after all? Going back to renting chairs from other hair-dressers? She was trained for nothing else and had never wanted to be. She'd have to start all over again from scratch.

But on the other hand, she knew her mother was right. She couldn't continue like this. She had to let go of her flat and her business somehow and start again, start afresh. And whenever she thought about starting again her mind went straight to Carybrook, to Butterfly Cottage and, surprisingly, to Zach.

Carybrook felt like somewhere she could start again, somewhere different – much more of a new beginning than going to Spain to move in with her mum and stepdad, however temporary that might be. But if she did give it all up, if she did manage to sell the business – or at the very least get out of the lease – what would she do and where would she live? Butterfly Cottage wasn't hers to just move into. Zach would want to sell eventually and she wouldn't have any money to buy him out – just as he didn't have the money to do the same for her. But maybe, with her half of the proceeds, she could afford somewhere in Carybrook – somewhere on the other side of the village.

She shook her head and drew her attention back to the list of things she needed to do that sat in front of her. She was kidding herself if she thought she'd be happy to leave London completely, but the words of the to-do list blurred and she found herself imagining what it would be like to cut the hair of the people of Carybrook. Was there a hairdresser in the village? Zach had mentioned needing a haircut. Was that just absent-mindedness or because there was nowhere to go? She was still thinking about it when Bernice placed a cup of tea on the desk beside her.

'You look miles away, love,' she said. 'Are you OK?'

'No, Mum, I really don't think I am. I...' She hesitated. Should she tell her mother what she'd been thinking about?

'Of course you're not OK,' Bernice said. 'Silly of me to even say so. But we've got a plan, haven't we?'

Meredith nodded.

'And I've written a cheque for that bloody Joe,' Bernice went on. Joe had dropped in her estimations to a point almost as low as Dennis and she spoke of him in the same tone of voice. 'So you can arrange to give that to him and get him off your back once and for all.'

'I'll post it,' Meredith said. 'I cannot face seeing him again and hearing about Jemma and the baby.'

'Do you know where he lives?'

She nodded. 'I've had to send all his post on.'

'You need to stop doing things for him, love, and stop meeting with him. This cheque finishes things.'

Meredith took the cheque. 'And I'll pay you back all of this, I don't care how much you protest.'

'Well, let's talk about that later. What about everything else? Have you managed to have a look through the lease, or call the bank about the loans?'

Meredith rubbed her hand over her head. 'No,' she said. 'I keep just looking at the list and thinking about…'

'What could have been?' Bernice asked.

'No. Not that. More like what might be now.'

'And?'

'I keep thinking about Carybrook, about Butterfly Cottage.'

Bernice looked at her daughter for a moment, her brow furrowed with either worry or thought – Meredith didn't know which.

'Would you like to know what I think?'

'Sure.' She had no idea what she thought herself, so why not see what her mother thought?

'You need a break. When did you last have a holiday?'

'Six years ago, but I can't take a holiday and leave all this mess behind me.'

'You've got a lot of decisions to make and I don't think you can make them sitting in this flat worrying about everything. You need to get away. Can you post-pone clients if you took a week off?'

'Of course, but that just sounds like less money coming in.'

'Just put a pin in that for the moment. I think we should pack up and go to Carybrook and work it all out from there. You have Wi-Fi at Butterfly Cottage, I suppose?'

'Yeah, Zach has everything set up.'

'Well, start packing then and we can be there for the fete you were telling me about. And I can finally meet the gorgeous Zach!'

* * *

They set off early on Saturday morning in a car Bernice had rented. As they drove out of London, Meredith was consumed by a sense of overwhelming relief and a feeling that, after this, nothing would ever be the same again. The cheque was in the post to Joe, she'd worked out the break clauses in the salon lease and she'd given notice on the flat. Hopefully, she could find the space she needed to work out where to go next. She hadn't ac-tually handed in her notice on the salon or spoken to the landlord to make arrangements to do so – she couldn't do that without talking to everyone who worked there, she owed them all that – but she was beginning to see it was the only option. She realised now that what she had taken on had become too big, too unwieldy for her to continue to manage on the shoestring she had.

How did big salon owners cope? How did they keep their heads above water? Meredith could only assume they had a better financial buffer than she had ever had. Maybe that was where she'd gone so wrong – by living on hope and credit.

As the fields of Suffolk passed by, she felt tears burn the back of her eyes. She knew her future was going to look very different, and in many ways, she welcomed that, but it didn't mean she wasn't going to grieve what could have been.

'Where do I go from here, love?' Bernice asked, and Meredith realised they were driving down the stretch of road where she had first met Zach out on his bike.

'Oh,' she said. 'We've come too far. I did this the first time I came out here.'

'Is that when you met the mysterious cycling Zach?' Bernice asked, looking over at her daughter.

'Yes, and keep your eyes on the road, please. You need to drive up to the next roundabout and go all the way around it and come back down this road. I'll direct you from there.'

They arrived at Butterfly Cottage at lunchtime and Bernice pulled the car up right behind Zach's truck, just as Meredith had done the week before.

'Johnson's Gardening Services,' Bernice said as they got out of the car and walked towards the cottage. 'So that's him then.'

Meredith sighed to herself. Her mother, rather typically, seemed to be far more interested in Zach than she was in the house itself. She was probably already marrying the two of them off in her imagination. She had a habit of doing that and Meredith knew that she must be devastated about her split with Joe, even though she pretended not to be. She wanted to be a grandma, Meredith knew that well enough.

But now Joe was having a baby with someone else.

'Mum,' Meredith said, trying to get her mother's attention which seemed consumed by Zach's truck. 'This is Butterfly Cottage.'

They stood in front of it and Meredith used the opportunity to take it all in – the gate at the end of the garden path that led to the green front door with roses growing around it, the flowerbeds under each window, the whitewashed walls. She breathed in. How did all this – well, half of all this – become hers? And now, as she looked at it properly for perhaps the first time, she wondered how on earth she could have been so hasty as to want to sell it immediately. She needed to rethink that decision in light of all the other decisions she had made since her mother's arrival.

'Wow,' Bernice whispered under her breath. 'I'm lost for words.'

Meredith found that very unlikely and sure enough within a minute her mother was rambling on about all the beautiful features of the cottage.

'And some great-aunt who nobody had ever heard of before just left you this?'

'Well,' Meredith replied, 'I'm assuming that Dad had heard of her before.'

'Oh, don't you talk to me about him. I'll—'

'And remember,' Meredith continued, interrupting the incoming rant. 'She didn't just leave it to me. She left it to Zach as well.'

'Oooh, yes, and when am I going to meet this Zach?' Bernice asked, Meredith's father seemingly forgotten.

'Now, if he's here,' Meredith said as she unlocked the front door and ushered her mother in. 'What would you like to do first? A rest, a house tour, or...'

'Let's look at this garden,' Bernice replied, striding to the back of the house as if she owned the place, cooing and gushing about everything as she went. 'Gorgeous kitchen,' she said. 'It'll need some renovation though, eventually. Oh, and I like this sunroom and oh...' She stopped at the French doors, looking out. 'And this is the garden.'

Meredith leaned in front of her mother to turn the key and open the glass door into the garden.

'You know,' Bernice said, 'those doors aren't very secure. You need to speak to your insurers about that.'

Meredith's stomach turned over. Insurance. Was there any? Why had she not asked Zach? Could she not get anything right?

'What's the matter?' Bernice asked softly.

'Oh, nothing. It's just this house. Whenever I see it I can hardly believe it's half mine.'

'It is astonishing,' Bernice said, looking out into the garden. 'It's so unexpected, so unlikely. There has to be a catch, surely.'

'Well, the fact that I own it with a man I hardly know is quite problematic,' Meredith replied.

'Look at this garden,' Bernice said. 'I always wanted a garden when you were little, you know, but as there were only two of us the council would only ever give us a flat.'

'But we had that lovely garden once you met Lloyd.' Meredith remembered the herbs that Bernice used to grow on the kitchen windowsill, and the park down the road where the swings were always broken by bigger children – the nearest things they had to a garden until Lloyd came along.

'Well, that garden was nothing like this!'

'Mum, I don't think many ordinary people on the Kent border have a garden like this.'

Bernice seemed to pick herself up from her reverie then and began to walk down to the bottom of the garden, striding in a determined manner. Meredith followed her, counting the butterflies as she went. She didn't think she'd ever seen so many in one place, not even on the bougainvillea that grew outside her mother's house in Spain.

As they walked around the dogleg at the end of the garden, Meredith saw Zach's caravan and then Zach himself, crouched down in one of the vegetable beds he had recently dug. When he saw them he stood up, taking off his gloves and wiping his hands on his shorts.

He caught Meredith's eye and grinned. 'You're back,' he said, and there it was again, that inconvenient feeling in her stomach.

Meredith watched as her mother approached Zach with her hand extended.

'I'm Bernice Collins, Meredith's mother,' she said.

'And you must be Zach Johnson.' Zach took the proffered hand, a rather confused look on his face. 'Hello, Mrs Collins,' he said.

'Oh, please call me Bernice. And don't worry, I'm not stalking you. I saw your name on your truck outside.'

Zach smiled and opened his mouth to say something but Bernice was off again.

'This must be your caravan then. Meredith tells me you live here. Is it comfortable? Why don't you live in the house?'

'Mum...' Meredith said.

'What? I'm just asking.'

'I prefer the van,' Zach replied. 'I'm just used to it.'

'Funny way of living,' Bernice muttered.

'Mum,' Meredith repeated, warning in her voice.

Bernice ignored her and turned back to Zach. 'Well, it's lovely to meet you at last. I feel like you're all Meredith talks about.'

'Mum!'

'Is that right?' Zach grinned and looked over at Meredith.

'Now, what are we doing about lunch?' Bernice asked.

'We could go to the pub,' Meredith replied. 'You could meet Alf and some of the locals.'

'That sounds lovely. I've always fancied living in a village.'

'You do live in a village, Mum!'

'Spain isn't the same. I mean an English village, like Miss Marple investigating where this great-aunt of yours came from.'

Zach watched this exchange in a slightly dazed way as if he wasn't quite sure what had hit his quiet and idyllic life.

'Perhaps you should freshen up, Mum?' Meredith asked. 'I'll take your things up to your room and put the sheets on the bed for you.'

'Oh, I can do all that,' Bernice replied. 'Just give me the car keys and I'll bring our stuff in.'

She took the keys and headed off back towards the house. 'See you later, Zach,' she called.

'I'm sorry about that,' Meredith said, turning to Zach. 'She's very excited and intrigued about this whole business – when she's not cursing my father, of course.'

Zach smiled that smile that seemed to melt Meredith every time she saw it. 'That's OK,' he said. 'The pub might be busy at lunchtime though because of the fete.'

'Oh, of course. Mum is very eager to see the fete.'

'But you don't seem so keen?'

'Is it that obvious?' Meredith asked. The thought of her mother at the fete was a bit exhausting. 'I'm just feeling a bit overwhelmed by things I have to do. I should have insured this house, shouldn't I? And I haven't so that's something to add to the list...'

'Meredith, the house is all insured. I just took over the insurance that Miss Samuels had taken out.'

'I should pay half then at least.'

'Meredith, are you OK?' Zach asked.

She realised she had been babbling, as she often did in situations that made her anxious like this one. Although she couldn't quite pinpoint what she was anxious about. She was glad to be back in Carybrook, glad to be away from London. But that didn't mean all her problems had disappeared.

'Yes, I'm fine.' She looked at him and smiled although it felt more like a grimace. 'What are you planting?'

'Pumpkins and squash. I've been growing them in pots but they're big enough to plant out now. They need a lot of space to grow.'

'I... Why are you doing this if you might not be here when the pumpkins are ready to harvest?'

Zach sighed. 'Because it's what I do,' he said. 'And it's what Miss Samuels wanted. She said there had been a vegetable patch here when her childhood friend lived here – not pumpkins though, nobody grew pumpkins then. But she wanted pumpkins now and...' He stopped and rubbed a hand over his forehead. 'I know it's stupid. I know we'll have to sell, but I have to do this, and once it's done there's only a few other jobs before we can put the cottage on the market so...' He trailed off, turning back to his pumpkins.

'There's no rush to sell,' Meredith said. 'Not any more.'

Zach looked up, squinting in the sun. 'But I thought...' He stopped.

It was then that she realised she was crying the tears that she had been blinking back on the car ride here, not wanting her mother to know how sad she was.

'Everything's fallen apart and I have to sell the salon and move out of my flat and my ex is having a baby with somebody else and unless I go back to Spain with my mother I have nowhere to go but here so I can't sell it until I've worked out...' She stopped, choking back tears. 'I'm sorry. None of this is your problem, I'll go and find Mum and...'

'No, wait. Come and sit down, talk to me. This is our house and if you need to live here for a while that's fine with me.'

Meredith let herself be led towards the caravan and sat down on one of the chairs outside. Zach stepped inside the van and reappeared with a box of tissues.

'Just let me put some of these pots away in the shed and I'll get you something to drink.'

Meredith nodded, sniffing into her tissue. As she waited for him to come back she found herself thinking about the salon and about that sense of relief that she'd felt as they'd driven away from London. It was almost as though she didn't want the salon, the only thing in her life that she was proud of. It was almost as if she would be glad to get rid of it if she did sell it or close it down.

Was it true that it was the only thing she was proud of? Was it even the salon she was proud of at all? She was proud of herself as a hairdresser and of the loyal client base she had built up, but the salon itself?

She had dreamed of her own salon for so long, but when it happened it hadn't felt as good as she'd hoped it would. When she really allowed herself to think about it the salon itself had always made her anxious, from the day she'd signed the lease. She knew she should have got a solicitor to look through it, but Joe had told her it was a waste of money, that he could do it himself. He worked in building management so Meredith had believed him, but it had been so complicated. When she and her mother had been looking for the break clauses it had taken over an hour to decipher them.

Joe had been the driving force behind the salon, constantly telling Meredith that it was the next step, the thing that would put her on the ladder to success. She had already felt quite successful at that point – she had loyal clientele and a healthy bank account. But that bank account had been wiped out by the overheads for the salon and she had never built the savings back up again.

She had been seduced by the idea of being in one place and not having to trek across south London to the various salons she worked in. She'd been seduced by plate glass doors and state-of-the-art equipment rather than relying on what had always been her bread and butter – her own hairdressing skills. At the time Joe had seemed so supportive, but now as she looked back she wondered if it was supportive to force somebody into something they weren't one hundred per cent happy with.

Her thoughts were interrupted by Zach walking back towards her.

'Meredith,' he said. 'I know that we need to talk

and we will, I promise, but I think you need to see this first.'

He was holding a rusty old biscuit tin that appeared to have pictures of the Queen's coronation on the side.

'Where on earth did you get that?' she asked.

'I found it in the shed. It's a total mess in there and I need to sort everything out. As I was putting the pots away I knocked over a spade which in turn knocked over a shelf and this fell off. I wouldn't have paid it much attention if it hadn't opened as it landed.'

'What's inside? Something horrible?'

'Not horrible, no,' Zach said, handing Meredith the tin. 'Take a look.'

Meredith prised open the biscuit tin and looked inside. There sitting at the bottom of the tin were a small pile of letters with handwritten addresses on the envelopes. All the addresses were made out to Butterfly Cottage and the stamps looked very old. The letters were tied up with garden twine.

'Oh my God,' Meredith whispered. 'Are these the letters that Delia Cheggers told me about?'

'I think so,' Zach replied.

PART II

PART II

21 June 1964

My Darling

It is Midsummer's Day and all I can think about is you. Both of you. Because of course I remember. How could I forget?

As I haven't heard back from you I think perhaps I should stop writing, that I should stop bothering you and leave you to your new life. I have no right to know anything after what I did, after how I was tempted, after what I let myself believe.

I went back to Carybrook last month. I parked outside Butterfly Cottage. But I never got out of my car. I was too afraid, too ashamed by what I had done to face you or anybody else.

But as I sat there, waiting for nothing at all and remembering everything, I noticed how shabby the cottage was looking, how over-grown the front garden was. And I wondered if you had left. Have my letters been delivered to an empty cottage? Have you not read any of them? You will never know how sorry I am.

But I don't deserve your forgiveness so perhaps it is for the best that you didn't read what I'd written – all those apologies, all that plead-

ing. Nobody needs to read that. For a moment, as I sat in the car outside Butterfly Cottage, I thought about breaking in and retrieving all the letters, setting fire to them.

And yet here I am writing just one more.

I should never have listened to Richard. I should never have taken the money.

Always,

JM

14

SUFFOLK, JUNE 2018

Meredith stared into the biscuit tin.

'I haven't read them,' Zach said. 'I haven't even looked at them. The postmark on that top one is June 1964 though and that's what made me think...'

'That they were the letters Delia Cheggers told me about.'

Zach nodded, sitting down next to Meredith.

'We should read them,' she said. 'But it doesn't seem right somehow. They aren't our letters. They're none of our business, really.' She looked at Zach. 'What would you do?'

'If Miss Summers had left the house entirely to me,' Zach said, 'and I hadn't heard Delia Cheggers' story, I'd probably just burn them – because they aren't any of my business. But it's different for you. This is your family – a family that until a few weeks ago you had no idea even existed.'

'Should I read them, then?' Meredith asked.

'Well, if it helps,' Zach replied. 'They have been opened, so Miss Samuels had read them. She did know what they contained before she died.'

'Do you think they were here, just sitting on the doormat when she came back from Australia?'

'Considering nobody had set foot in the house since she left, I'd say yes.'

'How weird it must have been for her,' Meredith mused, 'for this voice from the past to just be sitting there, waiting for her to return.'

She reached into the biscuit tin and picked up the letters. There were eight altogether and, according to the postmarks, they dated from November 1963 to the last letter in June 1964. 'I should read them in order,' she said, sorting them by date.

Zach reached out and touched her wrist. She felt that familiar tingle of electricity where his skin touched hers. 'Before you do,' he said, 'you were going to tell me something earlier. Do you still want to talk?'

Meredith sighed and dropped the letters back into the tin. Excited as she was to read them, they wouldn't change anything about her situation. Everything was still a mess; she would still have to sell the salon and find somewhere else to live and start again. She might even solve the mystery of Clara Samuels, but it wouldn't really change anything. She couldn't live on fresh country air.

She shook her head. 'It's OK,' she said. 'Things are a bit of a mess but they'll sort themselves out.'

'But you need the money from this house to help them sort themselves out, don't you?'

'Not straight away, Zach. I feel as though I need a bit of space to do nothing, to work out what I need to do next and, as Mum suggested, Carybrook seems as good a place as any.'

'You know we don't have a hairdresser in Carybrook.'

'Which explains the state of your hair.' Meredith smiled.

'I do need a haircut. We used to have a woman who came round in a van. She did Miss Samuels's hair for her and gave mine a trim now and then, but then she disappeared.'

'People seem to have a habit of doing that around here.'

Zach smiled. 'All I'm saying is that I reckon there's clients here if you want them.'

The thought had, of course, crossed Meredith's

mind too but it was too soon to be thinking about any-thing like that. She had a lot of loose ends to tie up before she could start something new.

She smiled at Zach. 'I'll think about it,' she said.

Bernice appeared, walking towards them.

'Hello, you two,' she said. 'Are you ready for some lunch and this fete then?' She stopped, looking at the biscuit tin that sat on Meredith's knee. 'What's that you've got there?'

'Zach found it in the shed over there,' Meredith said. 'Mum, do you remember me telling you that I met up with a woman called Delia Cheggers and she told me a little about Clara Samuels and Butterfly Cottage?'

'Is she the one who told you the story about those letters being delivered to the empty cottage?' Bernice asked. 'That's a tale that's grown legs over the years if ever I've heard one. As if that—'

'Mum,' Meredith interrupted. 'I think what we've got here is those letters.'

Bernice stared at her daughter.

'Really?' she said. 'But I assumed it was just a sort of village legend.'

'Well,' Zach interjected. 'Let's not get over-excited. We haven't actually read them yet, but the dates on the postmarks do add up to what Meredith was told.'

'Let's read them then,' Bernice said. 'What are we waiting for?'

But Meredith continued to sit with the biscuit tin on her lap, not moving.

'What's the matter, love?' Bernice asked.

'It doesn't seem right to read them. They're not my letters and this is not my story.'

'No,' Zach said. 'I get that they're not your letters, but this *is* part of your story. I knew Miss Samuels. I worked for her and talked to her every day. We became friends over time. But you never knew her and she never got in touch with you. There has to be a reason why and that is part of your story.'

'He's right, you know,' Bernice said. 'And short of finding your father, which is very unlikely, I think these letters might be all we have to go on when it comes to the mystery of Clara Samuels.'

Meredith looked at the small pile of letters sitting in the biscuit tin and picked them up, weighing them in her hand. They felt old to the touch as if they might crumble to dust if she didn't treat them carefully. She remembered that they would have been old when Clara had first read them herself. Had Clara been expecting them or had they been a surprise? She wondered how her great-aunt had felt when she read them.

But Zach and her mum were right; this was partly her story now. She'd had no idea that Clara had existed and she wanted to know why she had never been in touch, not to mention why she had left Meredith half of the house. The whole situation was bizarre, one of those stories you wouldn't really believe if somebody else told it to you. Just as her mother hadn't really believed the story about the letters. It was no wonder Joe had called it her 'mythical cottage'.

She wondered if Joe had yet received the cheque that her mother had written. She wondered how he would feel when he saw it.

'Meredith,' Bernice said softly now. 'What would you like to do?'

'We can just put them back in the shed,' Zach suggested. 'Pretend we never found them.'

Meredith laughed gently. 'As if any of us will forget now. No, let's read them.'

She sorted them into date order and opened the first one, slowly unfolding the blue writing paper. It was dated toward the end of November 1963, a few days after the assassination of President Kennedy. It was apparently this tragic event that had nudged the author to write. Whoever the writer was – and Meredith presumed from the language that it was a man, although that was far from clear – they had thought of Clara when they'd heard about the assassination and had wanted to talk to her about it 'just like we always used to'.

As she read on, she interpreted some sort of separation between Clara and the writer, one that had been the writer's fault entirely, something that they deeply regretted as it was clear the writer had very deep feelings for Clara. It was impossible to tell what had happened between them though, just as it was impossible to know anything about Clara's side of the story, although there was reference to Richard and Esther, there was no indication of what had happened.

When she had finished the first letter, Meredith passed it to her mother as she opened the second one. When Bernice had finished reading, she passed her letter to Zach and so it went on until they'd all read them all.

'Well...' Bernice said, breaking the silence. She never had been a fan of silence.

'They don't tell us very much, do they?' Zach said. 'I'm sorry, Meredith, I was hoping they might unravel a bit of the mystery.'

'They were never going to though, were they?' Meredith replied. 'They weren't written by Clara so whoever did write them back in the sixties would have no idea that I'd be born over twenty years later.'

'He does mention Esther, though,' Bernice said. 'And Richard.'

'What makes you think the writer is a he?' Zach asked, eyebrow raised.

'Well, because whoever they are they are obviously in love with Clara, aren't they? But you're right, Zach, I shouldn't presume that means they were a man. They have only signed the letter with their initials, after all.'

Zach sat back in his chair. 'So tell me about Esther,' he said. 'What was she like?'

'She was my grandmother,' Meredith explained. 'My father's mother. She was also Clara's sister, although obviously she never mentioned that to either me or Mum. I don't know if Dad knew anything about her though.'

'He must have been the one who told Clara about you, though,' Bernice replied. 'So he must have known about her, we're just not sure when he found out.'

'Anyway,' Meredith went on. 'Esther was married to a man called Richard but he died before I was born. Did you ever meet him, Mum? I can't remember.'

'Mercifully, no. He died a year or two before I met

Dennis and there was no love lost there. I've never been entirely sure what happened between your father and grandfather but Dennis really didn't like him, didn't even want to talk about him, really. He only visited his mother reluctantly. I have...' She paused for a moment, looking at Zach. 'I have issues with my own parents so I never pushed for answers. Anyway," Bernice took a breath, "Richard and Esther lived in a house in Stevenage, and after Richard died Esther moved into a bungalow nearby which is where Meredith and I used to visit her. She never mentioned Clara or Carybrook in the whole time I knew her.'

'But they were here,' Meredith said. 'Gary Molliner thinks that's the reason Clara moved here in the first place.'

'So from what I can gather from these letters,' Zach said, 'Miss Samuels and the writer – we'll come back to who they might be in a minute – were obviously in some kind of relationship and then the writer left Carybrook, probably suddenly, would you agree?'

Meredith and Bernice both nodded.

'Everyone seemed to just disappear at the same time,' Bernice said.

'And your grandfather seemed to have something to do with the writer leaving. They say here in the last letter "I should never have listened to Richard. I should never have taken the money".'

'What on earth happened here?' Meredith asked quietly.

'And why?' Zach responded.

'I'm sorry, love,' Bernice said. 'These letters just seem to have complicated everything even further.'

The trio lapsed into silence again until, after a few minutes, Bernice's stomach rumbled.

'Oh, Mum, we never did go and get lunch.'

'That's OK, love, I can afford to miss a meal.'

'I can warm up some soup if anyone's interested?' Zach said.

'Actually, that would be lovely,' Meredith replied. 'I suddenly don't feel like going out anywhere. Those letters have made me feel incredibly sad.'

Zach disappeared into his van and started clattering about with pans while Bernice and Meredith were left with their own thoughts. Something truly tragic had happened here, Meredith thought, a love affair gone awry and two people who were meant to be together had been torn apart. The fallout seemed to have meant that Clara ended up on the other side of the world and her sister had never acknowledged her existence again.

How on earth did that happen?

And who was the mysterious letter writer who had signed their letters with their initials only – JM in a curling script?

* * *

None of them spoke about Clara or the letters or the man in the photograph over lunch and, when the meal was finished, Bernice announced that she was going to go for a walk around the village to get the lay of the land. 'Maybe I'll pop into that fete you were talking about,' she said.

'Do you want me to come with you?' Meredith asked.

'No, love, it's OK. I can see that you don't really want to. You stay here and I promise I won't go asking nosey questions about Clara Samuels or the man in the photograph.'

Meredith smiled. 'Are you sure you won't get lost or anything?'

'I'll be fine, love. You know me, I'm sure I'll meet someone who can point me in the right direction.'

Bernice was one of those people who made friends wherever she went.

Zach and Meredith sat in silence after Bernice had left, neither of them wanting to speak or move.

'I brought my hairdressing scissors this time,' Meredith said after a while. 'You can have that haircut if you like.'

'You don't have to.' Zach smiled.

'Come on, it'll take both our minds off things,' she replied, although she suspected that was wishful thinking.

Zach went off to wash his hair while Meredith went to get towels. Once he was settled in a chair outside his van, she ran her fingers through his damp hair. Purely professionally, of course, not because it felt so nice.

'Do you mind not going to the fete?' she asked. 'I just didn't feel like seeing people. I feel strangely upset about those letters, as though I've stumbled into somebody else's tragedy.'

'I feel the same,' Zach replied, his voice soft as Meredith stood behind him, trimming the hair at the nape of his neck. In the silence that followed she listened to the sound of birds and felt the warmth of the sun on her neck. Other than the occasional dog bark there were no other sounds – no traffic, no shouting, no screech of tube train brakes. It felt like another world compared to London.

'I love it here, you know.'

'In the garden, you mean?' Zach asked.

'Yes, but also Carybrook itself. I know I've only been here for a few days on and off but there's something very special about it that I can't quite explain.'

'Could you see yourself living here?'

'You just want me to stay so you can get your haircut regularly!'

'I'm telling you, there's an opportunity there if you want it.'

Did she want it? She wasn't sure she wanted to open a salon again anytime soon but hadn't Zach said the previous hairdresser had been mobile? Not that Meredith had any sort of vehicle to be mobile in, but still – the opportunity was there.

She continued carefully trimming Zach's hair in silence, trying to ignore the warm feeling she felt every time she touched him.

'Why do you think Clara left the house to both of us?' she asked as she moved around to face him.

'Maybe it was her way of telling us something,' Zach said. 'As though we're supposed to work out what to do together.'

'Work out what to do about what?'

'Our futures, I suppose.' As he spoke he turned his head slightly to look at her. 'Neither of us is in the best place, are we?'

Meredith smiled but looked away. She felt suddenly very close to this man who only a week ago she'd been trying to get arrested for trespassing.

'I wish I could have met her,' she said. 'I wish she'd found me when she came back to England.'

'Maybe she just couldn't face it,' Zach replied. 'Neither of us knows what she went through, or what she was going through on her return.'

Meredith closed her eyes for a moment to blink back the tears that were inexplicably there. She gently turned Zach's head away from her to cut the hair around his ears and so he couldn't see her.

Everything was changing so quickly. She already knew that her mother was right, that she had to leave the life she had behind, that it was becoming increasingly unsustainable now that she was by herself. By August she would be essentially homeless. Yes, she'd still have Butterfly Cottage – or half of it, at least – but that didn't seem like a long-term solution unless she wanted to have Zach living in her garden forever. He'd want to sell eventually anyway.

'I haven't been entirely truthful with you,' she said. 'Or at least, I haven't told you the real reason why I wanted to sell the cottage straight away.'

'I'm guessing it has something to do with why you were so upset earlier. You said your business wasn't doing well?'

'As I said, I own a hair salon – or at least, I own the business, I rent the actual premises. I've got myself in a mess with the finances and my first thought when I heard about Butterfly Cottage was that I could sell it and the money would sort out the mess.'

'But then you found out about me,' Zach said.

'Well, yes, that was the first spanner in the works.' Meredith smiled. 'But to be honest, everything was much more complicated than I was letting myself believe. My fiancé moved out a few weeks ago and I can't really afford the rent on our flat on my own, plus I'd borrowed a lot of money off him to start up the salon but he wanted it back because...' She realised she had stopped cutting and was standing with her hand on Zach's shoulder, staring into space. She felt his hand come up and touch hers, just for a moment.

'You don't have to tell me,' he said.

'His new girlfriend is expecting a baby and he wants his money back. I was desperately hoping that Butterfly Cottage was the answer, but of course it wasn't. There is never one easy answer to a complicated mess like that.'

'Do you know what you are going to do?' Zach asked.

Meredith told him what she and Bernice had done so far – giving notice on the flat and paying Joe off.

'But in a few weeks I won't have anywhere to live. I think my mum wants me to go back to Spain with her, which is lovely of her but I'm not sure it's what I want or need right now.'

'You can live at Butterfly Cottage,' Zach said. 'I'm in no hurry to sell, you know that. But I know that doesn't help you with your salon. That must have been your dream.'

'It was, for many years,' Meredith replied. 'Or at least I thought it was.'

Zach's brow furrowed as Meredith walked in front of him to cut the hair around his other ear. 'How do you mean?'

'I love hairdressing,' she said. 'It was what I wanted to do from the very first time Mum took me to the tiny hairdressers at the end of our road when I was about ten. I've never really thought about doing anything else. But the salon with all the plate glass windows and state of the art everything…' She trailed off, shrugged.

'So this may be a stupid question, but why did you do it?'

'It felt like the next logical step,' Meredith said, echoing what Joe had said at the time. 'And it felt like the answer to everything because before that I'd had to travel about a lot to see my clients in different salons in the area. I thought it was what I wanted but now I wonder if maybe it was what Joe wanted. Joe was – still is, I suppose – very into image and appearance. He earned a lot more money than me too and he always wanted to put on a sort of united front. Me being a common or garden hairdresser with a lot of elderly clients didn't do that, but me having my own salon did.'

'That's no excuse to put you in a position where you are doing something that you don't really want to do,' Zach said, turning his head to face her and nearly getting his ear cut off in the process.

'You need to keep your head still,' Meredith said, moving his head back into position before continuing. 'I thought it was what I wanted but I have been a fool not to put my foot down earlier and an even bigger fool to get in such a financial mess without asking anyone for help. I can't believe I've only just worked all this out – that the salon was Joe's dream more than it was mine. I suppose that's why he put money into it.'

'Money that you've now had to pay back.'

Meredith groaned. 'I've been such an idiot. Why did I not see any of this earlier?'

'Sometimes you need to move away from a situation to see it clearly,' Zach said. Meredith wondered if that was why he'd come to Carybrook in the first place.

'Look, I'm sorry,' she said. 'None of this is your problem. All you wanted was a haircut.'

She stood in front of him and ran her fingers through his hair again, checking the layers. 'I thought I might go to Ickbury Manor tomorrow,' she said. 'I did email them about their records but I haven't heard anything.' She squatted in front of him, her eyes almost level with his as she checked the two sides of his hair were even.

His eyes met hers.

'I'll drive you,' he said softly.

'You don't have to...'

'Yes, I do. I'll help you however you need me while you work this all out.' His fingers touched her cheek and for a moment she thought he was going to kiss her. She also thought that she wouldn't stop him if he did.

But instead, he jumped up suddenly, sending the towel flying.

'I've got it,' he said. 'I've worked out where I've seen JM written like that before. It's Jimmy Mack.'

15

SUFFOLK, JUNE AND JULY 1963

When Clara arrived at Carybrook School on the Monday morning after the church fete, there was a huge commotion in the staff room and Betty was at the centre of it.

'There you are, Clara,' Betty called, beckoning her over. 'I've been waiting for you.' As Clara approached, Betty held out her left hand to show a small but beautiful diamond ring.

'Oh my goodness, Betty,' Clara said, leaning over to kiss her friend on the cheek. 'Congratulations! When did John pop the question?'

'On Friday night in the car, just after we dropped you off. He was so nervous, bless him, as if I'd say anything other than a resounding "yes"!'

'So, when's the wedding?' Clara asked.

'Well, we're hoping for next spring but we're also planning to move away from Carybrook after we're married so it does depend on staffing at the school. I'm dreading telling Miss Cheggers.'

'Oh, she'll be happy for you,' Clara said, swallowing down the sense of disappointment that the friend she had managed to make in Carybrook would be gone by next spring. Spring was a long way away yet and besides, she'd found James again now so anything was possible.

'And I think you've got something to tell me too,' Betty said. 'Who was that gorgeous man you were with on Friday night?'

'Oh, that was James,' Clara said, feeling that sense of warmth in her belly that she always seemed to feel now whenever she thought of him. She explained to Betty about how she had known James when they were children, how he'd moved away and now suddenly was back at the same time she was.

'Isn't that just amazing?' Betty said.

'It's quite the coincidence.'

'And I saw that he came to the fete with you on Saturday too.'

'Oh, you should have come and said hello. I'd have introduced you.'

'I didn't want to disturb. You looked so lovely together eating your cream teas and staring lovingly at each other.'

'Betty!' Clara could feel herself blushing now. 'That's not how it was at all.'

'I think it's a little bit how it was,' Betty replied and Clara thought about James's lips brushing against hers as he had said goodbye on Saturday afternoon and told her that he'd see her soon.

'When are you seeing him again?' Betty asked.

'I think probably at the weekend.'

'Oh, I think you might see him again before that,' Betty said with a smile, just as the bell for first class rang.

It turned out that Betty was right, and that Clara would see James sooner than the weekend. He was waiting for her outside the school when she finished for the day that Monday afternoon.

Betty nudged her as James walked up to them, introducing himself to Betty while Clara tried to collect herself, unable to think about anything other than that kiss on Saturday and how much she wanted to kiss him again.

'Well, I'll leave you two to it,' Betty said, heading off towards John's car. 'I've got a fiancé to plan a wedding with.'

'Hello, you,' James said as Betty walked away.

'Hello,' Clara said, her voice sounding strangely strangled.

'I wondered if you'd like to see where I work and maybe have a bite to eat with me.'

Clara hesitated. She'd been intending to do some preparation for her lessons that week and maybe have an early night.

'Sorry,' James said. 'I shouldn't have sprung this on you, I...'

'No,' Clara replied, reaching over to touch his arm. 'I'd love to.'

His smile, when it came, was like sunshine and Clara couldn't believe she'd even thought about hesitating.

'My car is just around the corner,' he said, taking her hand as they walked.

On the way to Ickbury Manor Clara told him about the excruciating Sunday lunch she'd had with Esther and Richard the day before.

'They asked a lot of questions about you,' she said.

'None of them good ones, I'll bet.'

Clara laughed. 'They wanted to know your intentions,' she said. 'And why it was that we were suddenly being seen together all over the place.'

'All over the place?' James queried. 'Just at the village fete, surely.'

'That is all over the place in their view.'

'I take it they disapprove.'

'They can both be very concerned with things like appearance and so on. I think they believe a gardener is beneath me.'

'But if I were a vicar, it would be OK?'

'I'm sorry,' Clara said. 'She always was a horrible snob. I shouldn't have said anything, should I? I've offended you.'

'Don't be silly.' James turned to grin at her. 'I don't really mind what your sister thinks of me. But I do mind what *you* think. Do you think a lowly gardener is beneath you?'

'Of course not,' Clara insisted. 'But I am interested in what your intentions are.'

'Are you now?' James chuckled. 'Well, you'll have to wait to find out.'

He turned the car into a side gate that led onto the grounds of Ickbury Manor. Clara hadn't been here since a school trip just before the war. Since then it had been in the hands of the army who had not left it in a very good state.

'We're trying to get it back to the way it was,' James said. 'Obviously, the grounds had been used as an army training centre for years and the Ministry of Defence only gave it back to the family in the late fifties so there has been a lot of work to do.'

When they arrived he guided her around the grounds of Ickbury Manor, showing her the different parts of the garden and how the team of gardeners had brought them back to life – the rose garden, the kitchen garden, the orchard.

'And you've worked on all of them?' Clara asked.

'At one stage or another, but my favourite is the kitchen garden. I love growing vegetables. I'm always astonished by how many people we can feed from a small packet of seeds.'

Clara who, other than looking at the Butterfly Garden, had no experience of growing anything, relished in James's enthusiasm even if she wasn't always sure what he was talking about, especially when he got on to the tricky subject of cross-pollination and harvesting seeds.

'The bees help a lot, of course, and we have our own beehives on the estate – they sell the honey in the gift shop.'

Later he took her back to the bothy where he lived and introduced her to some of the other gardeners who were all preparing an outdoor cooking fire.

'We're having steak tonight if you'd like to join us,'

James said. 'From one of the bullocks that graze on the land right here at the Manor.'

She agreed to stay, feeling a little more comfortable when she realised that James intended for them to eat alone at a small table a little away from the others. She already sensed the teasing that would take place later, once she had gone. Thankfully all the gardeners seemed too polite to make any ribald remarks in front of her.

The steak was delicious and tasted of the woodsmoke it had been cooked on. They also ate fresh bread and vegetables that had been grown in the kitchen garden.

After dinner, he made coffee and brought it out to the table. They talked about their days, about the news, the Profumo affair, and the Labour Party whilst Clara watched him smoke, blowing smoke rings into the summer air.

'You asked about my intentions,' he said.

'I don't expect any of them are good.' She smiled.

'Hopefully not, but I'd like to keep seeing you, Clara, if you'd like that too.'

Of course she would like that too; how on earth could she say no?

When he drove her home that night he kissed her in the car and it was nothing like the gentle brushing of lips they had exchanged after the church fete. This kiss was passionate and deep and left Clara with the feeling that everything she had been missing was returning to her.

* * *

From then on James and Clara became almost inseparable, or as inseparable as they could be without risking losing their jobs. They saw each other three or four times a week – going to the cinema in Ickbury, to the dance when it came around, occasionally a concert in Ipswich or they would eat together, sometimes at the bothy but more often in the garden at Butterfly Cottage. They enjoyed each other's company and Clara had never felt so content in her own skin, so much herself.

She had never really known herself, she came to realise, and had lived a somewhat chameleon-like life fitting in with her surroundings, trying not to be noticed too much, trying not to put anyone out. At the school in London and at the boarding house she had always kept a low profile, obeying the rules and working hard, and she hadn't been miserable by any account. She had always had company and she loved her work and the children she taught. But neither had she been happy. Not really. Not like this.

She had always been wary of attaching her happiness to anyone other than herself. Since leaving home when she was eighteen to go up to Cambridge, she had had nobody but herself to rely on anyway so it was easier to be independent. But sometimes that independence leaned towards loneliness, especially as the girls at the boarding house left to get married or to move on to bigger and better things elsewhere. She had become so used to being lonely that she had stopped realising that she was until James walked back into her life. And she noticed that, rather than relying on James for her happiness, or attaching that emotion to him, she was happy in herself even when he wasn't there.

They were both long past the first flush of youth, long past the grand giddy romances that Clara read about in books. The attraction had been instant, from the moment she saw him for the first time at the dance, really, but the love and affection had grown slowly over the weeks that they spent together and it was something more than just physical.

After the cinema, they would go to a small bar in Ickbury and talk about the film. It was a rather trendy bar that sold Spanish wine, played jazz and, unlike the bar at the Ickbury dance, always had both ice and Vermouth. Clara had been surprised that such a place existed in a Suffolk market town.

'We're not completely stuck in the past out here in the sticks, you know,' James had said, smiling at her surprise.

When they had exhausted the subject of the film, they would talk about politics and religion, the war and whether or not Britain should join the EEC. They talked about art and books and life and love and Clara realised that the memory she had always held of James Mackenzie wasn't a completely fabricated one. He was different from the other men she knew, the men she had dated in London, the men her friends were married to. He was interested in people and how the world worked, he was interested in art and nature, he was well-read and thought about things from different viewpoints all the time. Esther and Richard sniffed and changed the subject whenever Clara mentioned him, thinking him a common vicar's boy turned gardener, thinking him beneath them, but he was so much more than that.

After the bar owner closed for the evening, they would carry on talking in James's car, or back in the living room at Butterfly Cottage and Clara would end up going to bed far too late and yawning her way through the next day's lessons. Not that she minded, though; tiredness was a small price to pay for the positive changes in her life since moving out of London. She wondered sometimes what would have happened to her if Butterfly Cottage had not gone up for sale, or if Esther had not told her about it. Would she still be in the boarding house watching her life pass by?

It was her newfound contentedness that got her through to the end of term listening to Betty's never-ending wedding plans. She knew, were it not for James and Butterfly Cottage, that she would be dreading hearing about Betty's wedding and would have been listening with a sense of envy. She didn't like to admit this, even to herself, but it was how she had felt whenever any of the girls in the boarding house had left to be married. She had never had any particular dreams of getting married herself, and yet the envy was there anyway. It was important to acknowledge the dark side of ourselves, Clara thought.

'It'll be you next,' Betty would say. 'You and James planning your happy ever after.'

'It's a bit soon for that,' Clara had replied, pushing the thought away, not wanting to discuss it because she didn't want to jinx anything. She had never imagined herself as anything other than a teacher and James lived a life very different from Betty's fiancé. As a journeyman gardener, he would be off to the next job as soon as this one came to an end. And then what would happen?

She could only enjoy the moment, what they had together now and how, this time, he always stayed in touch.

'I should teach you to drive,' James said one evening. 'Then you could come and see me at lunchtime, bring me sandwiches.' His eyes sparkled as he joked about it.

'I'm not running around bringing you sandwiches,' Clara teased back, 'especially when you have all this amazing produce right on-site at the Manor, but I wouldn't mind learning to drive. Richard did say he'd teach me, but he's had such a time teaching Esther that I daren't ask.'

'So she's not picking up driving well, then.' James seemed almost pleased that Esther wasn't good at something. He never admitted it but the snub that Esther had given him at the church fete still seemed to smart.

'I thought she'd be good at it, as she seems to be good at everything, but it turns out that she's a liability. I just hope she never passes her test.'

Her time with James was making the summer fly

by and as term ended they were able to spend more time together.

They celebrated the start of Clara's summer holidays with a trip to London – the steam train to Ipswich and the diesel to Liverpool Street, the reverse journey of the trip she had made when she first saw Butterfly Cottage. They took the tube to Sloane Square and walked down the King's Road as Clara pointed out Peter Jones, Mary Quant's Bazaar, and the boarding house she had lived in. It looked dirty and shabby and depressing, and she wondered who slept in her old room.

They ate lunch in an American-themed restaurant which had a Wurlitzer jukebox and a photo booth machine.

'Let's get our picture taken,' James said, pulling Clara into the booth and putting a coin in the slot, pulling a series of faces at the camera with each flash. The strip of photographs was ridiculous and only two were in focus.

'One each,' James said, as he went off to ask the barman to cut the photographs for them.

'Do you want to see where you used to live?' Clara asked after lunch.

'God no,' he replied. 'Let's not spoil a nice day with that.'

They got back to Ipswich just in time to see the last Carybrook train leave the station. They tipsily took an expensive taxi back to the village, and the driver couldn't believe his luck.

'Made as much as I usually make in the whole night,' he said as he dropped Clara off at Butterfly Cottage.

'I'll be over first thing,' James said to her before the taxi took him on to Ickbury Manor. 'Help you hang that wallpaper.'

At home, Clara took out the photograph they had taken in the photo booth and looked at it, at James's funny face, at her own huge smile. She couldn't remember when she was last this happy.

She took the photograph to her desk where she kept the old locket that she had inherited from her mother when she died. It was the only thing she had of her parents – the locket with her father's photograph inside. She slipped the picture of her and James over the one of her father and closed the locket, dropping it back inside the drawer in the desk. She smiled to herself as she did so.

As the summer went on, Clara felt herself falling in love in a way that surpassed the physical attraction, the kissing, the carefully controlled passion in James's car late at night. She felt a connection that couldn't be broken, despite losing touch, and that wouldn't be broken even if he had to leave, to move away and take a gardening job elsewhere. She was sure that he felt it too although she didn't dare ask and he never said anything until the night he said, 'I love you.'

Each July the gardeners were given a week off and most went to see their families or to the seaside. James, however, decided to stay behind.

'Where would I go?' he asked when Clara questioned this. 'A week in dreary Lincolnshire with my father, neither of us knowing what to say to each other? I'd rather stay here with you.' He reached over and ran a finger down the side of her face.

They ate together every evening in the bothy, which he had to himself for the week, sitting outside enjoying the evening sunshine and the gentle birdsong. She would stay far too late and he would drive her home, picking her up again the next day, until the day she didn't go home.

When he asked her if she wanted to stay, she didn't hesitate, and when he took her to bed she knew that whatever happened James Mackenzie was her past, her present and her future and they would find a way.

Afterwards, as he held her he told her he
loved her.

'I think I always have,' he said.

16

SUFFOLK, JUNE 2018

'Jimmy Mack?' Meredith echoed, staring at Zach. 'Why does that name sound familiar?'

'Come with me,' Zach said, taking her hand and pulling her towards his caravan.

'I need to check the back of your hair,' she said.

'I'm sure it's fine, better than it was, anyway. I want to show you something.'

She had never been in his caravan before. The time they had spent together had been either in the pub or the cottage garden. It was cosier inside than she'd imagined, and larger, like the Tardis in *Doctor Who*. There was a kitchenette, tiny dining area and two small banquettes that faced each other. Each had a bookcase above it, and this was where Zach led her.

'So, basically, this is like a little house you can pull along with your car and go wherever you want?' Meredith asked. She had never really thought about the inside of a caravan before.

'Well, not exactly. I have to put away all the loose stuff, like the books, before I move, and disconnect the gas, electricity and water. Plus, I can't just turn up any-where. There are laws in this country about where you can and can't camp. Scotland is a bit easier.'

'So where do you sleep?' Meredith peered towards the back of the caravan.

'The banquettes turn into a bed,' he said, ges-turing vaguely. 'Now, you said the name Jimmy Mack rang a bell.'

'Sort of,' Meredith said, sitting down. 'But I can't remember where from.'

'Did you ever watch that children's TV show *Everyday Adventure*?'

'I loved that show! I used to watch it every day when I got home from school. I remember they had this woman on once who was a weightlifter and it was the only time I considered not being a hairdresser. I would go around our flat lifting bags of sugar above my head and—' She stopped suddenly, realisation dawning. 'Oh my God!'

'Yup,' Zach said, reaching up to the bookshelf and

pulling down some of the books, most of which Meredith had already noticed were about gardening. 'Jimmy Mack was the gardener on *Everyday Adventure.*'

'And you think Jimmy Mack is the same person who worked at Ickbury Manor and dated Clara and maybe wrote those letters.'

'I do,' Zach said, sitting down next to her. 'And I think he might be the man in the photograph too. Can I see the locket again?'

Meredith looped the chain over her neck from where she had taken to wearing it every day and passed it to Zach. 'Do you remember that time when vandals got into the garden and he cried live on air? That was so sad.'

'He was quite a famous gardener, you know,' Zach said. 'He was on all sorts of TV programmes in the eighties and nineties and he owned a chain of garden centres in Lincolnshire. He also wrote some excellent gardening books.' He showed the pile of books he'd collected off the shelf to Meredith, each one of them written by Jimmy Mack.

'So he was pretty famous outside of children's TV then?'

'His fame was rather niche,' Zach replied. 'But yes, I'd say he was fairly famous in his own way in his

fifties and sixties. He was always unveiling new cre-
ations at the Chelsea Flower Show and obviously he
was on television. I think he had a column in a newspaper too.' He stopped and opened the locket, looking
at the photograph again. 'It's impossible to tell if it's
him,' he said eventually, shaking his head. 'He's so
much younger and it's such a small photo. Plus you
can only really see half his head.'

Meredith remembered the feeling of recognition
she'd felt when she first saw the man in the photograph but she didn't think that feeling had anything to
do with Jimmy Mack, who she hadn't seen on TV
since she was a child.

'I met him a few times,' Zach went on, 'but he was
much older then and I just can't tell.' He handed the
locket back to Meredith.

'How did you come to meet him?' Meredith asked.

'My dad was a huge fan and we used to go and see
him talk sometimes when I was a kid. He usually did a
little tour every time he had a book out and all of
these copies are signed.'

Zach opened one of the books to show the inside
page where Jimmy Mack had signed a dedication to
somebody called Carl, whom Meredith assumed was
Zach's father. But more important than that was *how*
the book had been signed.

To Carl, with best wishes, JM.

The way the J and the M were written was very distinctive and very familiar, the letters curled together in exactly the same way that they had been at the end of each of the letters.

'It's him!' Meredith said.

'I knew I recognised how the J and the M were signed on those letters,' Zach said. 'Sorry it took me all afternoon to work it out. I'm surprised it took me so long, to be honest. I read these books a lot...' He trailed off, running his hand over the page that Jimmy Mack had inscribed to his father.

'So, whoever wrote those letters was definitely Jimmy Mack,' Meredith said.

'Although we can't be a hundred per cent sure that he was the same person who worked at Ickbury Manor in 1963.'

'It's one hell of a coincidence if not though, surely? Unless Great-Aunt Clara was dating two gardeners that summer, in which case fair play to her.'

'It is unlikely though.'

'In a village this size where everyone talks about everyone else?' Meredith said. 'Extremely unlikely. Delia Cheggers would have known about that for sure!'

'So there we go,' Zach said, closing the book and putting the pile on the seat beside him. 'Miss Samuels was dating Jimmy Mack in the summer of 1963.'

'And something happened that drove them apart, something that Jimmy Mack clearly regretted if those letters are anything to go by.'

'Something that drove Miss Samuels out of the country for most of the rest of her life,' Zach mused.

'Maybe,' Meredith said quietly. 'We don't know they are connected. She might have left the country for another reason entirely. After all, it doesn't seem like Jimmy Mack knew she'd gone.'

'We might never know what happened,' Zach said. 'That secret may well have died with Miss Samuels.'

'Unless my father knows more about it,' Meredith said. 'Wherever he is.'

Zach didn't say anything for a moment but Meredith noticed that he glanced towards the books and rested his hand on them as though thinking about his own father. Meredith wanted to know more about Zach, about his father, about his life. And she wanted to know what that kiss would have felt like if he hadn't had his big revelation before it even began.

'What happened to him?' she asked, mostly to take her mind off kissing Zach. 'To Jimmy Mack?'

'He died of a heart attack in 2004,' Zach replied. 'A few months later my dad died of the same thing.'

'I'm so sorry,' Meredith said.

Zach turned to look at her and smiled sadly. 'Don't be,' he said. 'It was a long time ago and he set me up with a great little gardening business I was able to carry on after I finished college. But these books of Jimmy Mack's are all I have left of Dad, really, and like I said, I read them a lot. He was very proud of them, always showing people the signed front page. That's why I'm surprised I didn't recognise the signature earlier.'

She remembered that he'd told her his mother had died when he was young and she wanted to ask him how he coped on his own. She'd barely been able to cope when Bernice and Lloyd moved to Spain, but she knew it was an intrusive question. Besides, most people managed to cope with things better than she did. Joe had always been telling her that.

'Do you think Clara knew about Jimmy Mack's gardening career?' she asked, bringing the subject back to the puzzle of Butterfly Cottage.

'Impossible to say, but at a guess I'd say no.'

'Why?'

'The world was a much bigger place in the eighties and nineties and Australia was a really long way away, and it's not like Jimmy Mack was a rock star or any-thing. He was just an English gardener.'

'Yeah, I see what you mean,' Meredith said. 'But maybe later, after everyone had access to the internet, she might have looked him up?'

'She might have done, but if she did she never mentioned it.'

Meredith sighed. Clara hadn't mentioned much, it seemed. 'I should go,' she said. 'See if Mum's back from her walk.'

'You don't have to,' Zach said. 'I can make a cup of tea.'

Meredith shook her head. She was suddenly ner-vous to be with him, wanting to but not sure she was ready for what that almost-kiss might lead to. 'I'm probably going to take Mum to the pub for dinner if you want to join us?'

'That would be lovely,' Zach replied. 'And don't look so forlorn – you never know what we might find out at Ickbury Manor tomorrow.'

Meredith smiled even though she felt that it was all a bit hopeless and that the secrets had died with Clara and Jimmy Mack.

At the door of the caravan, she hesitated and turned around.

'One more question,' she said. 'Jimmy Mack surely wasn't his real name, was it?'

'No, I think it must have been a nickname that he turned into sort of stage name. His full name was James Mackenzie.'

* * *

Zach and Meredith set off for Ickbury Manor the next morning, full of Bernice's pancakes. They had filled her in on the latest Jimmy Mack developments over breakfast. Bernice, apparently, had been a big fan of the TV gardener.

'It says here that parts of the Manor date back to Tudor times and that Elizabeth I was a regular visitor to Ickbury,' Meredith said, reading from the website as she sat in the passenger seat of Zach's van.

Zach chuckled. 'Every old house says that on the website – either some Tudor monarch or Shakespeare. It gets the punters in. What does it say about the gardens?'

'"The grounds were originally designed in the style of Capability Brown during the 1780s",' Meredith read. 'Oh, I've actually heard of him. Didn't he invent the ha-ha?'

Zach looked at her briefly. 'I'm impressed,' he teased. 'Although the ha-ha was first used in French gardens, I think, but Capability Brown brought it to England.'

'Mum and I used to watch a lot of gardening shows to live vicariously through others as we were in an eighth-floor flat with no balcony.' She paused for a moment, remembering the days before Lloyd came along when she and her mum had muddled through in that horrible, damp council flat.

'Anyway,' she went on, looking at the Ickbury Manor website again. 'It goes on to say "During the Second World War, the grounds and gardens of Ickbury Manor were given over to the war effort. They were used as a training camp by the army in the war. In the 1960s a team of journeymen gardeners were hired to help return the grounds to their former glory".'

'And Jimmy Mack would have been one of them,' Zach said.

'Although I couldn't find anything specific about that online.'

'You looked him up?'

'I couldn't sleep last night,' Meredith admitted, not admitting that part of the reason she couldn't sleep was because she was thinking about how much she'd wanted Zach to kiss her even though it seemed like that was the last thing she needed right now. 'I had so many thoughts swirling around in my head so I thought I'd read up on Jimmy Mack, or James Mackenzie. There's plenty of stuff about his later life – his TV career, his garden centres and his writing – but hardly anything about how he got there. Even his Wikipedia page just says that he worked on various gardens in Essex, Suffolk and Norfolk.'

'It does say that he was a vicar's son,' Zach said.

'You looked him up too?'

'I couldn't sleep either.' Meredith wondered why.

'It said that his father moved about a lot.'

'I know how that feels,' Zach said, his eyes on the road ahead. 'It can be quite unsettling and it makes it hard to make friends.' He stopped for a moment and Meredith was trying to decide whether to ask more about it or change the subject when he carried on. 'I'm sorry I haven't told you very much about my dad, but he was the modern equivalent of a journeyman gardener, like the young Jimmy Mack, and we moved from place to place as he worked on big landscaping projects. I changed school a lot and never really settled anywhere. I guess that's why I'm still more comfortable in the van than the house, even though Butterfly Cottage is the longest I've been in one place since college.'

'That must have been hard,' Meredith said.

'No harder than growing up without a garden at all.'

'I was lucky. Mum met Lloyd not long after my dad left and they got married when I was thirteen. We always had a garden after that and I got a brand-new family, which made up for the disappearance of my actual father.' Meredith had found herself thinking of Dennis a lot over the last few days, wondering where he was, wondering what she could have done to help them have a better relationship, how she could take back the things she said on her eighteenth birthday, and wondering if she could find him. Since she'd first heard about Great-Aunt Clara, she'd been thinking about how much she wanted to talk to her father, find out what he knew and where he'd been.

'I was twenty-one when Dad died,' Zach said. 'I'd just graduated and I had no idea what to do. He had a job in Gloucestershire lined up so I wrote to them and asked if they minded if I took the job. They said yes although they paid me less than they would have done a more experienced gardener like Dad. Over time I started to work all over the country.'

'And how did you end up in Carybrook?'

'That really was just a happy coincidence. I was in between jobs and was passing through when I saw the advertisement that Miss Samuels put in the post office. I was intrigued and when I found out it was a full landscaping job, I took it on.' He paused for a moment. 'We're here,' Zach said as they turned off the road into a gravelled car park.

* * *

'What do you want to do first?' Zach asked after they'd paid their entrance fees and acquired a map of the grounds.

'Do you mind if we just walk around the gardens for a while first?' Meredith asked. 'I'd like to get a feel for the place before we start asking questions. Besides...' She trailed off.

'Besides what?' Zach asked.

'Oh, I'm just a bit nervous about asking any questions in case we come to a dead end or somebody tells us it's none of our business.'

'We won't know if we don't ask,' Zach said. 'But I wouldn't mind a wander about myself. Where shall we start?'

Meredith looked at the map. 'Let's start with the kitchen garden,' she said, striding off towards it.

It was breathtaking. Rows upon rows of beautiful-looking vegetables grew in perfectly squared-off beds

– onions, leeks, potatoes, cabbages, kale – bordered by soft fruit bushes, tomato vines, peas and beans. Around the edges were fruit trees, mostly apples and pears – although Zach pointed out quince and crab-apple – their fruits like tiny little balls where blossom had once been.

'We've had such a warm spring,' Zach said. 'It'll be a good year for apples.'

'Does that make a difference?' Meredith asked.

'If there's frost after the apple blossom blooms then you can end up with very little crop. The warmer the spring the better the apples on the whole.'

In between the fruit trees were bushes of lavender, rosemary and thyme – even Meredith could recognise them and she inhaled the smell of the lavender.

'What do you think?'

'I'd love to work somewhere like this,' Zach replied, staring at the rows of onions. 'On a big estate garden. Imagine what it must have been like in the sixties with an army of gardeners putting everything back together again after the war.'

'And Jimmy Mack was one of them.'

Zach nodded, seemingly transfixed by the garden, and Meredith found herself wondering if there were any gardening vacancies at the Manor that Zach could apply for. That way he wouldn't have to leave when the Butterfly Garden was finished.

She stopped herself there. What did it matter to her when he left Carybrook? She lived in London, after all, and they had both agreed they would have to sell the cottage eventually.

They began to walk again, out of the vegetable garden and through some trees into a rose garden which took them towards the house itself.

'What do you prefer?' Meredith asked. 'Vegetables or flowers?'

'My favourite thing is landscaping,' Zach said. 'Turning an overgrown or out of control garden into something special, like I hopefully have done at Butterfly Cottage.'

'I don't know what it looked like before,' Meredith said, 'But the garden is truly beautiful. You've done a wonderful job.'

'But if I had to choose, I'd say vegetables. There's something really special about planting some seeds and, a few months later, being able to eat what you have grown. And then you can harvest seeds for the next season and create hybrids and...' He looked over at Meredith and laughed. 'I can see I've lost you.'

'Hybrids?' she asked.

'It's when you cross-pollinate plants to make them more resilient to pests, for example.'

'OK,' Meredith replied wondering how on earth you went about doing that.

'Look,' Zach said, pointing across the main lawn in front of the house that they were now drawing nearer to. 'There's your ha-ha!'

From this angle, you could just about make out the line where the ground dipped away into a small ditch which acted as a fence. From the front of the house you wouldn't be able to see anything and the lawn would look as though it went all the way down to the meadows below without interruption – except that, thanks to the ha-ha, the sheep grazing in the meadow would not be able to wander up to the house.

'I wonder why it's called that?' Meredith mused.

'Apparently, because the optical illusion makes the viewer say "Aha!"' Zach replied.

'You are such a know-all,' Meredith teased, nudging him gently, and he slung an arm over her shoulder. Meredith thought about the day before, just before he remembered Jimmy Mack. At least his leaping up like that hadn't ruined his haircut. It looked really good if she did say so herself.

'Only about gardens,' he said. 'I'm pretty ignorant about everything else.' He stopped outside the house.

'Shall we go in and see what we can discover?' He stepped away from her and towards the steps leading inside.

Meredith could still feel the warm and pleasant sensation of Zach's arm around her shoulders and didn't answer for a moment.

'Meredith, are you OK?'

'Yes,' she said. 'Sorry, it's just...' She paused, shrugged.

'I know, but we want to find out for sure, don't we?'

Meredith nodded and walked towards the house entrance.

The main entrance hall was tiled with black and white tiles and there was a huge sweeping wooden staircase leading upstairs. Meredith noticed signs to a portrait gallery and a display of Chippendale furniture as well as an exhibit on the garden designs of Capability Brown.

'Let's head to the garden exhibition,' she suggested. 'See if anyone there can help?'

They followed the signs until they reached a huge plan of the grounds, which marked the beginning of the exhibition. Meredith realised then just how big the Ickbury estate was and just how many gardeners it must have taken to bring it back to life. She wondered how big the team that Jimmy Mack had worked with was. She also wondered how many people it took to keep everything looking so beautiful now. She hadn't seen any gardeners. It was as though the grounds were maintained by invisible hands.

She noticed Zach had cornered one of the guides – an elderly woman wearing a red blazer. Meredith followed him.

'Hello,' he said. 'I wonder if you can help us.'

'I'll try.' The woman smiled. Meredith noticed that her name badge read 'Ivy'.

'We think somebody we knew once worked here, back in the sixties,' Zach continued. 'He worked as a gardener.'

'One of the team that brought the grounds back to life after the war?' Ivy asked.

'We think so,' Meredith said. 'We're fairly sure he was here in the summer of 1963.'

'It's really the archive department that you need,' Ivy said.

'I did email them last week,' Meredith replied. 'But I never got a reply, so we thought we'd visit on the off-chance.' She crossed her fingers behind her back, hoping that Ivy knew something that would help.

'I am sorry about that, dear,' Ivy said. 'We are very short-staffed at the moment – we often are in the summer, but I can see this is important to you. Was this man a relative?'

'Not exactly, but he had a connection to a relative that I've only just found out about.'

Meredith saw Ivy's eyes widen a little. 'How intriguing,' she said. 'And luckily for you, this exhibition isn't just about Capability Brown and how he changed gardening forever. It's also about how the garden was put together again in the sixties using Brown's techniques and, as luck would have it, we have brought up some of our old record books as part of the display.'

'Really?' Meredith said, her stomach contracting with excitement. It couldn't be this easy, could it?

'Really,' Ivy replied. 'Follow me.'

Ivy led and Meredith followed. She reached out for Zach's hand as she did so and her stomach contracted even more as she felt the callouses of his skin against her palm. She didn't let go until Ivy stopped in front of a display cabinet with some old-fashioned-looking ledgers inside.

'This one is the budget for the garden,' Ivy said. 'That would have been kept by the head gardener and would have included all outgoings including pay, although I don't think individual names are recorded in that one.' She moved across to the other end of the cabinet. 'This one, however, is a record of the gardeners who worked on the project.'

Meredith and Zach both peered into the cabinet but the open page was marked '1964'.

'Did you say the person you are looking for worked here in 1963?' Ivy asked.

Meredith looked at the ledger, scanning the names which appeared to be in alphabetical order.

William Lloyd

Robert Lund

Albert Mace

Ronald Mercer

There was no James Mackenzie in 1964.

'That's right,' she said, looking up at Ivy. 'And it doesn't look like he was here in 1964.'

The older woman hesitated for a moment, looking around her.

'We're not very busy this morning,' she said. 'Just wait here whilst I go and fetch the keys.'

While she was gone, Zach and Meredith stared at the ledger book.

'Do you think he's in there?' Meredith asked.

'Yes, I'm pretty sure he is.'

Ivy wasn't gone long and she returned with the keys and two pairs of white gloves. She put one pair on and handed the other to Meredith. 'Put these on,' she said. 'I'd be in so much trouble with archives if I let anyone touch the books without gloves on.'

Meredith did not want Ivy to get into any trouble and suspected that she was already pushing it so put the gloves on immediately. Ivy unlocked the cabinet and carefully lifted the ledger. She turned the page back to show a list of names under the year 1963.

Zach and Meredith scanned the list.

William Lloyd

Jonathan London

Robert Lund

Albert Mace

James Mackenzie

Ronald Mercer

'There he is,' Meredith whispered, her finger hovering over the name, not daring to touch the page even with gloves on. She looked over at Ivy. 'Would there be any other information on James Mackenzie, do you know? An address or date of birth? Any references.'

'Well, we wouldn't have an address for him as the gardeners then would have lived on-site and travelled from job to job. I imagine there will be a record of his date of birth and national insurance number along with references.' She paused. 'I shouldn't really show you the personal records,' she said but began to carefully turn the pages of the book anyway.

'Here we are,' Ivy said eventually. 'This is obviously very important so I'm going to show you this even though I shouldn't. James Mackenzie, born 10 March 1930 – oh, he was a bit older than most of the travelling gardeners who worked here then.' Ivy showed her the page but had covered all the other information besides James's name and date of birth with her gloved hand.

'When you say he was older, what do you mean?' she asked.

'Well, usually the travelling gardeners, or journeyman gardeners as they were called at the time, would be in their twenties. It's not unheard of for them to be in their thirties – and your Mr Mackenzie was thirty-three that summer – but it would have been more unusual as many men that age would have married and had families and wouldn't have wanted to be away for months at a time.' She paused, cleared her throat. 'That's a terrible generalisation of course, but I think you know what I mean.'

'We don't think James Mackenzie was married,' Zach said. 'In fact, we don't think he ever married.' He stopped and looked over at Meredith for a moment.

She felt his look was asking her if she wanted to tell Ivy about who they thought James Mackenzie was.

'Well, thank you so much for your help,' Meredith said, taking off her white gloves and handing them to Ivy. She realised that she wasn't even remotely ready to tell a stranger that James Mackenzie and Jimmy Mack were probably one and the same. 'I do really appreciate you letting us look at the book, but we've taken up enough of your time.'

'Not at all. I hope it helped.'

'It really did, thank you.' Meredith smiled as Ivy started to put the ledger back in the cabinet.

They walked back the way they'd come.

'You know,' Zach said as they stood in the tiled entryway, 'I've read all those books that Jimmy Mack wrote and lots of them have biographical information in them. He talks about the early jobs he worked on and how much he learned from them – he even mentions some of the gardens he worked in but he never once mentions Ickbury Manor.'

'He also never married and neither did Clara which feels unusual to me,' Meredith said. 'Especially for that generation. Like Ivy said, it's a huge generalisation, but what if...' She stopped and shook her head. 'I'm totally over-romanticising this I think, but what if they broke each other's hearts so badly that neither of them fell in love again?'

Zach laughed. 'Yeah, I think you're over-romanticising it. But what would I know? I'm like Jimmy Mack – well into my thirties and still travelling around with no responsibility.'

'Has there never been anyone?' Meredith asked. 'Anyone you'd want to settle down with?'

Zach looked down at his feet and shook his head. 'Do you want to look at anything else or shall we walk back to the van?'

'Let's go home,' Meredith said, without realising. 'Oh, and by home I mean Butterfly Cottage.'

'It's funny,' Zach said as they walked back toward the car park, 'but Butterfly Cottage does feel like home, or at least the garden does. I'll be sad to say goodbye when the time comes.'

'I feel strangely settled at the cottage too. I know a couple of weeks ago all I wanted was to sell up and cash in but... Well, things change, don't they?'

Zach nodded. 'I never expected to be in Carybrook so long. I certainly never expected it to feel like home.'

'A couple of months ago I wouldn't have been able to tell you where Suffolk was let alone Carybrook and now it feels like the closest thing to home I've got.'

They stood by the van now and Zach unlocked it.

'Have you thought any more about what you're going to do?' he asked as they got in.

'I have absolutely no idea. I don't want to go back to Spain with Mum but I may have no other option.'

'And what about your salon? You said you realised that it wasn't your dream any more.'

'I'm going to break the lease at the end of the summer,' Meredith said. 'I'm going to see if any of the hairdressers who already work there want to take it over, but if not I'll break the lease when the next break date comes up and I'll either sell the business or all the equipment and move on.'

'Wow.'

'I know.'

It was the first time that she'd said the words out loud but they had been going round and round in her head for days. She had realised that she had the power to stop this big thing that felt so out of control in her life; she had the power to move on and start again.

But it would leave her without a home and without a job.

'You know, you could just stay at Butterfly Cottage,' Zach said. She turned in her seat to look at him and as her eyes met his she felt that fizz of electricity again. 'I still have work to do in the garden, but even when it's finished we don't have to sell straight away if you just need somewhere to stay and work out what to do next. And you could think about all the hair that needs cutting in Carybrook.'

'I do feel as though I want to stay in Carybrook for a while, and not just because I want to find out more about Clara. I feel safe there. I feel as though I could start again but...' She paused, looking away from Zach. 'There's inheritance tax to pay and we still don't know how much.'

'There's always a way, Meredith. You asked earlier about whether I'd ever met anyone who I'd settle down with and the answer is no. Since Dad died I've felt this need to keep moving, to not let the grass grow under my feet but Carybrook has given me a reason to settle.'

Meredith opened her mouth to ask an inevitable question, but Zach just smiled.

'Not a person, just the place itself. When I took the job on at Butterfly Cottage I never expected to stay so long, I never expected to make a friend in Miss Samuels and I certainly never expected to inherit half a house.' He paused as his eyes met Meredith's. 'In other words, I'm in no hurry to leave either. I'm happy where I am for now.'

'But you can't keep living in the garden while I

swan about in the house like the lady of the manor,' Meredith protested.

'You're hardly that and I've told you I'm happy in the caravan. I'm used to it.'

'But what about when the weather gets colder?' It was almost impossible to imagine the weather getting any colder ever again as they entered the second hottest week in fifteen years but still, winter would come. It always did.

'I survived last winter,' Zach said, but he must have seen the look on Meredith's face because he added, 'But I promise to use one of the spare bedrooms if I need to.'

'Good, well, that's settled then. We'll both stay for a while. Gary Molliner will be disappointed that I'm not putting the cottage on the market, but I think we both need time to work out what's next. And I'd love to find out more about Jimmy Mack and his connection with my great-aunt, but it looks like we might have reached a dead end.'

'You never know what might happen,' Zach said, his eyes holding hers. This time neither of them looked away and neither of them jumped up out of their seat. Instead, they leaned towards each other across the front seats of the van, and when Zach's lips brushed hers Meredith didn't pull away.

17

SUFFOLK, AUGUST 1963

In early August three important things happened.

Firstly, Stephen Ward – the osteopath who had organised the parties where John Profumo first met Christine Keeler and who had been on trial all summer for prostitution offences – died after an overdose of barbiturates. The gossip in and around Carybrook picked up pace again after Clara had hoped people were growing tired of the whole thing.

Secondly, five days after that, the gossip switched when a gang of fifteen men held up the Glasgow to Euston post train, making off with over two and a half million pounds in cash and leaving the driver with serious head injuries.

And thirdly, Clara and James made an important

decision, one that was unconventional but made them both happier than they thought they could ever be.

It felt like an ordinary Thursday night. They had been to see *Billy Liar* at the cinema in Ickbury.

'Have you read the book?' Clara asked.

James nodded. 'A few years ago, but I thought the film was better.' He smiled. 'You probably didn't though, did you?' He knew, after a summer of cinema visits, how Clara always preferred books.

'This time I actually agree with you,' she replied. 'I think Julie Christie makes everything better.'

James laughed, and as Clara walked towards where he had parked he took her arm, gently steering her in a different direction.

'Come for a walk by the river with me,' he said.

It was a warm night and Clara was glad to not be going home yet. Since the men James lived with had returned from their holidays it was harder for her and James to find any privacy and she dared not take him back to Butterfly Cottage for fear of village gossip.

They walked away from the town square and over the bridge to the footpath that ran alongside the river. The sky was clear and the moon was almost full and they walked in comfortable silence for a while.

'Do you ever think about the future, Clara?' James asked.

She didn't know how to respond at first because the truth was that she didn't, really. She hadn't been able to in London because, until Esther mentioned the sale of Butterfly Cottage, she hadn't been able to see a way out of the routine and the boarding house and the fact that she was always going to be alone. And she hadn't thought about the future since moving back to Carybrook because the present had been so wonderful.

'I think about my career,' she said carefully. 'I wonder if one day I'll be able to take Miss Cheggers' job, but I've never been one for planning.'

'No,' James said, 'me neither, but I do have to think about the next gardening season, the next job. I have to think about where I'll be next spring.'

Clara's stomach dropped.

'You mean you'll have to leave soon,' she said.

'It had been my plan.' He paused then and stopped walking, turning Clara to face him. 'But then I met you.'

'Oh,' Clara said, unable to articulate her thoughts, unable to get a grasp on what James was saying.

'I have no real idea what I'm going to do,' he went on. 'There are overwinter jobs at Ickbury Manor with better accommodation and I'm hoping to be considered for one of them and after that, I don't know...' He paused again as though stopping for breath and Clara didn't dare to interrupt. 'Perhaps we can work that out together but before I do anything else I have to ask you something.'

He stopped again, fishing something out of his pocket. Clara suddenly felt breathless, nervous.

'What's going on...?' she began.

He showed her what he was holding – a diamond ring, subtle but beautiful. 'It was my mother's,' he explained. 'She wasn't wearing it on the day she died. She left it along with her wedding ring by the kitchen sink. She must have been washing up and forgot to put it back on, but at least it meant that Dad had something to remember her by. When I was twenty-one, he gave it to me and I've been carrying it around ever since. Whenever I looked at it I thought of you...' He trailed off, looking away from Clara for a moment but she understood. She had felt the same.

'I thought of you too,' she said. 'When I was in London, I thought of you.'

'I want you to have the ring,' he said, holding it out to her. 'I want you to wear it. I want to ask you to marry me but I can't promise you anything, I can't even promise that I'll have a job locally, but I can promise to love you, always.'

Clara felt happiness surge inside her. 'That's all I

want,' she said quietly as he took her left hand and slipped the ring onto the third finger.

'I'm sorry that none of this is very conventional,' he went on, holding her hand in his. 'But I want us to be together and...'

'Since when have I ever wanted conventional?' she asked as she stood on tiptoe to kiss him.

She felt his arm around her waist, drawing her towards him as they walked back the way they had come – along the river and back to where James's car was parked. They didn't speak until they were back in the centre of Ickbury, wrapped up instead in their own quiet bubble of happiness.

'We have a lot to talk about,' James said eventually as he unlocked the passenger door and held it open for Clara. 'As I was saying, I don't know what I can do for work yet, or how I can support you. I'm sorry I don't have a more steady sort of job.'

Clara smiled. 'Don't be ridiculous, none of that matters so long as we're together. We'll work something out.'

'We need to make a plan,' he insisted.

But Clara shook her head. 'I don't really believe in plans,' she said. 'I believe that the right thing happens at the right time. Just as it has tonight.'

But there was a thought in the back of her head

that sat there long after James had dropped her off, long after their passionate kisses goodbye in his car. A thought that stayed in her head late into the night and was still there when she woke the next morning.

If she married, no matter how unconventional that marriage may be, everything would change and everything she had worked so hard for would disappear.

As she boiled the kettle for tea and made toast under the grill she looked around at the kitchen, the sunroom, the French doors, the garden beyond where another beautifully warm and settled day beckoned. This was all hers – each brick, each floorboard, each stick of furniture (although some of it she would like to change when she had the time and money – the tastes of the diocese did not exactly match hers). She thought of the wallpaper that now adorned the walls of the front room. She thought of the writing bureau – the only piece of furniture she owned, taken from her parents' house after their deaths and heaved up the stairs of the boarding house to her room when Mrs Benyon wasn't looking.

If she married, none of it would be hers alone any more. It would be theirs – hers and James's. None of it could be taken away from her these days, which was something, except her hard fought for independence and her career.

She could keep working after the wedding of course, but if there were children things would change. She would leave her job, stay at home with the children and give up all rights to any income of her own.

Could she do that?

Did she want to do that?

Was she too old for children anyway?

She made herself sit down, made herself drink her tea and eat her toast, and she made herself think rationally about her independence, her loneliness and how often she had wanted exactly what was happening to her back when she lived in the boarding house.

And she thought of James, his smile, his kindness, the way he had looked at her when she had said yes to his proposal.

Because of course she had said yes. She had been thinking about him since they lost touch, wondering what had happened to him, wondering what he was doing. She had built up a fantasy in her head of him that a woman of her age should know better than to do, and that fantasy hadn't been far from the truth.

James didn't want to take her house from her or try to control her. He probably didn't want children either and there were plenty of ways of stopping that happening – they'd been careful so far, after all. It was clear from what he'd said the previous evening that he would probably still be travelling a lot for his job and she would be here, teaching at the school. But she would know that he would always come home to her and he would know that, in the long school holidays, she could travel with him, see a bit more of the country than she had so far. And she also knew that if she wanted to be with James and stay in Carybrook and keep her job at the village school, she would have to abide by some of society's rules. She wasn't in London any more.

She had been on her own for too long, had become too used to her own company and that fierce independence that blurred boundaries of loneliness. She didn't want to be alone any more. She wanted a different future, one she had hardly dared dream of.

And last night by the river that future had been offered to her. She loved James, of that she was sure, and he loved her. Or at least she believed he did to the extent that anybody can know how another feels. She was simply nervous of the changes that were inevitably going to happen. That was normal. It didn't mean that the change itself was wrong.

Clara allowed her shoulders to relax down her back and sipped her tea.

Everything would be fine, she told herself.

But there was something she had to do first.

* * *

She waited until she was sure that Richard would be safely on his way to his office in Ipswich before she left Butterfly Cottage and walked across the village to see her sister.

When Esther opened the door she raised her eyebrows in surprise. 'Clara,' she said. 'I wasn't expecting you.'

'Is this a bad time?'

'No, not at all. I'm free this morning. Come in, I'll make some coffee.'

Clara went through to the sitting room and perched on the edge of the upholstered chair that she always sat on when she came to Esther and Richard's on Sundays. Esther followed a few minutes later with a tray of coffee and a plate of biscuits.

'To what do I owe the pleasure?' Esther asked, pouring the coffee into porcelain mugs.

'Oh, don't be like that,' Clara replied. 'I see you every Sunday, it's not like I'm avoiding you. I know how busy you are in the week with your committees and meetings and so on.'

Esther added milk and sugar to Clara's mug and passed it to her.

'So, this is just a social call, is it?'

Clara had thought she and Esther got on better these days and she'd felt, since the move to Butterfly Cottage, that they were growing closer. But since the summer fete when Esther and James had met again, things had been different, and Clara sensed a cold front coming from her sister.

'Well, I do have some news,' Clara said. She had deliberately not worn James's ring that morning so that Esther wouldn't see it immediately. She wanted to tell her sister the whole story before she got to the engagement part.

Well, perhaps not the whole story. Perhaps she would leave out those summer nights spent at the bothy. And perhaps she would play down the fact that James would probably still have to travel a lot for work.

'I presume this is about you and that gardener,' Esther said, a touch of the childhood bitterness in her voice.

'Um... Well, yes, I...'

'The whole village knows you are going about with him. Barely seen apart, so I've heard.'

'The whole village?' Clara queried. 'Really? I can't imagine that most people care.'

'Well, maybe not the whole village,' Esther replied with a sniff. 'But you've been seen around together, gallivanting in his car, coming back at all hours of the night.'

'If you mean we've been spending time together and going to the cinema or for a drink or to a dance like most normal men and women then yes, that's true.'

'And you never thought to tell me.'

'You seemed upset when you met him at the fete, I didn't want to upset you further if it was only going to be a temporary thing. James is a journeyman gardener and he sometimes moves for work so...' She stopped, looking at her sister. 'Besides, you never said you knew anything about it.'

'Well, I didn't want to cause upset in front of Richard. I'm assuming as you're here to talk about it that things are quite serious between the two of you.'

Clara decided to just say the words. 'Last night he asked me to marry him and I said yes.'

Esther sniffed again and took a sip of her coffee. 'Well,' she said eventually. 'It's about time. You were on the brink of becoming an old maid like Jean Cheggers.'

Clara suppressed her smile. An old maid? Her sister talked like a character from a melodramatic Victorian novel.

'Thank you,' she said instead.

'But doesn't he travel for work a lot?' There was no hiding anything from Esther. 'It's no life for a married couple, always being apart like that. And what about your job? And the cottage – that cottage is yours, bought with Daddy's money.'

Clara squeezed her fingernails into her palms to stop herself from snapping. 'The cottage is mine,' she said, pushing down her own doubts from earlier. 'He's not going to take it away from me—'

'Are you sure about that?' Esther interrupted. 'It was his childhood home.'

'For two years,' she replied. 'He lived in London a lot longer than he ever lived here. Besides, I'm hoping we'll have a marriage of equals, like you and Richard, and we'll work together for the best outcome. Isn't that what you do?'

'Well, yes, of course.'

'And if James has to travel for his job we'll make it work, but he's also considering a more permanent role at Ickbury Manor.'

Esther seemed to relax a little then. 'So he is taking this and you seriously then?' she asked.

'Very seriously,' Clara confirmed. 'But you are aware that I don't need looking after, aren't you?'

Esther sniffed again. 'You never have.'

She wished she could talk to her sister about the other thing that was bothering her. Not the travelling that James would have to do, not the rather unconventional marriage they might have, but the fact that she was certain she didn't want children. She wanted to tell James and, even though part of her was fairly sure he wouldn't mind, she didn't know how to broach it. But she couldn't talk to Esther, who had always wanted children more than anything, about that, could she?

She would have to deal with it by herself and for some reason that thought made her feel nauseous.

'Clara,' Esther said, her voice sounding as though it was coming from far away. 'Are you all right?'

'Yes, sorry. I think I'm just a bit hot. I'm fine, really.' The strange nauseous feeling disappeared as soon as it had come and Clara was left feeling very hungry. She reached across for a biscuit. 'I haven't eaten much today either.'

'Well, you make sure you look after yourself. Would you like to stay for a bite of lunch?'

'No, no, I should get on really.'

'Speaking of lunch,' Esther said. 'Richard and I

should welcome James to the family if you're serious about marrying him.'

'Of course I'm serious,' Clara replied. 'What makes you think I'm not?'

'It just seems a bit sudden.'

'Well, as you pointed out, time is ticking along and I don't want to be an old maid, do I?' She smiled as she said it so as not to cause any more animosity, but she didn't feel much like smiling.

'I shouldn't have said that,' Esther said. 'Times are changing, I know that and women want careers and independence. I'm actually very proud of you, you know.'

Clara was momentarily taken aback. It was a rare thing to get a direct compliment from her sister. 'Thank you, Esther,' she said. 'I appreciate it.'

'So, bring James for lunch on Sunday,' her sister went on. 'How about that?'

'That would be lovely,' Clara replied, secretly thinking that James would probably not be able to think of anything worse.

* * *

James arrived at Butterfly Cottage on Sunday morning dressed in his best suit, his hair slicked back. He looked positively un-James like dressed up like that and Clara couldn't help a chuckle.

'For the record, I hate wearing this thing, and these are the lengths I'll go to for you,' he said, ducking his head to kiss her. 'Because I love you.'

'I love you too,' she said. She didn't want to tell him that even Richard didn't wear a suit on a Sunday and a jacket and tie would have been fine. Besides, Esther would appreciate the effort.

They walked slowly across the village together. Everywhere was quiet as people returned home for lunch after church or retired to the pub for an hour before closing time. They didn't bump into any of the curious villagers bubbling with gossip about her and James that Esther had talked about. It was an exaggeration, anyway. Nobody was really interested in them. And nobody would be that interested in their marriage either.

Richard greeted them warmly at the door and for a moment Clara dared to hope that everything was going to be all right, that they would accept James for who he was.

'Take off your jacket and loosen your tie,' Richard said to James. 'It's too hot to stand on formality.' And it was hot in the house, despite the windows being open. Clara felt that strange sensation of nausea and hunger wash over her again. It seemed to be happening a lot lately and she thought it was because she wasn't really eating enough – hadn't been since James had proposed. Her mind had been full of so many thoughts, her body running on nervous excitement.

'Now, what can I get you all to drink?' Richard asked. 'G&T for you Clara, and for you James?'

'Do you have a beer?'

Richard paused, blinked, looked at Clara. 'Oh, well, no. I'm sorry, no, we don't.' Clara closed her eyes for a minute. She knew Richard never bought beer in cans, he thought it was common. 'We've got whiskey, wine... um...' Richard was trying to think of alternatives, trying not to be rude and dismissive, which was something at least.

'Wine will be fine,' James said but Clara knew he didn't like wine. It gave him a headache.

Things didn't really improve from then on as an awkward silence descended. James, never really content to sit still for long, took his glass of wine to the window and looked out over the garden. Richard looked at Clara and raised his eyebrows. Clara looked away.

It was far too hot for a roast dinner, and everyone had a sheen of sweat across their foreheads by the time they sat down. Richard carved the chicken and handed out the plates and everyone helped themselves to vegetables from the tureens on the table.

'So,' Esther said with a rather obviously fake bon-homie. 'When's the big day?'

'Oh,' James began. 'I'm not sure we've decided, have we...' He looked hopefully over at Clara.

'Not until next summer,' Clara said, very aware that Esther and Richard would be expecting some sort of plan. 'My friend Betty is marrying in the spring and I don't want to trump her. Besides, we don't want anything very formal, do we?' She smiled encouragingly at James. 'I think just a Register Office job should do.'

'Your wish is my command,' James said.

'A Register Office?' Esther queried.

'And you'll continue to work as a gardener, will you, James?' Richard interrupted, his face red and his mouth full of roast potato. 'After the wedding, I mean.'

'Well, that is my profession,' James replied. 'I will probably still have to travel a lot but I've applied for the assistant head gardener position at Ickbury Manor. If I get it, I'll be here much more.'

'If you get it,' Richard echoed. 'You can't support a family on ifs and maybes.'

Clara choked on a piece of chicken, coughing into

her napkin. 'Sorry,' she said. 'But who said anything about supporting a family?'

'It's a man's job to support—'

'No, Richard, marriage is a team effort. I'd have thought you'd have known that by now.' Clara knew it was rude but she was sick to death of this old-fashioned attitude to marriage. 'I've got a very good job and I own a house. Everything will be fine.'

'This has always been your problem, old girl,' Richard said, pointing his knife at her. 'Always assuming everything will be fine with no plan or anything like that.'

'Well, it's worked out so far,' Clara said, turning back to the food that she did not want to eat. She noticed James across the table from her had his head down, his cheeks red with frustration or embarrassment.

'And what will you do if you don't get this job?' Richard asked, turning back to James. 'Because if—'

'For goodness' sake, Richard,' Esther said loudly and Richard stopped mid-sentence. Clara sent a look of thanks in her sister's direction. 'Not everyone is obliged to live their lives exactly like you,' Esther went on. 'Now, can we please talk about something else?'

There was another uncomfortable silence while Esther cleared the plates, refusing Clara's offer of help. When she brought in the sherry trifle, Clara thought they would have to eat it in silence with nothing but the clinking of spoons to accompany them. But James saved the afternoon.

'Your garden is beautiful,' he said.

Clara saw her sister blush. She knew how much Esther loved her garden. She also knew that James wasn't much of a fan of such perfectly manicured spaces, but at least he was trying.

'Thank you,' Esther said. 'I wouldn't mind your advice on a shady patch where I can't get anything to grow.'

It wasn't going to be easy, Clara thought to herself, but maybe they could all find some common ground eventually. Even if they did have to talk about gardens whenever they met.

18

SUFFOLK, JUNE 2018

The atmosphere in Zach's van felt charged as they drove back to Carybrook, the energy of that kiss lay between them and for a few minutes neither of them spoke. Meredith had been thinking about what it would be like to kiss Zach since the previous afternoon and, when he finally had, she'd been only too glad to kiss him back, but was that a good idea? If they were to share the cottage, if they were to get through this complicated legal situation, then it seemed to Meredith that throwing kisses into the mix wasn't the best idea. And besides, it hadn't been that long since she and Joe had split up and only a couple of weeks since she got the shocking news that Joe and Jemma were expecting a baby. Had she thought, up to that point, that she and Joe would get back together?

Not that any of those arguments stopped her from wanting to kiss Zach again though.

'Soooo,' Zach said eventually, drawing the word out.

Meredith could feel herself blushing. 'So,' she replied.

'I'm sorry, I shouldn't have kissed you like that, out of nowhere.'

'It wasn't out of nowhere though, was it? And besides, you don't need to apologise. I kissed you back.'

When she looked at him he was grinning. 'You did, didn't you,' he said. 'Perhaps you'd let me do that again sometime?'

'Perhaps,' Meredith replied. And perhaps, she thought to herself, she didn't need to overthink everything.

'And what next on the Jimmy Mack front?' Zach asked, changing the subject.

'Is there anywhere else to go?' Meredith replied. 'I think we can be pretty sure that the James Mackenzie that worked at Ickbury Manor in 1963 is Jimmy Mack – the birth dates are the same and that would be way too much of a coincidence if they weren't the same person.'

Zach nodded. 'And I think we can be equally certain that the James Mackenzie of Ickbury Manor was the same person that Miss Samuels was seeing during that same summer. And the same person whose photograph is inside that locket.'

'But what happened that autumn?' Meredith pondered, her hand wrapping itself around the locket which had become a sort of talisman to her, a tangible object that proved to her that her great-aunt had been real. 'We know they both left the area and we know that Clara ended up in Australia and James ended up being a minor celebrity. But we have no way of knowing what happened in between.'

'There are places we could check,' Zach said. 'Jimmy Mack's publishers, for example, although I suspect there is a confidentiality clause so they couldn't tell us anything.'

'Who gets the money for his books now?' Meredith asked.

'His estate, but who he left it to I couldn't tell you. If he had a will it will be on the public record so we could see if we could find that, but nobody is obliged to talk to us.'

'Would there be a record for Clara?'

'Yes!' Zach said, slapping his hand on the steering wheel. 'I can't believe I never thought of it. I know she went to Australia in 1964 and I know she went by ship – she told me that much herself. She went as part of the Ten Pound Pom scheme.'

'What was that?' Meredith asked.

'It was an initiative after the Second World War that encouraged people to emigrate to Australia, especially skilled workers like doctors, nurses and teachers.'

'And what happened between her leaving Carybrook and going to Australia the next year, do you know?'

Zach shook his head. 'No idea,' he said. 'I feel that Miss Samuels only ever told me snippets of her life.'

'So if she left Carybrook in 1963 and went to Australia in 1964 where was she in between? Do you know when in 1964 she sailed?' Meredith asked. 'Or the name of the ship?'

'She sailed in the autumn,' Zach replied. 'She was there for that Christmas, I remember her saying how it had been her first Christmas in the sun but that after many years summer Christmases felt normal.' He stopped for a moment. 'I don't know the name of the ship though.'

'There would be passenger lists of the ships, I guess,' Meredith said. 'But without a name...'

'It's another fruitless search.'

'Not necessarily. Just harder. But even if we do find out, we've still got this missing year. Where was she between November 1963 and the autumn of 1964?' Meredith wondered how far she would take this. How badly did she need to know? And at what point did natural curiosity give way to prying into somebody else's past?

'I can look into it tomorrow maybe,' Zach said, sounding downhearted. 'But for now, we'd best go and tell your mum what we've found out.'

She reached over and touched Zach's wrist. 'Don't mention the kiss to Mum,' she said.

It was Zach's turn to blush. 'I had no intention of telling her!'

'It's just if she gets even a whiff of it she'll get over-excited and I need to take this, whatever this is between us, slowly. My life is still complicated.'

He moved his arm from under hers and held her hand. 'I know,' he said softly. 'You take it as slowly as you need. We can just stay friends if that's what you want.'

Meredith wasn't sure what she wanted, but she did know that her life was changing and she hoped for the better. But she had to go slowly, take everything one step at a time and not rush into any decisions she might end up running away from later.

Bernice insisted on making lunch when they arrived back at the cottage.

'You sit in the garden and I'll bring everything out,' she said. 'I walked up to that lovely-looking deli near the pub and bought all sorts of goodies.'

They did as they were told, sitting at the wrought iron table on the patio as Bernice brought out fresh bread and cheeses, olives and salads, pickles and cold meats and an exotic-looking fruit salad, along with glasses of fizzy elderflower cordial.

'This looks amazing, Mum,' Meredith said. 'I hadn't had a chance to check out that deli yet.'

'When I saw it, I couldn't resist! I could have bought the whole shop.'

As they ate they told her everything they had discovered at Ickbury Manor – the exhibition about the gardens during the war, the staff log book that Ivy had so kindly let them look at, James Mackenzie's name on the list for 1963 but missing for 1964.

'And it's definitely him?' Bernice asked. 'Jimmy Mack?'

'The dates of birth add up,' Meredith replied.

'So, mysterious Great-Aunt Clara used to date Jimmy Mack. Well, well. Imagine that.'

'Except it was before he was Jimmy Mack,' Zach clarified.

Bernice nodded, cutting herself another piece of cheese.

'Do you think Clara knew?' she asked. 'That he became Jimmy Mack?'

'We were wondering that,' Meredith said. 'But I think it's unlikely. He was only on British TV, as far as we know, and programmes weren't syndicated all over the world then like they are now.'

'Do you think she ever tried to find him again?'

'Maybe that's what she was doing in that missing year?' Zach said.

'What missing year?' Bernice asked and Meredith explained.

'Perhaps she went back to London,' Bernice said. 'Back to her old life before she moved here. And when that didn't work out either she left the country.'

'I don't see how we'll ever know. In fact, I'm not sure that we'll ever find out more than we already have. Zach suggested contacting Jimmy Mack's publishers or looking through the passenger lists for all the ships that departed for Australia in the autumn of 1964 to see when Clara left, but what will it tell us? Even if they tell us exactly when she left, they won't tell us why. I feel as though we'll never know why Clara and my grandparents left Carybrook so suddenly. There aren't any records that will tell us that.'

'Perhaps not,' Bernice said, a strange look on her face.

'What are you thinking, Mum?'

'Oh, nothing. I'm a nosey old woman who can't stand an unsolved mystery, but this is real life, isn't it? Real people's lives. Real lives don't have neat endings where everything is tied up in a bow and we don't always know the truth about each other. It's such a shame your grandmother never mentioned she had a sister.'

'That's another weird thing,' Meredith said. 'Why on earth didn't she tell us?'

'Well, they'd obviously had a falling out, hadn't they,' Bernice replied. 'And without wanting to speak ill of the dead, your grandmother was a miserable old bag. I had a few fallings out with her too.'

Zach chuckled to himself and wiped his mouth on a paper napkin. 'Sorry,' he said. 'I shouldn't laugh. But I should get on with that pumpkin patch if you don't mind. Thanks so much for lunch, Bernice.'

As he stood up he looked at Meredith and she felt that charged feeling that she had felt in the van after he'd kissed her. They looked at each other for a little too long before Zach moved away again.

'What's going on there?' Bernice asked when Zach was out of earshot.

'What are you talking about, Mum?' Meredith looked away, and not in the direction Zach had gone, hiding her face from her mother.

'I saw the way he looked at you just then,' Bernice went on. Her voice was kind but teasing – Meredith knew that her mother wanted nothing more than for her to be happy. The news that she'd given to Bernice over the last week – the failing salon, the inability to pay her rent, Joe's betrayal – must have been a shock. Nobody wants to see their daughter unhappy and un-ravelling. But Bernice hadn't judged or even shown her shock or sadness, she'd just been practical, helping Meredith get things back on track. And now she saw an opportunity for some fun in her daughter's life. That was all.

'There was a moment earlier,' Meredith admitted.

'A moment?' Bernice raised her eyebrows sug-gestively.

Meredith didn't want to elaborate. 'I don't know if I'm ready,' she said simply.

Bernice sighed. 'You know, we all screw up some-times. I know that you blame yourself for what has happened with the salon and with Joe. We don't al-ways have control over everything. We can try our best and it never quite works out. Look at me and your dad, I blamed myself for years over not being able to keep him at home. I so wanted us to be a proper family but it wasn't really until I met Lloyd that I re-alised none of it was my fault. If your father wanted to leave he would leave, nothing I could have done would have stopped it. It's the same with you and Joe. What Joe does is his decision.'

'The salon is all me though.'

'Not necessarily,' Bernice said. 'I've seen how hard you've worked, I've seen how well you budgeted. But hard work and good intentions don't always mean everything will work out. The important thing is real-ising when it's time to move on.'

'Mother, are you suggesting that I should move on with Zach?'

Bernice shrugged. 'Why not? He's a good-looking young man, you seem to get on well and he clearly likes you.'

'And right now it would make everything so much more complicated.'

'Because of this house?' Bernice asked.

'Partly, yes. I told him that I wanted to stay for a while, just until I worked out what to do.'

'So you're not going back to London?'

'Well, I'll have to eventually,' Meredith said, feeling rather reluctant about the idea. How much she had changed in just a few short weeks. 'I'll have to sort everything out properly, actually have a conversation with my salon manager and the other hairdressers rather than just asking them if they can cover for one more week. But I'm not sure I want to go back to London permanently. Part of me feels I could be happy here.'

'I never thought I'd leave London,' Bernice said. 'I'd lived there my whole life. I couldn't imagine a version of myself anywhere else. But then I met Lloyd and moved to the suburbs and then Spain.' She turned to look at her daughter. 'And I have no regrets. It's been good for me to live a quieter life and I think it would be good for you.'

'But I'd still need to sell this house.' Meredith felt sad at that thought. A far cry from the person who couldn't wait to sell it. 'And split the proceeds with Zach so we can each decide where to go from there.'

'Is that what he said when you told him you wanted to stay a while?' Bernice asked.

Meredith shook her head. 'No, he said I could stay as long as I needed. You know, he wants to finish the garden before we think about selling. He said he was happy living in his caravan too, which feels weird to me. I'd like him to live in the house. He said he'd think about it.'

'Everyone's different, love,' Bernice said. 'Not

everyone wants to live conventionally. Look at your father.'

Meredith couldn't help but laugh. 'Really, Mum? First, you say I should date Zach and then you compare him to Dad? Make up your mind.'

'I didn't mean it like that,' Bernice said, playfully swatting at her daughter. 'I just meant that we all have to find our own way of being happy – and that isn't always in the way society tells us it is. For the record, he's nothing like your father. He's much surer of himself, much more settled in his own body.'

'He told me he's been travelling all over the country for work, that he'd never been able to settle anywhere until he arrived in Carybrook. He said this is the first place that has felt like home in years.'

'Well, it seems to have had that effect on you as well.'

'Maybe,' Meredith said quietly, thinking about what it would be like to live here permanently. 'Maybe.'

'Well,' Bernice said, standing up. 'I'd better get these lunch things tidied up.'

'Let me help you, Mum.'

'No, you sit there and enjoy the sun. It sounds as though you've got a bit of thinking to do.' Bernice began to stack the plates. 'Speaking of which, do you think there's anywhere else you can go to find out the answers to this Jimmy Mack mystery?'

'I'm not sure where else we can look. I know Zach suggested the passenger lists of the ships and Jimmy Mack's publishers, but I can't see that either of those will really tell us anything.'

'I agree that it's a bit of a dead end. Perhaps we'll all have to be content with never really knowing the truth.'

After Bernice had gone back into the cottage Meredith settled back into her chair and closed her eyes, feeling the warmth of the sun on her face, hearing the gentle clatter of dishes from the kitchen. She felt inexplicably content in a way she hadn't for many years. She tried to remember. She hadn't felt this way the whole time she'd been running the salon or any of the time she'd been with Joe. She hadn't felt like this since she was a child, since Bernice had met Lloyd and they'd moved to Kent and finally got the garden that her mother had been craving for so long. Meredith could remember sitting in that garden with the sun on her face just as it was now. She could remember hearing birdsong and the gentle sound of the neighbours mowing their lawns. It must have been the summer she had turned fourteen. Had she really not felt true contentment since then?

She wished she could bottle this feeling and keep it forever.

Maybe living in Carybrook could be the next best thing.

And she realised then that it didn't matter if she never found out what had happened between her great-aunt and the man who went on to become Jimmy Mack. She could guess most of it anyway and her heart went out to Clara. She had been let down by a man and been left heartbroken, then for whatever reason the man regretted his actions and tried to find her again, sending letters that Clara finally read decades later. There was some comfort in knowing that her great-aunt had died knowing that James was sorry for whatever it was he had done.

There was more to it than that though, wasn't there? The mention of money that James Mackenzie wished he hadn't taken. Was he paid off in some way? And then there was the way Clara was never spoken about, as though she had been wiped off the surface of the earth. Whose decision had that been? Clara's, or Esther and Richard Bradshaw's?

But Meredith may never know and, as her mother had said, she would have to be content with that. Right now, sitting in this garden with the sun on her face, she felt that she could be content with anything.

Besides, she had much more important things to worry about, like what she was going to do about the salon, when she was going to have a serious conversation with the staff, where she was going to live, what she was going to do for a living when she got there.

But all she could think about was that she didn't want to leave Carybrook and that despite not feeling ready she wanted to spend more time with Zach.

The warmth of the sun and the lack of sleep the night before must have made her drift off because the next thing she remembered was her mother gently shaking her awake.

'Meredith, love, are you OK?'

Meredith looked up and smiled. 'Sorry,' she said. 'I must have nodded off. I've not been sleeping that well, I suppose.'

'Only,' Bernice bit her lip and looked over her shoulder at something or someone who was standing in the sunroom, 'there's somebody here to see you.'

Meredith stood up, peering over her mother's shoulder.

'Nobody knows I'm here, I don't think,' she said, watching as a man stepped out onto the patio.

'Hello, Meredith,' he said.

'Dad! What are you doing here?'

19

SUFFOLK, SEPTEMBER AND OCTOBER 1963

Clara started the new term at Carybrook School a bundle of nerves. She hadn't really seen anyone other than James, Esther and Richard since her engagement as there had been no Ickbury dances during the last part of August and many people had decamped to the seaside for a week or two before term and the busyness of September began. As she stepped into the staff room with that shiny ring on her finger, she felt as anxious as she had done on her first day in June.

'I told you that you'd be next,' Betty squealed when she saw Clara's ring, which she spotted from across the room like a magpie. 'That James is a fast worker, isn't he? When did this happen?'

'Oh, only a couple of weeks ago,' Clara replied. 'I would have told you but you were at the seaside.'

'I'm so happy for you!' Betty grinned.

'So am I, Clara,' John said, passing her a rather weak-looking cup of tea. 'But I'm not sure Miss Cheggers is going to be delighting in three of her teachers leaving this academic year.'

'Oh, I'm not intending to leave,' Clara said adamantly. Her career was still important to her. 'We're staying in Carybrook so I can keep teaching.'

'Well, until you hear the pitter-patter of little feet, anyway,' Betty said.

Clara smiled at Betty in that same benign way she used to smile at Mrs Benyon back in London. She was used to having different opinions about life than those around her and knew when not to say anything. But she had come to a decision. She had spoken with James and told him that she was certain that she didn't want children and that she understood if that meant he wanted to change his mind.

He didn't exactly say he was relieved to hear it but there was a look that passed over his face that told Clara exactly that – so much so she almost burst out laughing.

'We're probably a bit too old for all that anyway,' he'd said.

'You make it sound like we're eighty-three not thirty-three,' she'd said, squeezing his arm, as relieved as he had seemed to be, delighted they were on the same page.

Since the disastrous Sunday lunch, things appeared to have settled down between Clara and her sister as well. She knew Richard and James would never see eye to eye – they were too different – but Esther at least seemed more on her side now.

'I just want you to be happy, Clara,' her sister had said to her. 'Or as happy as any of us can be.'

'Thank you,' Clara had said, silently acknowledging the elephant in the room that she knew made her sister not quite happy – the fact that she hadn't had children. How different they both were as well. 'I hope Richard can be happy for us too.'

Esther had rolled her eyes. 'Oh, you leave Richard to me. He likes to show off in front of new people, make sure they all know his opinions on everything, but I've spoken to him. I told him that his opinions are already known by us all and don't need any reiteration and they certainly don't need to come up in conversation again. If James ever wants business advice he knows where to come.'

'Thank you,' Clara had said again, smiling to herself. Her sister could stand up for herself when she needed to and it was good to see.

James had been harder to calm down.

'I can rub along with Esther if we talk about gardens and food,' he'd said. 'She's not so bad and has certainly mellowed since we were at school but I'm fairly sure Richard doesn't like me.'

'Does it matter whether Richard likes you or not?' Clara had replied. 'Plenty of families have factions that don't get along. Surely me liking you is the most important thing.'

James had smiled then. 'I'm glad you like me,' he had said, pulling her towards him. 'But I don't know, Richard really dug the knife in.'

'About your work?'

'I know you don't care about this either, but he always makes me feel I should be more steady in my work, more secure.'

'But I have a good job, James, and I don't need looking after. And we have this house. Everything will be all right. Times are changing, we don't have to live exactly like everyone else, you know. Besides, we won't be getting married until next year – a lot could have changed by then.' There was a very good chance he would get this gardening job at Ickbury Manor and then none of this would matter any more.

He'd reluctantly agreed and did genuinely seem to be looking forward to getting on with the Butterfly Garden.

'Maybe I'll actually get it finished next summer when I'm living here,' he'd said. His progress over the summer had been slow and distracted, for obvious reasons.

Things had settled down, simple wedding plans were tentatively made and by the time term started Clara hoped that everything was back on track.

And yet, that wasn't quite how it felt.

'Oh, after the initial excitement of the engagement wore off I felt a bit uncertain,' Betty had reassured her. 'I kept questioning everything – was John the right person, did I want to be with him for the rest of my life, what if somebody better came along. On and on it went. But after a few days, I knew I was being ridiculous. It's normal to feel nervous about big life changes. Don't worry about it.'

Clara tried to take Betty's advice, tried not to worry. But there was a lot on her mind.

She had assured Miss Cheggers, when she'd told her of the engagement, that she had no intention of giving up teaching, that being married would change very little and that children had never been a top priority for her in the way they were for Betty.

Miss Cheggers had looked at Clara over her reading glasses. 'Hmmm,' she'd said. 'Well, I do want to believe you and you do seem more career-orientated than most.' She had paused. 'You know, Clara,' she'd continued after an uncomfortable moment. 'You may wish to consider taking the contraceptive pill. Many women sing its praises. It gives them the freedom, you see; freedom to live their lives as they see fit.'

Clara had felt her face burn with embarrassment. Was Miss Cheggers really talking to her about contraception? She had wanted the ground to open up and swallow her. Although the headmistress was right, it was something Clara had been considering. A few of the girls in the boarding house in London had talked about taking it as soon as they were married – it wasn't available for unmarried women, which Clara thought rather defeated the point of the little miracle pills.

'Anyway, I wish you a lifetime of happiness, my dear,' Miss Cheggers had said and Clara felt relief flood through her body that the subject seemed to be closed.

Clara had hurried from the headmistress's office before the conversation could get any more embarrassing. She hadn't wanted to sit there any longer because she had a feeling that she had been lying to Miss Cheggers and lying to herself.

She had a feeling that the contraceptive pill would come too late.

The strange dizzy, nauseous feeling that had plagued her during those hot days of August hadn't stopped as the weather got cooler and as far as she could remember – she wasn't very good at keeping track – she hadn't had a period since July.

She may not have babies at the top of her agenda, but it seemed that it was a little late to worry.

Clara was fairly certain she was pregnant and soon she would have to pluck up the courage to make a doctor's appointment and find out for sure.

* * *

The doctor's waiting room in Ickbury was hot and uncomfortable and Clara hid behind her newspaper hoping that she wouldn't see anyone she knew or who knew her sister. The last thing she needed right now was gossip going around about her. Luckily she was called into the doctor's office before she bumped into anyone.

Dr Franks was an intense-looking man who ushered Clara to a chair before asking what he could do for her this morning.

'I think I'm pregnant,' she said. The words sounded like they were being spoken by somebody else. When she said them out loud all their implications that she hadn't allowed herself to think about came crashing down on her.

'How long have you been married?' Dr Franks asked.

Clara took a breath. 'I'm not. I'm getting married next year but that seems as though it will be too late.'

Dr Franks smiled kindly. For some reason, Clara had been expecting disapproval and a lecture on morals but really, she realised now, Dr Franks must see much worse than this on a daily basis. They talked a little about dates and Dr Franks confirmed that the baby would be due in April. He said she could make another appointment for a couple of months down the line and, in the meantime, he would book her a hospital bed.

'Will Ickbury Hospital be all right for you or would you like somewhere further afield?' he asked. It took Clara a moment to realise that he was asking if she wanted to have the baby somewhere else, away from friends and family.

'Ickbury is fine,' she replied.

'Perhaps you could bring the wedding forward,' he suggested, as though that hadn't crossed Clara's mind and then he asked her to leave a urine sample before she left. 'Just to be sure,' he said.

She emerged from the doctor's surgery into a beautiful late September afternoon, but even the sunshine couldn't lift her spirits. Even though she had already known that she was probably pregnant and that the baby would be due in April, she felt the doctor's confirmation as a terrible blow. She'd been so careful when she'd been with James, but nothing was ever completely free from risk, she knew that. Not even the new contraceptive pill that Miss Cheggers was so excited about.

The doctor had said the urine test would take up to two weeks to come back with the definite result and she found herself hoping that it was all a mistake, that there was something else wrong with her.

She had always assumed, as the other women in the boarding house had come and gone to their new jobs and – more often – their new husbands, that this would never happen to her. She had always assumed she would never meet anyone and she would go on to be an unmarried headmistress herself, like Miss Cheggers. Yet here she was, only three months after moving away from the boarding house herself, engaged and pregnant.

She hadn't seen it coming. And she certainly didn't feel happy.

She should feel happy, she knew that. But she didn't.

She loved James, of that there was no doubt. Having him back in her life again had allowed Clara to blossom, to become the person she always knew she was capable of being – a person who smiled a lot, who wasn't short or irritable with the children in her class. A person who went to the cinema and to dances, who sat in wine bars discussing films and politics. She liked this version of herself.

But they'd had plans – even if James got the job at Ickbury Manor they still planned to travel in the summers, to live their own lives and have their own careers, to be happy both together and apart.

Clara being pregnant changed everything for both of them.

And so she decided, as she stood outside the doctor's surgery in the September sunshine, that she would say nothing and tell nobody until the test results came back. Because nothing was certain until then.

Even if deep down Clara already knew the truth.

* * *

It was James, of course, who she told first when the doctor's test was confirmed.

Clara asked him to meet her after work, to come to Butterfly Cottage.

'Do you want to see a film or something?' he asked.

'No, I'd just like to stay at home and talk if that's OK with you?'

She cooked chicken for them both, which they ate in Clara's kitchen in what felt to her as a rather oppressive atmosphere, although she suspected James hadn't noticed anything as he talked as normal about the garden, about the weather, about his job offer at Ickbury Manor which had been confirmed the week before, which he was surprisingly happy about.

'Much as I love travelling about for my work,' he said, 'I didn't really relish being away from you for months at a time. This way I'm much nearer although I will have to stay on-site a couple of nights a week.'

Then he asked about the wedding, if she'd had any ideas about dates or venues yet. 'I know it's a while away yet but I was talking to your friend's other half, John, and it sounds like there's a hell of a lot we have to do.'

This was Clara's opportunity and she couldn't let it slip through her fingers.

'Do you think we could bring the date of the wedding forward?' she asked.

'I'd marry you tomorrow if I could,' James grinned. 'But I thought you wanted to wait until after Betty and John had tied the knot?'

'I do,' Clara swallowed. 'At least I did... I...' Her mouth felt dry and she thought for a moment that the chicken was about to make a reappearance. 'Could you get me a glass of water?' she asked.

James jumped up, getting a glass from the kitchen cabinet and filling it from the tap. When he came back to the table he moved his chair closer to Clara's.

'Are you not feeling well?' he asked.

'I'm not ill,' Clara replied. 'But I have been to the doctor's recently.'

'Why didn't you tell me? I could have—'

But Clara pressed her hand against his before he could go on guessing at what might be the problem.

'It seems that I'm pregnant,' she said.

She closed her eyes and the words felt as though they hung above her head like a speech bubble in a comic strip. James didn't say anything.

'I know this isn't ideal,' she went on into the silence, her eyes still closed. 'I know what we talked about…' She trailed off then because she didn't know what else to say. She remembered the look of relief on James's face when she'd told him she didn't want children and the joy she'd felt when she realised they both wanted the same thing. And yet here they were and they had to face it together.

She opened her eyes then. 'What do you think?' Clara asked, as though she was asking him if they should have daisies or lilies at the wedding.

'I think it's wonderful news,' he replied. 'And of course we can bring the wedding forward.'

He was smiling but Clara could see that his smile didn't reach his eyes. This wasn't what he wanted, none of this was, she could tell. He must feel as Clara had felt outside the doctor's surgery.

And there was somebody else who wasn't going to be over the moon about this either.

* * *

Esther had gone pale, her mouth a thin line. Clara watched as her sister's knuckles whitened from gripping the counter. She wished now that she'd gone more gently with her news and hadn't just blurted it out while Esther was making tea. She could have at least waited until they were sitting down.

'You're pregnant?' Esther repeated quietly.

'Oh God, I'm so sorry. I shouldn't have told you like that, I should have...'

Esther straightened herself up then, her face relaxing, the colour returning a little.

'No, Clara, it should be me saying I'm sorry. I have to learn to stop reacting like this when people share their good news. I just...' Her voice faltered for a moment again and she turned to pour the hot water into the teapot. She picked up the tray. 'Shall we go and sit down?'

Clara waited for Esther to speak when they sat down. She didn't want to say the wrong thing and upset her sister again.

'I'm sorry,' she said again.

'You don't have to be, I understand.'

'I've tried so hard not to turn into them but I think I'm failing.'

'Them?' Clara queried. 'Who?'

'Mother and Father,' Esther replied. 'They were always so angry and bitter, so superior. I didn't really realise how bad they were until you went to university.'

'Did something happen?' Esther had been twenty when Clara had left and still living at home waiting for Richard to propose.

Esther nodded. 'They did something that made me realise that they weren't nice people.'

Clara wondered how it had taken Esther so long to work that out but didn't say anything.

'When you were away they tore up your post,' Esther went on. 'Your letters from James, they just ripped them up and put them in the bin. I thought it would be all right because you would write to him and give him your college address. But the letters kept coming so that can't have happened.'

'He moved,' Clara said. 'And I didn't know where because I didn't get his letters.'

Esther pressed a hand to her forehead. 'I know I should have done something. I was a grown woman and I should have stood up to them, or at the very least taped the letters back together and sent them on to you. But I was afraid of them I think, especially—' She stopped suddenly.

'Especially what?' Clara asked. She didn't know how she felt about this revelation. She'd worked out that her parents must have got rid of the letters when James had told her he'd kept writing, but she hadn't realised her sister had known about it for all this time.

'I overheard them talking one night,' Esther went on. 'About how they had finally managed to stop this ridiculous friendship between you and James and how they thought he was beneath you. I heard them say that it was because of them that his family had moved away when war broke out. Mother had put in a complaint about Reverend Mackenzie to the bishop and...'

'But why?' Clara asked. 'Why go to all that trouble to make someone else's life unhappy? Why did they dislike the Mackenzies so much?'

'Because you were happier with them than you were with us,' Esther said.

Clara didn't respond to that. She didn't know how, without saying something she might regret.

'But I don't want to be like them,' Esther said. 'I want you to be happy.'

But you don't really, do you? Clara thought to herself. *And you are like them, you do think James is beneath you.*

'Are you happy?' Esther asked.

Clara nodded because even after this she couldn't be so cruel as to tell her childless sister that she was struggling to be happy about the baby and that she was terrified about the future, about the idea of giving birth and she was frustrated about the career she had worked so hard at.

She also kept thinking about the way James had looked at her when she'd told him, that smile that didn't reach his eyes and the way he'd turned away from her not long afterwards to do the washing up and go back to the Manor.

Could they carry on pretending that this was what they both wanted? If they did, would they settle into the rhythm of family life in time?

Clara didn't see that they had a lot of choice.

'If you're happy then I'm happy,' Esther said, patting Clara's thigh in an unusual display of affection before turning to pour the tea.

'I didn't mean to upset you.'

'You didn't,' Esther smiled, but Clara could see the sadness in it. 'Nobody's life goes exactly as they plan it, does it?'

'You're going to be a brilliant aunt,' Clara said, trying hard to be normal, to not show her unhappiness and her shock at the cruelty of her parents. 'As long as...' She hesitated.

'As long as what?'

'Well, you're not disapproving, are you, because...'

'Because you're not married, you mean?' Esther finished with a short laugh. 'Oh, of course not. It's 1963 after all, and you're bringing the wedding forward aren't you, so there's no problem.'

'We're hoping to get married next month, but it will be a quiet affair at Ickbury Register Office. Just the four of us – if you and Richard will come.' Clara had thought about asking Betty and John as well once she broke the news of her pregnancy at school. She was intending to tell Miss Cheggers on Monday morning.

'Of course we'll come,' Esther replied.

'And you think Richard will be all right about everything? He won't disapprove?'

'Oh, Richard will have a pink fit about it all, no doubt!' Esther chuckled. 'But you leave him to me. By the next time you see him, he will be nothing but sweetness and light.'

* * *

Telling Miss Cheggers was even harder than telling her sister. While the headmistress pretended to be happy for Clara and James she visibly disapproved of the obvious elephant in the room – sex before marriage. If Clara had thought the conversation about contraception had been awkward it held nothing to this and she was relieved when the bell rang signalling the first class of the day so she could scuttle away from the headmistress as fast as possible.

Betty, though, was delighted when she heard, and

wasn't remotely put out by the fact that Clara's wedding would now come first.

Clara felt Betty's hand on her arm. 'I completely understand why you need to bring the wedding forward. I'd be the same in your position.'

Clara nodded, realising she would be eight months pregnant by the time Betty married. Would she be able to go? Or would her 'almost geriatric pregnancy' mean she would have to stay at home on bed rest?

'Well, we'll definitely be at the Register Office,' Betty went on. 'Me and John. We'd be happy to.'

'Thank you,' Clara said, glad it wouldn't just be her and James, Esther and Richard, glad that somebody would be there as a buffer so that Richard didn't quiz James all day about the future.

'What are you two whispering about?' John asked, coming over and slipping an arm around Betty's waist.

Betty batted him away with a laugh. 'Not in here, John,' she said. 'And we're talking about weddings. I'll fill you in later.'

'Lucky me,' John said rolling his eyes.

* * *

For the next couple of weeks, life continued as normal in Carybrook. People began to hear about Clara and James's Register Office wedding and congratulated her when they saw her, but if any of them knew, or guessed, the reason behind the haste they certainly didn't say anything. The wedding banns were posted and the Register Office itself was booked for November and Richard – who, true to Esther's word, was nothing but kind about the situation, unusually so, Clara thought – had offered to pay for a meal and champagne afterwards. James, meanwhile, was getting ready to start in his new role as assistant head gardener at Ickbury Manor. Clara didn't see as much of him as she had been doing over the summer and when she did he seemed nervous and jittery and distant somehow. She kept telling herself that everything would be all right. Just because neither of them had planned for this didn't mean it wouldn't work out. People must have to do this sort of thing all the time. They would both settle into it.

What choice did they have?

Her life was about to change into something almost impossible to imagine. Until this summer she had always thought of herself much like Miss Cheggers or Miss Higgs, the headmistress at her London school. She thought she would never marry, never become a mother, and spend her life dedicated to teaching. There were exciting reforms ahead in British schooling and she had been interested in being a part of them, but she knew now that wasn't to be. A different future lay ahead of her and just because it wasn't the future she expected, didn't mean that it wasn't going to be rewarding and delightful, filled with love and happiness.

But she was overwhelmed by a feeling of doubt that sat in her stomach, making her almost as nauseous as the pregnancy. However much she tried to convince herself otherwise, nothing about this situation felt right.

'It's just nerves and hormones,' Betty reassured her, but it felt like more than that. As though something was about to happen.

So when she came back from school one Friday afternoon, laden down with groceries to make a meal for James that evening, she wasn't surprised to find the hand-delivered letter sitting on the doormat. As she picked it up it felt almost inevitable. Her name was written on the front in handwriting as familiar to her as her own. She watched her finger slice open the envelope as though it was separate from herself. She pulled out the single sheet of writing paper.

My Darling

I am so sorry but I can't do this.

I know you will be safe and looked after by Esther and Richard, I know they will be able to give you and the baby a much better future than I can. Don't turn away from them as I'm turning from you.

This is the right thing to do and I should never have let this get so far. If I could go back to the night I first saw your beautiful face at the dance in Ickbury I would do things differently.

But life is not like that is it?

Always

JM

Clara looked at the sheet of notepaper and thought about the look in James's eyes as he'd pretended to smile when she'd told him she was pregnant. She thought about all the conversations they'd had about the future, all the plans for travel – to Scotland, to Cornwall, to everywhere in between. She had wanted to do all of that with him, but they were James's plans and she should have known then that he would never be able to stay in one place forever.

She folded the sheet of paper and put it back in the envelope which she in turn put in her pocket as she sat down on the bottom stair and gave herself over to tears, just for a moment. She was alone again.

Except she wasn't alone, was she? She had a baby to think of now, and no career to support them both.

There was only one place she could turn.

She hoped that James was right and that Esther and Richard would help her. Because she had nowhere else to go.

20

SUFFOLK, JUNE 2018

Meredith stared at her father, hardly able to believe he was there. It had been fifteen years since she'd last seen him and he looked older of course, and significantly more tanned.

Dennis stepped down onto the patio towards his daughter. Bernice stood very close behind him with her arms folded like a bodyguard, although Meredith wasn't sure who she was guarding.

'I heard you'd inherited a house,' he said, gently squeezing his daughter's shoulder. 'I thought I'd come and see it.'

'Oh, you heard, did you?' Bernice said, straightening herself up as Dennis turned towards her. 'I'd say you've got a lot of explaining to do, Dennis Bradshaw.'

Meredith watched as her father visibly slumped at Bernice's harsh but true words.

'I'm sorry,' he said to nobody in particular.

She stood up. 'Dad, did you know Clara Samuels?' she asked gently.

'I did, love, and your mum's right – I do have a lot of explaining to do. But not right now, eh? I need to find somewhere to stay and...'

It was then that she noticed it, the twang in her father's voice, the hint of an Antipodean accent. 'Dad, have you been in Australia all this time?'

Dennis held up his hands in submission. 'You've got me,' he said. Pieces of a puzzle started to come together in Meredith's head.

'You can stay here,' Meredith said. 'We've got a spare room, Mum and I can go and make it up for you.' She looked over at Bernice who was giving her the sort of look that said she would rather walk over hot coals than make up a bed for her ex in the same house she was sleeping in. 'Why don't you sit down here and Mum and I will go up and sort things out for you. Do you have any bags?'

'Still in the car, love,' Dennis replied. 'I'll get them later.'

'Can I make you a cup of tea or something?' Meredith said before her mother, who looked like she was going to burst, started chastising him again. The last thing she needed was for her parents to have one of their ridiculous spiralling arguments. Although it did look like only Bernice was up for a quarrel. Dennis seemed much calmer than she had ever seen him. She watched him sit quietly in the chair she had just vacated and realised that more than just the passing years had changed him.

'No tea, love, I'll just wait here for you.'

* * *

'What on earth were you thinking, asking him to stay?' Bernice stage-whispered as they walked up the stairs. 'I suppose I'd best get back to Spain and—'

'Mum,' Meredith turned around on the stairs and held up her hand. Bernice miraculously stopped talking and followed her daughter into the smallest bedroom in the house.

'This will do for Dad,' she said. 'Can you get some spare sheets? There's a pack of brand-new ones in my room.' Meredith had brought new sheets with her as part of her intention to stage the cottage as though people lived here for a quick sale. She couldn't believe that was only a couple of weeks ago. The idea of selling the cottage now seemed impossible. She loved it here. She didn't know yet how she was going to make things work but Carybrook, and hopefully Butterfly Cottage, were going to play a part in her future one way or another.

'I don't want you to go back to Spain, Mum,' she said as Bernice unfolded the sheets. 'We're all grown adults. Surely we can live together for a few days? I've asked him to stay because he's my father and he clearly doesn't have anywhere else to go. I don't know why he's here but it's pretty clear Dad knew Clara and maybe he can help us find out what actually happened back in 1963. Maybe he already knows.'

'Maybe,' Bernice said. 'I just don't trust him. How do we know anything he tells us is the truth? He had a very strange relationship with the truth when you were a child, telling us he'd be back at dinner time and not coming back for a week. You know that.'

'I do know that,' Meredith replied. 'But there must be a reason and I think that reason has to be connected to Clara and Australia.'

'I also noticed that he's not the same man who walked out of your eighteenth birthday party.'

Meredith felt that familiar sweeping dip in her stomach when she thought of that night and what she had said to him as Bernice tucked the fitted sheet under the mattress.

'He used to be all swagger and confidence, could charm the birds from the trees, you know?' Meredith did know; Joe had been exactly the same until he'd gone and charmed a different bird. Was that what Dennis had been doing to her mother when he disappeared for days? She shook the thought away. If her mother didn't want to tell her, it wasn't her business. 'It's the reason I took him back over and over again.' Bernice stopped, looking out of the window. 'I loved him once, you know. But all that charm and swagger has gone.' She turned back to Meredith. 'Something has happened, that's for sure. Something that has knocked the stuffing out of him.'

'Only one way to find out,' Meredith said. 'I'll just have to ask him.'

'And take what he says with a pinch of salt, OK? I can see he's changed but we don't know how much yet.'

Meredith rolled her eyes. There would never be much love lost between her parents now. 'OK, Mum,' she said.

* * *

When they got back downstairs Dennis was sitting at the garden table with Zach. They each had a beer in hand and were laughing at something.

'Hello,' Meredith said. 'You've met Zach then.'

'I have indeed,' Dennis replied. He seemed a little cheerier now, which probably had something to do with the beer. He always did drink a bit too much but that wasn't something Meredith was going to address right now.

'I don't know if he told you this, but Clara Samuels left this house to both me and Zach – half each.'

'I did explain who I was,' Zach said. 'But he already seemed to know.'

'You did?'

Dennis nodded. 'Clara wrote to me about Zach,' he said. 'She told me that she was going to leave half the house to him. She wanted to ask me if that was all right.'

'You?' Bernice snapped. 'What's it got to do with you who Clara Samuels leaves her house to?'

'Mum,' Meredith warned. Bernice sighed and sat down on the opposite side of the table from her ex.

'Why did she want to ask you, Dad?'

Dennis put down his beer bottle and wiped his mouth on the back of his hand. 'Originally she was going to leave Butterfly Cottage to me,' he said. 'But I asked her not to. I asked her to leave it to you.'

'You did...' Meredith looked over at her mother whose eyes were nearly popping out of her head with the effort of not saying anything. She tried again, 'You did that? You were the one who told Clara about me?'

Dennis nodded again.

'But why?' Meredith felt suddenly very self-conscious that she was the only one standing and sat down on the only available chair next to her father. 'What's going on?'

'I should go,' Zach said, standing up suddenly. 'This is a family matter. I only came over to talk to you about the garden, Meredith, but it can wait. I'll catch up with you later.'

'Stay,' Dennis said, his voice suddenly authoritative, so much so that Zach sat straight back down again. 'Clara told me what a good friend you'd been to her in her last months, how well you'd looked after her. This is part of your story as well.'

Zach looked over at Meredith. 'Is that OK with you?' he asked.

'Yes, stay. This is your house too and Clara was your friend. Whatever is going on it involves you as well.' She turned back to her father, placed her hand on top of his. 'Dad, I know you're tired and you've had a long journey but can you tell me how you knew Clara?'

'It's complicated,' Dennis replied. He closed his eyes for a moment and Meredith realised that he was trying to stop himself from crying. She felt him squeeze her hand. 'I've been a fairly rubbish father,' he went on. 'I don't need Bernice to tell me that. I was never able to settle at anything, I always had itchy feet, always thought the grass would be greener some-where else. When Bernice first told me she was preg-nant I was delighted but also terrified. I loved you, Meredith, from the moment you were born, but you deserved so much better than me.'

'Dad, that's not…'

'It is, love, we both know that. I barely know you. I have no idea what you've been doing since you were eighteen, no idea where your life has taken you. Are you married? Do you have kids of your own?'

Meredith swallowed, remembering Joe, remem-bering the mess she'd made of her own life, a mess that still needed sorting out. Maybe she was more like her father than she cared to think about. 'No to both,' she said. 'And life hasn't taken me anywhere very ex-citing except a load of debts and nowhere to live.'

Dennis looked at her then, his brow furrowing.

'Long story,' Meredith said. 'For another time.'

'Well, I don't know,' Dennis said with a sigh. 'I was always off looking for the next break, the next dodgy job, the next big thing. I never really found it. And then I went to Australia and started to find myself.'

'Why did you go?' Bernice asked. She'd done well to stay quiet for so long. 'And when?'

'I left England in the late summer of 2003, not long after I last saw you both at Meredith's party. My mother died around that time. I don't know if you remember?'

Meredith wanted to interrupt, to apologise for what she'd said all those years ago, but before she could her father continued.

'Well, before she died she summoned me to the hospital, said she had something she wanted to tell me, something she wished she'd told me earlier.'

'And that's what took you to Australia?' Meredith asked. She didn't want to rush her father but she couldn't help herself.

Dennis closed his eyes again, just for a moment.

'I found out that Clara Samuels was my biological mother.'

PART III

PART III

21

SUFFOLK, OCTOBER 1963

James stood awkwardly in the reception of Richard's office building in Ipswich. He'd never been anywhere like this before, with its wood-panelled walls, quiet sense of busyness and perfectly spoken receptionists. He was wearing his best (his only) suit, which he'd had for over eight years, the same suit he'd worn to that terrible Sunday lunch back in the summer. The fabric was scratchy and it was too tight across his chest and shoulders these days. He felt as though he could hardly breathe.

'Please do take a seat, sir,' the receptionist said.

He'd never been called 'sir' before either. Did they think he was a client? Did he look like he needed an accountant? He had two pound notes in his wallet and a few coins – he didn't need an accountant to tell him he was as poor as a church mouse or to work out that even with the new job at Ickbury Manor he wouldn't be much better off. It certainly wasn't enough to look after a family, even if he didn't have to worry about rent thanks to Clara's purchase of Butterfly Cottage.

Not that he felt particularly comfortable about that either. He would never tell Clara, he knew he was wrong to think the way he did – if not wrong, at least very old-fashioned. It was 1963 and times were changing, thank God. Women deserved far more agency and control over their lives than they had, he knew that. But the voice inside his head, the same one that criticised him endlessly for abandoning his father in the cold, leaky vicarage in Lincolnshire, the same voice that told him what a failure he was, kept telling him now that he should be looking after Clara and the baby, not Clara looking after him.

'Can I get you a cup of tea or coffee?' the receptionist asked. She was standing right next to him and he hadn't noticed because he was too busy mentally wringing his hands and tearing out his hair.

'No,' he replied. 'No, thank you.' His voice sounded like it didn't belong here. He didn't belong here. None of this was right.

He loved Clara, he had fallen in love with her as a

teenager through the letters she wrote to him, but he felt as though that was all he was sure of right now. His head was swimming and he felt completely over-whelmed. He wanted to love Clara but he wanted to do it on his own terms, without the judgements of Richard and Esther, without the house and baby and the conventionalities of life that were suddenly before him. He'd asked her to marry him so they could be together and he wished more than anything that he could have met her when she was still in London, when she was still free, before Butterfly Cottage and Carybrook and all that that entailed.

When he was with Clara he thought it would be all right. The idea of being a father wasn't the problem – he could imagine himself teaching his child how to tend a garden, how to bring things back to life season after season. The idea of being Clara's husband, waking up with her every morning wasn't the problem. But as soon as he stepped out of But-terfly Cottage or out of the gardens at Ickbury Manor the reality of the situation would hit him. He felt overwhelmed by the closeness of the people of Cary-brook, by the gossip. It made him feel dizzy and claustrophobic and he knew that people looked down on him, in the same way that some of his fa-ther's parishioners had looked down on the Reverend Mackenzie when Butterfly Cottage was the vicarage.

He didn't know if he could do it, he didn't know if he could even live in a house – he hadn't done so since he was twenty-one.

And he hated himself for being such a coward.

Because he should talk to Clara about all of this. She would understand, surely? She would help him. Together they could find a way forward.

But he never did.

He heard the tap of shoes on the wooden floors of the accountancy practice and he looked up to see an older lady in a tweed skirt and cream blouse, her hair stiff and permed and steel grey, standing in front of him.

'Mr Bradshaw will see you now,' she said as James stood up. 'Please follow me.'

He followed the steely grey hair down a maze of corridors and up a flight of stairs to Richard's office.

He had received the summons a few days earlier – a letter addressed to him at Ickbury Manor, formally typed on thick cream paper, the words *Pocklington & Shaw, Chartered Accountants* printed on the back. James had thought it was a mistake at first, a letter addressed to the wrong person until he opened it and started reading the neatly typed script and Richard's signature at the end. Had Richard typed it himself? Surely he had somebody to do that for him. Probably this steely-haired woman he was following now. Which meant that she knew his business. He felt prickles of discomfort at the thought, reminding himself that professional secretaries took confidentiality very seriously.

The letter had asked James to make an appointment to see Richard for a 'chat'.

There are matters we need to talk about before things go any further. Perhaps indeed they shouldn't go any further.

The wording was cryptic but James wasn't stupid, he got the gist of it. He already knew Richard wasn't exactly welcoming him into the family with open arms. There was a sinister edge to Richard sometimes, especially when Esther and Clara weren't looking, and James had no doubt that he was a man who always got what he wanted in the end.

So James called the telephone number and made the appointment, hating himself for the little voice in the back of his head that kept telling him that Richard was about to give him a way out.

He shouldn't want a way out. He should want to be with Clara no matter what.

But he also knew he couldn't be the man Clara needed him to be.

Richard stood as the woman, who was most probably his secretary, ushered James into the room.

'James,' Richard said, holding out his hand, his eyes sparkling with something that felt unpleasant and something that made anyone around him feel inadequate. 'Good to see you.'

James took the proffered hand, his mouth dry. He was unable to think of a thing to say.

'Well, take a seat,' Richard went on and James sat down as ordered. 'Good man, good man.'

The steely-haired secretary closed the door with a click and the smile immediately dropped from Richard's face. Nobody spoke.

'What's all this about?' James said eventually. He planted both feet firmly on the floor and leaned forward, elbows on knees, determined to play a part in the conversation that was about to take place, even though he knew Richard was in charge.

'I think you know,' Richard replied. 'I think you just need someone to say it out loud to you.'

Any confidence or control that James had trickled away then. Richard was going to ask him to leave and he knew that, if that was the case, he would. He would run away, just as he'd run from his father, just as he'd run from every job and every potential relationship he'd ever had. He'd always told himself he was looking for something, for home, for Clara. But now he had Clara and he even had Butterfly Cottage and he was ready to run again.

Because that's who he was, who he'd always been. He could never settle, never sit still, never save money, never stick to anything. If meeting Clara again hadn't changed that, nothing would.

'There's a job,' Richard said. 'In Essex, not far from Saffron Walden. Do you know the area?'

'I know Saffron Walden,' James replied. He'd worked once, a long time ago and only for a few months, in the grounds at Audley End. He'd run from there too, of course. Run away from a girl who'd got too keen.

'It's a privately owned house,' Richard said. 'Have you heard of the Coverdale family?'

James had. The Coverdales had opened a garden centre – shops and greenhouses for all your gardening needs, appealing particularly to the middle classes whose love of gardening, in these days of peace and prosperity, was on the rise.

'They have two garden centres at the moment,'

Richard said. 'But if I know the Coverdales they will have more before long.'

James agreed. He hated to admit it, but his interest was piqued.

'They are looking for a head gardener,' Richard went on. 'Someone to oversee both the garden centre and the grounds of Coverdale House, which as I'm sure you know is open to the public one day a week, not unlike Ickbury Manor, although much smaller and not as old.'

James nodded. Why could he not find his voice? Why was he not stopping this?

'I've recommended you for the job,' Richard said. 'The family are clients of mine. They'd like you to start as soon as possible.'

'But they don't know me.'

'My recommendation is enough so please don't let me down. This is what you want, isn't it? A head gardener's position? It comes with a small cottage in the grounds, very private. You'd be set up. You won't get anything like this at Ickbury until Old Man Percy dies, we both know that he'll never retire.'

James did know that, it was another thing that had been bothering him. He would be stuck as assistant head gardener for a long time at Ickbury Manor.

'Does Clara know?' he asked. 'Is she all right with the move away from Carybrook? We'd planned...'

Richard laughed then, an awful hollow sound. 'Oh, I see,' he said. 'We're still pretending that everything is perfect between you and Clara, are we? We're still pretending that this wedding is going ahead next month?'

'I don't know what you—'

'You do,' Richard snapped. 'Neither you nor Clara are happy, especially Clara. I'm fairly certain this baby has come as a blow to both of your plans. Am I right?'

James didn't say anything. He knew Richard was right. There was no point confirming it. Clara was as uncertain about the future as he was. The whole thing was a mess and neither of them could make it go away.

'I don't understand...' James began, but he understood completely and that part of him that was always running felt relieved.

'My wife and I have never been blessed with children,' Richard said, holding up his hand to prevent James from interrupting. 'A niece or nephew will be the next best thing. Esther is very excited about it, already knitting booties and cardigans.'

James wondered then what Richard was planning, what he'd do to keep his wife happy, how far he'd go.

'Clara will never know about any of this,' Richard went on. 'She will never hear of this conversation or know where you are going. You'll write her a note, a note that I will approve and deliver myself so you don't make any last-minute changes, and you will disappear to Essex. Do I make myself clear?'

'No,' James said, finally standing up for himself. 'This is all wrong. Clara and I can manage, just as we were planning. She's carrying my baby, what will she do if—'

'Look me in the eye,' Richard interrupted, 'and tell me that this is what you want. Tell me you want to be tied down with a wife and a baby, living a respectable life in a village fuelled by gossip, raising a baby – possibly more than one – and unable to be free to roam about the country as you have done for the last God knows how long?'

'How do you know how I've spent my life?'

Richard placed his hands on the desk that sat between them and leaned forward. 'Look me in the eyes and tell me that village life is what you want.'

But James couldn't, because it wasn't what he wanted. What he wanted was to buy a caravan and to run away into the sunset with Clara, living off the land, off whatever work they could both get. But he knew that wasn't what Clara wanted, he knew it was a fantasy that would never become reality. He'd known that really since the first night he'd met Clara again at the dance and seen her Mary Quant dress and listened to her talk about her career. He couldn't look Richard in the eye and say it, so he looked down at his own feet instead, shame rushing through him.

'I thought not,' Richard said. 'There's something else as well. It's not just the job and the house that you'll get when you leave. I can also let you have a little sweetener, some money to get you started. You can learn as much as you can from the Coverdales and then you can strike out on your own venture. How does this sum suit?'

Richard slid a piece of paper across the desk towards James with a figure written on it. An amount of money that James wouldn't be able to save in his wildest dreams.

'I do love Clara, you know,' he said.

'I know you do,' Richard replied. 'And don't you worry about her. Esther and I will look after her and the baby.'

James's fingers twitched over the piece of paper with the sum of money written on it. He could take this now and be set for life. He could walk away from the woman he loved and the life he felt would suffocate him. Or he could stick it out, support Clara.

He cleared his throat and snatched his hand back. 'No,' he said. 'I think I'll stay where I am.'

Richard took a sharp breath. James suspected that very few people ever said no to him.

'This isn't a choice,' Richard said quietly. 'If you don't take the money and my offer I will speak to old man Percy at Ickbury and by this time tomorrow your job offer will have been retracted and you will have nothing. Do I make myself clear?'

James knew then that he would take the offer and do what Richard wanted. He thought perhaps most people did. He knew he would take it because it was the best thing for Clara. Without a job, everything would be much worse than it already was and he couldn't see that he could travel across the country and leave Clara with a baby, no job and very little money coming in. If he left now Clara and the baby would have everything they needed. Esther would make sure that Richard saw to that.

But he also vowed to himself that this time things would be different. That he would stay at Coverdale House and learn everything he could and he would do something with this money that would make a difference, that would make him proud of himself for the first time in his life.

22

THE INDIAN OCEAN, NOVEMBER 1964

Clara looked out over the endless expanse of ocean. She had lost track of what day it was or even what month. It almost felt as though she had been at sea for her whole life. With each nautical mile they travelled she felt her old life slip away a little more until it seemed as though everything that had happened before she had boarded the ship in Southampton three weeks ago (or at least she was told it was three weeks, she had no idea) had become a sort of blur.

She ran a finger around the waistband of her skirt. All her clothes felt tight from the copious amount of food and drink that was provided on board. If one planned one's day correctly you could eat five meals if you wanted to, not that Clara did want to. What she really wanted was to be alone but there was little opportunity for that – someone was always roping her into another game of cards, or another go at skittles, all accompanied by a drink or two. She'd stopped drinking gin and tonic after the first day because every time it was offered to her it would remind her of Richard – 'another G&T, old girl' – and to remember Richard meant remembering everything she'd walked away from and the whole point of being here was to forget. The Babycham that many of the women drank reminded her of that first night she'd met James again in Ickbury, as did the after-dinner dancing. So she allowed herself a couple of glasses of brandy and dry each evening before creeping off to her cabin when everyone else was occupied. She didn't feel ready to allow herself to have fun just yet. All she wanted to do was get off this damn ship and get on with her life.

They'd had stops along the journey. Clara had particularly enjoyed the day she spent in Lisbon where the cathedral had taken her breath away. But the stopover in Durban had been confronting. She'd read about the apartheid system in South Africa but seeing it in action had broken a piece of her heart. How could human beings be so cruel to each other? She'd felt when she'd got back on the ship as though her life thus far had been extremely sheltered, and that living in London on her own for so long hadn't been the grand adventure she thought it had been.

Perhaps this wasn't either, but she'd had to do something.

Not long after James had disappeared from Cary-brook, Clara had moved to the newly built town of Stevenage in Hertfordshire with her sister and Richard. She hadn't had much choice in the matter, she couldn't have stayed in Carybrook for much longer as it had been getting harder and harder to hide her pregnancy. She had told Miss Cheggers that there had been a family crisis, that she would be away indefinitely and that she would have to leave her post with immediate effect. She didn't mention James or their wedding or the baby and Miss Cheggers didn't ask what had happened. Part of her had wanted to tell the headmistress the real story, in all its gory detail. She trusted Miss Cheggers and she wanted to tell the truth more than anything, but in the end, her own shame and her sister's warning words stopped her.

'Don't tell anyone what we're doing or where we're going,' Esther had said. 'People surprise you with their judgements sometimes.'

Instead, she had left the headmistress's office with burning cheeks from the guilt of telling such a lie and she had avoided Betty and John and her other friends, slinking back to Butterfly Cottage to pack what she would need over the next few months. She hadn't realised, when she'd locked the door behind her, that it would be the last time she saw the cottage for an extremely long time. She hadn't realised what would happen next.

Richard and Esther had been planning a move to Stevenage for a while, it turned out, although it had been the first Clara had heard of it. Richard was being promoted again, transferred to Stevenage to run the firm's new branch there, set up just a few years ago when the Queen had officially opened the new town of Stevenage. But from snippets of conversations she heard between her sister and brother-in-law, Clara felt there was more to it than that. She felt they had been wanting to leave Carybrook for a while, away from the gossip and the questions about why it was that they didn't have children of their own.

They had offered, when they first moved to Stevenage, to bring up Clara's baby as their own. They had made the suggestion as though Clara had a choice in the matter, but she knew she didn't. She hadn't had a choice about what happened to her since she found out she was pregnant and she knew that her child would have a much better start in life with her sister.

'Richard and I will bring the baby back from the hospital,' Esther had said. 'We'll tell people we'd been looking to adopt for a long time but hadn't wanted to say anything in case we jinxed it. People will understand, don't you worry.'

Clara had been pretty sure that a lot of people would guess exactly what had happened but that was of no concern to her now. She had been living in a grey cloud of despair and had done since the day she had found the note that James had left. She had been such a fool. She had known he wasn't happy, that he hadn't wanted to settle down. She hadn't been exactly over the moon about it all herself, but she had thought that between them they would have found a way. She should have seen it coming. How could a man who'd lived his adult life like James, roaming about the country, flitting from job to job, possibly be happy tied down by responsibility in a small village like Carybrook?

In those rare moments when the clouds of depression had broken she'd known that in an unbearably cruel way, James had done them both a favour.

And he'd done Esther a favour too. Now she could have the child she had wanted for so long. She knew she was doing the right thing, she wanted the best for her baby and this way she would get it. She was sure

Esther wouldn't be like their parents had been. She had told Clara herself that she didn't want to be like them.

Besides, Clara had no real choice. Women did bring up babies on their own, but she knew it wasn't easy and required money, of which she had very little of her own unless she sold Butterfly Cottage – but then where would she bring up the baby? No, this was the only option. Her sister had always been desperate to be a mother and she, Clara, had the opportunity to give her what she wanted. Something good should come out of this dreadful, heartbreaking mess.

She had given birth to a son in a hospital for single women somewhere in the Hertfordshire countryside. She had never been completely sure where it had been as the cloud of despair had descended so heavily by then that she couldn't bring herself to care. After the birth, which had been long and painful, the baby had been taken away and Clara had lain in her hospital bed staring at the ceiling until she was discharged. She went back to the house in Stevenage and a few days later Richard and Esther returned with the baby they had adopted.

'We're going to call him Dennis,' Esther had said, and Clara had thought it an extremely unsuitable name for a baby. But then all the Dennises in the world must have been babies once.

In those first months after she'd had her baby, Clara felt as though her life was over forever. She barely left the house, barely spoke to anyone, and lost all interest in everything. Some days would pass and she wouldn't be able to remember what she'd done, or how she'd spent the day. At night she would hear the baby crying and her sore breasts would leak milk, but still she couldn't cry the tears she wanted to release.

Esther had suggested that she go to the doctor. 'Perhaps they can give you a tonic or something,' she'd said. But Clara knew she didn't need a doctor and that after she'd had the necessary post-natal appointments, she would be trying very hard to never talk about the last few months again with anyone.

But she'd also known that she couldn't keep living with Richard and Esther, forever watching her own baby – her and James's baby – being brought up by someone else. She'd had no doubt that she was doing the right thing by giving her son (she couldn't quite bring herself to call him Dennis) up for adoption, but she had to do something with her own life, preferably far away from Stevenage.

And far away from Carybrook too. She couldn't go

back, not now, to the place where she had briefly been so happy.

She'd seen the article about Ten Pound Poms in one of the supplements that came with *The Sunday Times*. Esther had been in the kitchen cooking a roast that Clara had no desire to eat and Richard had been grumbling about the new Labour government that Clara had no interest in when it jumped out of the page at her. The answer to all her problems.

The Ten Pound Pom scheme was the nickname for the Assisted Passage Migration Scheme, which Australia had initiated after the war in an attempt to increase the Australian population and boost industry. For just ten pounds, British people could disappear to the other side of the world. Clara had remembered the woman she'd known in London who had emigrated to Australia with her new husband to start a new life. She'd wondered what had happened to her, how that new life was going.

Clara was a good teacher, she knew that, and she'd always known that teaching was where she wanted to be, what she wanted to do. She wanted to be back in a classroom full of children eager (and perhaps not so eager) to learn. For the first time in many months, she had felt a spark of something – not excitement exactly but a nudge of purpose, a reminder that there was still a lot of life left to live and she had to get on with living it somehow. She had to find a new kind of normal, a way of healing from the last year.

But the thought of getting a teaching job in England had been almost too much to bear. She would have to explain where she had been for the last year, why she had left Carybrook School so quickly. And what would she say to that? She couldn't think of anything plausible. If she'd stayed, she'd known that she would be tainted with a sense of shame that she didn't deserve.

And yet, for just ten pounds she could get on a boat to Australia and leave the shame behind.

'Don't be so ridiculous,' Esther had exclaimed when Clara had first put the idea to her. 'You can't just up and leave for the other side of the world on a whim.'

'It's a bit much, old girl,' Richard had said from behind his newspaper.

'You'll miss out on Dennis growing up.'

'Esther,' Clara had replied. 'That's exactly the point.'

Neither Esther nor Richard had come to Southampton to see her off, neither of them had really spoken to her again after she'd insisted that this was what she wanted. She'd thought they would have been pleased to see her go so they could carry on as the family they were meant to be, but instead, Clara had left under a cloud of anger and bitterness. She'd almost capitulated, almost given up the whole idea just to please them, but she'd known she had to do something to get herself out of this mess.

And Australia was all she'd had.

Clara looked out to sea one last time before retiring to her cabin to change for dinner. Leaving Stevenage had been a terrible wrench, and she felt endless waves of guilt and shame for leaving her son behind, for walking away. But she knew that she had done the right thing, that Dennis (she still wondered where that name had come from) would have a much better life with Richard and Esther than he would ever have growing up in a bedsit with a single mother.

She had no choice. She never had.

The first few nights on board had been dreadful but she had finally cried those tears that she had wanted to cry for the last few months since she'd given birth. Eventually, she had come out of her cabin and started to tentatively talk to people even though she would much rather be alone. Most of the other passengers were couples or families, but she found a small group of single women who were all on a mission similar to hers, she thought, although none of them asked questions or talked about anything that had happened before Southampton.

And now the journey was coming to an end. They had left South Africa behind a few days ago and were well on their way to Fremantle on the west coast of Australia. From there they would go on to Sydney where her new life awaited her.

23

SUFFOLK, JUNE 2018

'He's nothing like I thought he'd be from how you and your mum described him,' Zach said.

'He's not how I remember either,' Meredith replied.

They were sitting outside Zach's caravan, the late afternoon sun quietly dissecting the day, their fingers gently curled around each other's.

What a day it had been – from their early visit to Ickbury Manor and the discovery that the James Mackenzie who worked there in 1963 was probably the same man who went on to become Jimmy Mack, to Dennis's sudden arrival and the revelations he had brought with him. Not to mention that kiss, a kiss that had been repeated once they were alone again.

'How do you mean?' Zach asked.

'He used to have all this confidence and swagger,' Meredith said, echoing her mother's words. 'He was always looking for the next dodgy deal, always on the hunt for greener grass like he said, but that part of him seems to have gone.'

'Maybe that's what happens as we get older, as we gain experience.'

'There's something else about him too, though. He used to be full of this weird energy that stopped him being able to sit still or stick to one thing. I mean, I haven't really known him since I was eleven, but it always felt like he had to be constantly moving. But now he seems so much more patient, as though he's found his own inner peace.'

'He is remarkably Zen,' Zach agreed, 'for a man who has found out everything he believed about himself was a lie.'

They had all stared at Dennis in silence when he'd dropped his bombshell about Clara Samuels being his biological mother. But after he had said it, Meredith had realised how much sense it made, had realised that Clara must have been pregnant when she left Carybrook in the autumn of 1963 and that Esther and Richard must have adopted the baby and raised Dennis as their own. Her generation looked back on the sixties as some great time of revolution – culturally and sexually – but that was unlikely to be the case in a sleepy village like Carybrook where everyone knew everybody's business. There were some people who even now frowned on single mothers so in the early sixties it would have been something Clara would have needed to hide. That must be why she'd left.

And then she'd realised that Clara Samuels wasn't her great-aunt at all, she was her grandmother.

It had been Bernice who had broken the silence, of course. 'You mean to say that dreadful woman wasn't your mother after all?'

Dennis had smiled softly at that. 'No Bernice,' he'd said. 'I'm delighted to inform you that she wasn't.'

'All that time I spent with her, allowing her to get to know her granddaughter and…'

'Mum,' Meredith had said, touching her mother's arm.

'Sorry, love, it's just a shock.'

'Are you sure you wouldn't rather I left?' Zach had asked then. He'd looked uncomfortable to be there.

'I'd like you to hear this,' Dennis had said. 'I'm surprised Clara hadn't already told you to be honest. The way she spoke about you in her letters made me feel that she'd taken you into her confidence.'

Zach had shaken his head. 'No, but I'll stay if that's what you'd like.'

Meredith had wondered then if Zach had been thinking about the other letters that sat in an old biscuit tin in his caravan – letters from the man who must be Dennis's father.

Her grandfather. Her hand itched to clutch the locket around her neck, the locket that held a photograph not only of her great-grandfather in his army uniform, but a photo of her grandparents as well.

Dennis had gone on to talk about his childhood then, how unhappy he'd been, how he'd never lived up to his parents' expectations.

'Dad was never really there,' he'd said. 'Always at work or playing golf, and as for Mum, well...' He'd paused and Meredith had watched as her mother, in an uncharacteristic thawing of hostilities, had reached over and squeezed Dennis's arm. Both Bernice and Meredith knew what an unpleasant and difficult person Esther Bradshaw had been. Was she always like that or had the severing of the relationship with her sister caused it?

'I was never good enough for Mum. Nothing I ever did was right, which I suppose makes more sense now I know what I know, but at the time it was just so painful. And then, as I grew older, my father became...' He'd paused for a moment. Meredith remembered her mother saying that something had happened between Dennis and his father. 'Richard Bradshaw was a very angry man. He hid it well, always full of smiles and handshakes, but at home he was different and when I was a teenager he became violent. He'd take his belt to me over any slight misdemeanour, any below-average mark at school. It went on until the day I hit him back.' Dennis had stopped again.

'Dad, I...'

'I'm not proud of what I did but I snapped, I suppose. After that, I gave up trying to please them or trying to do well. I gave up on school, gave up on everything, really, except booze and drugs and having a good time. I never told Clara about that. I didn't want her to blame herself. She thought she was doing the best thing for me when Richard and Esther adopted me.'

He'd left home at sixteen and found work whenever he could – bars, building sites, whatever he could get. After Richard had died he'd tried to make amends with Esther and, while they had never had a comfortable relationship, he visited occasionally. By the time he'd met Bernice, he'd been in a good place, working for a good construction company, even taking some trade qualifications. The foreman, Clive, had taken Dennis under his wing, said he'd shown huge potential. Things had been steady for a while, which was just as well as Bernice was only eighteen when she realised she was pregnant.

It was after Meredith had been born that things fell apart. Dennis started drinking again, not showing up for work. Eventually, Clive had had no choice but to sack him. As a child, Meredith had blamed herself for her father's periods of absence, but now she understood a little more why he'd been unable to cope with fatherhood. He'd left for good when Meredith had been eleven and at that point, he'd completely severed his relationship with his mother as well. Even though Bernice had been to see Esther occasionally, Dennis had stopped visiting.

'I hadn't seen Mum... Esther for years when she finally got in touch again,' Dennis had continued.

'How did she find you?' Bernice had asked.

'She sent a letter to the foreman of the building company I was with. You remember Clive? We'd stayed in touch over the years, he'd always helped me find work, always seen the good in me when I couldn't see it myself. So when the letter came, Clive knew where to find me. The letter took a long time to get to me though and by the time I got in touch with Mum, she was in a hospice on end-of-life care. She had no-body by then, just the woman who'd lived next door who came to see her now and then. I'd felt sorry for her, dying alone like that.'

'I did try,' Bernice had said, sadness in her voice. 'But my God, Dennis, she made it very difficult.'

'I know this isn't your fault. Or yours, Meredith,' he'd added, looking over at his daughter. 'She spent a lot of time pushing people away. I don't know why. Whatever the reason, I saw her in the hospice just once. She told me I was adopted, that she'd had a sister who had "fallen". That was the exact word she'd used – fallen. As though having a baby was the greatest sin on earth. As though *I* was the greatest sin on earth.'

Meredith had been able to see how upset her father was. He'd looked as though he was going to cry.

'Dad,' she'd said. 'We don't have to talk about this right now, you know.'

'It's OK, Meredith. I'm OK.'

He hadn't looked OK though.

He went on to tell them a story that explained that missing year between Clara leaving Carybrook and sailing to Australia. A few months after she had bought Butterfly Cottage she had found out that she was pregnant. The father of her baby had disappeared, leaving nothing but a note and she had been left with no choice but to leave Carybrook and have her baby in a hospital for single mothers to be given up for adoption.

'Esther and Richard had never had children,' Dennis had said. 'And they offered to adopt me, bring me up as their own. But they didn't, did they? Not really. They knew I wasn't theirs and, looking back, they always treated me as though I was some sort of cuckoo in the nest that they didn't understand.'

Meredith had felt desperately sorry for her father then and knew now why he had been the way he had been when she was a child.

'What happened to Clara?' she had asked.

'She lived with Esther and Richard for a while afterwards, but according to Esther she just left one day and went to Australia.'

'Nobody leaves and goes to Australia on a whim,' Bernice had interrupted.

'Clara told me that she'd been part of the Ten Pound Pom programme,' Zach had said. 'That teachers had been in high demand and she had wanted to start afresh. I can understand why now.'

Dennis had nodded, agreeing with Zach.

'And what about your father?' Meredith had asked. She'd wanted to know how much Dennis knew before she produced the biscuit tin, which she would obviously have to do because it seemed James Mackenzie's disappearance wasn't as cut and dried as it seemed.

'All Esther told me was that he was a gardener. She called him "common" and "ill-educated". She didn't have a good word to say about Clara or the man who was my father. She told me that if I wanted to know anything else I'd have to ask Clara herself.'

'Did she know where Clara was?'

'Yes, she gave me an address, scrawled on a scrap of paper. And then she told me to leave and not to come back.'

'Horrible old bag,' Bernice had muttered under her breath.

Dennis hadn't really wanted to talk any more then. He was tired, he'd said, would they mind if he rested. Bernice had gone inside to phone Lloyd while Meredith and Zach had wandered to the bottom of the garden where they sat now.

'This changes everything though,' Zach said. 'This house, it's not mine, it's nothing to do with me. It's yours and your father's. I need to find a way to give my half back to him. Alexander Maddison will know.'

'But it sounds as though Dad didn't want it,' Meredith replied. 'He said that he told Clara to give the house to me and then approved half of it going to you.'

'It's weird though. Why did she give me half the house?'

'Because you were a good friend to her in her last months, because she cared about you and wanted to make sure that you were provided for in the future? I don't know, and we'll probably never know for sure, but it's what she wanted. Dad might know more when he's ready to talk again.'

'And what about you, how do you feel?'

'I honestly don't know. Clara was my grandmother, but it doesn't change anything, really, does it? I still never got to meet her, to know her.'

She felt the warmth of Zach's hand in hers, the gentle squeeze of support. 'I'm so sorry about that, Meredith,' he said.

'I don't really understand why Dad never told us, never got in touch from Australia or introduced us to Clara.'

'Perhaps she didn't want him to,' Zach suggested. 'You could ask him?'

'I don't want to push him. When he was telling us about finding out he was adopted he seemed to close up somehow. It almost felt as though he was telling a story about someone else.'

'There's guilt there,' Zach said. 'And shame. Trust me, I can spot both a mile off, I've carried enough of it around with me over the years. Guilt over my dad's death, shame over not doing more with my life.' He shrugged, looked away. 'He will tell you in time.'

'Do you think he knows about his own father?' Meredith asked. 'Do you think Clara told him?'

'I wonder if she told him about the letters.'

'The ones from Jimmy Mack?'

Zach nodded.

'I wondered that. Whether he knows or not, we should give Dad the letters. They're his legacy. He can decide what to do with them.'

24

HOBART, TASMANIA, SEPTEMBER 2003

Clara sat down at her kitchen table and looked through her retirement cards once more. When she had qualified as a teacher in 1952 she hadn't imagined she would teach for so long. While she had never dreamed of marriage and babies in the way so many of her contemporaries had done, she hadn't thought she would teach until she was seventy-three! That she was seventy-three was also a shock. Where had the years gone?

Inside she still felt like the woman who had left London and bought a cottage in a Suffolk village.

Life had gone very differently, in so many ways, to how she had imagined it would. How could she ever have imagined that she would move to an island at the very end of the world and be happier there than she ever thought possible?

It had been quite by chance that she'd ended up here – a chance meeting, a flurry of off-the-hoof job applications. She had been teaching in Sydney at a large primary school in one of the northern shore suburbs. It had been hard work with so much to get used to – the heat, the different curriculum, the accents of the children, not to mention the need to flip the year on its end with the long summer holidays coming over Christmas – and she had wondered, often, if she had made a terrible mistake.

One hot January day – all these years later that still felt like a strange thing to say – a colleague had told her she was moving south. 'I can't stand the heat here any more, Clara, I need more temperate climes.' Susan was also an émigré from England, sweating her way through the teaching days. She was going, she said, to Tasmania. 'There are so many teaching jobs there. The money isn't as good but it'll be cooler for most of the year at least.'

Susan had sent Clara the Tasmanian job listings and Clara had started to apply. It had felt like a rushed decision, but moving to the other side of the world had been a rushed decision so what was moving to another state in comparison, really?

She had fallen in love with the island state the moment she had stepped off the ferry at Devonport on a crisp clear June morning. The air had smelt like autumn in a way that felt familiar and by the time she'd taken the bus south to Hobart, she knew this was where she wanted to be, where she needed to be.

She'd met up with Susan after her job interviews and she had shown Clara around Hobart.

'It's a bit behind the times in comparison to Sydney,' Susan had said. 'Which is behind the times in comparison to London, of course, so it's about 1950 here, but I like it.'

'I think I do too,' Clara had replied.

She'd started a teaching post at Sandy Bay School in the September of 1967 and she had been there ever since, until today – thirty-six years of service and she had loved every minute of it. She had made friends and joined clubs and thrown herself into the Tasmania way of life. She had done everything she could to distance herself from the person she used to be and the life she used to have. Tasmania had felt a good place to do that, right on the edge of the world, as far away as possible from that life, from Carybrook and Esther and Richard and Butterfly Cottage.

As far away as possible from her memories.

She had risen up the school ranks and bought a

small house in Sandy Bay. She had erased the months between leaving London and arriving in Sydney, telling people she just wanted a new adventure and was growing tired of London. She was promoted to headmistress in 1979 and had stayed in the post until five years ago when she'd finally admitted it was a bit too much for her and had stepped down to a part-time role focussing on literacy skills. She thought occasionally of Miss Cheggers, especially when one of her staff resigned. She often wondered what had happened to Miss Cheggers after she and Betty and John had all left.

Once a year she sent a postcard to her son via Esther on his birthday – a postcard of Tasmania so he knew she was thinking of him. She had written her address on them, but nobody had ever written back so Clara had thrown herself into her new life, into her career.

And now Clara's teaching life was over and a new phase of her life had to begin. She wasn't sure what it would be yet, but she knew she was looking forward to it.

There was a knock on the door then, disturbing Clara from her thoughts. Who could it be at eight o'clock in the evening? Nobody ever called so late these days – another sign of her increasing years.

She opened the door just a little at first and saw a man standing on her doorstep in the gloom. She flicked on the porch light so she could see him better.

'I'm looking for Clara Samuels,' the man said.

'I'm she,' Clara replied, 'And who are you?' But she already knew. The sweeping feeling in her stomach told her who he was.

'I'm Dennis,' the man said. 'And I think you might be my mother.'

25

SUFFOLK, JUNE 2018

It was evening when Zach and Meredith walked back up the garden to the house. Bernice and Dennis were sitting on the patio with glasses of wine in front of them. They both raised a hand in greeting.

'Your father is taking us out to dinner tonight,' Bernice said, eyebrows raised.

'You don't have to do that, Dad,' Meredith said. 'If you haven't got—'

Dennis held up his hand. 'Things have changed, love,' he said. 'I know I was always the broke one, who was always on the scrounge, but things have changed. I've had a job in Hobart for years now. I'm the manager of a restaurant there. Clara had a house in Sandy

Bay, which she left to me, although I haven't decided what to do with it yet.'

'Is Sandy Bay in Hobart too?' Meredith asked.

'Just on the outskirts. I live a few streets away with Nicola, we've been together a few years now.' He stopped, grinned, held out his hands. 'Seems like I've finally settled down.'

'I'm pleased for you, Dad, I really am.'

'I learned who I really am,' he replied. 'It makes a big difference. Perhaps you can come and visit us sometime?'

'Perhaps,' Meredith said, putting the coronation biscuit tin on the table between them. She still wasn't sure how she felt about the fact that her father had been in Australia all this time, living this new life with his real mother and his new girlfriend and had never thought to tell her about it.

'What on earth is that?' Dennis asked, pointing at the tin. 'It looks ancient.'

'It's a biscuit tin from the coronation so it's older than any of us,' Meredith said. 'But before I get on to that I need to tell you something, Dad.'

'What's the matter, love?'

'I should never have said what I said to you on my eighteenth birthday. I'd been drinking and I was trying to be someone I wasn't in front of my friends, and when you turned up I was angry and—'

Dennis held up his hand. 'You were angry and you were right. I wasn't a good father to you and Lloyd was. I wish I could turn back time and change things but I can't.'

Meredith sat with her hands on top of the biscuit tin, the weight of the locket around her neck and the sense of the secrets that had been kept for so long all around her. Nobody could change the past, but they could make their own futures. Maybe that is what both she and her father needed to do.

'So what's in this old tin?' Dennis said, clearly wanting to change the subject.

'I don't know how much you know about who your father was,' Meredith began.

'Clara never told me very much about him,' Dennis replied and then smiled softly. 'I always called her Clara, never "Mum". She wanted to tell everyone that I was her nephew from England and I went along with it. She still thought people would disapprove of her if she told them the truth.' He stopped for a moment, looked away. 'I went along with it because it was her life I had barged into. I just wanted to get to know her and really it didn't matter to me, considering she allowed me to start my life again. We told everyone an almost truth, that Clara and Esther had fallen out before I was born and I'd only found out about her existence when Esther died. People love a story of reunited families.'

He stopped again and Meredith remembered what Zach had said about guilt and shame. She saw both those emotions in her father now and she didn't rush him or interrupt his thoughts. She saw something else too. Love and peace – things she had never really associated with her father before. Finding Clara had helped him still the restlessness that had driven him his whole life.

'Can I ask a question?' Zach asked.

'Of course,' Dennis replied, inclining his head.

'You found out about Clara in 2003?'

'That's right.'

'Had you not needed your birth certificate before that?'

Meredith felt herself tense a little. She understood why Zach was curious, but it felt intrusive to ask this somehow, even though she was curious herself. But Dennis didn't seem bothered by the question.

'You'd think I would have done, wouldn't you?' he said with a smile. 'But I never did. I left school at sixteen without any qualifications, so I never went to college, I never had enough money to go abroad and I had my National Insurance card for any jobs I needed, and to be honest, a lot of them were cash in hand, no questions asked. I'm not proud of that but it was how my life was. The first time I needed any paperwork as such was when I was planning to go to Australia.'

'Thank you for telling me,' Zach said. 'I realise it's none of my business.'

Dennis spread his hands. 'No secrets amongst us any more, I think,' he said. Which brought everyone's attention back to the biscuit tin. 'Anyway, you were asking about my father. Clara spoke very little about him, as I said. She confirmed he was a gardener and that his name had been James. She told me he was someone she'd known when she was a kid, before the war, but they'd met up again when she moved back to Carybrook in 1963. She told me that he'd had to leave, that he'd gone before she knew she was pregnant and that she'd never been able to find him again.'

Meredith and Zach exchanged a glance. The lies we tell to protect those we love.

'I need to show you something, Dad,' Meredith said. 'When I first found out I'd inherited Butterfly Cottage and that I had a great-aunt that I'd never known about I was understandably confused. And then I found out Zach inherited half the cottage too and... Well, after I'd got over the shock of that Zach and I started trying to find out a bit about who Clara was and what had happened to make her move away. I knew that you must be the connection, that the only way this long-lost great-aunt could have known about me was through you but...'

'She's not your great-aunt, love,' Dennis said.

'My grandmother,' Meredith said softly. *The grand-mother I never met,* she thought to herself. A woman who sounded much nicer than the person she thought had been her grandmother. There was a lot here that she needed to unravel herself, but it could wait until she was alone, until she'd unravelled the other complications in her life.

'I'm sorry I didn't come back sooner,' Dennis said. 'I thought about coming back for the funeral – Clara's doctors kept me updated about her health after she became too ill to write or phone – but it felt too much somehow.' He shook his head. 'I wanted you to inherit the house, to see it and come to terms with it before I came back. I thought that if I turned up too soon you'd be too angry with me to accept the house. Truth is, I had no idea what to do.'

Meredith's initial reaction was to tell her father that she wouldn't have been angry, but was that true?

She had been so angry with him for so long – furious that he'd abandoned her, furious that he'd just shown up at her eighteenth and then disappeared again, seemingly forever. Despite her guilt at what she had said to him she had been angry for a long time when she was younger. And all that time Dennis had been battling with his own demons, his own sense of self. It really was true that you never understood the battles other people were fighting.

'You did a bit of digging, you said,' Dennis said.

Meredith told him then about meeting Delia Cheggers and the things that she had told her, the rumours of letters being delivered to an empty house. And then she told him about the letters Zach had found in the shed.

She pushed the biscuit tin over to her father, who opened it and looked inside.

'And you think these were letters my father wrote to Clara after she left Carybrook?'

'We're fairly sure they are.' She paused. 'Would you like us to leave you to read them? They are your letters now, after all.'

Dennis shook his head, placing the lid back on the tin. 'No,' he said. 'I will read them, but not right now. Why don't you tell me what you found out from reading them?'

'From what we've worked out and from what Delia told me the letters were from a man named James Mackenzie. He was a journeyman gardener and in the summer of 1963 he was working at Ickbury Manor, which is just in between here and Ickbury – it's an old Tudor manor house with these incredible gardens that had to be restored after the war.'

She told him about their visit to Ickbury Manor, about the record books that Ivy had let them look at and about how James Mackenzie did not come back to work at Ickbury in the summer of 1964.

And then Zach told Dennis about the signature on the letters and how the writing matched the inscriptions in his father's gardening books.

'Jimmy Mack?' Dennis said with surprise. 'The guy on the TV?'

'You remember him?' Bernice asked.

'Yeah, he did that gardening show that you liked. You always wanted a garden.'

'I got one in the end,' Bernice smiled. There was no anger or frustration in her voice and Meredith wondered if her mother would find her peace eventually too.

Meredith took the locket from around her neck and opened it, looking at the picture again. It was at that moment that she realised where that strange sense of recognition had come from when she'd first seen the photograph – a feeling that had pushed her to find out more. It wasn't that the man in the photograph looked like anyone in particular, it was more the face he was pulling. When she was a little girl and had been crying, that was the face her father pulled to cheer her up.

She didn't say anything though as she handed the locket to Dennis. 'This is the only photograph I have of him,' she said. 'Well, at least Zach and I presume it's him. It's hard to tell.'

'And he left before I was born without knowing about me,' Dennis said, looking at the photo inside the locket. 'I suppose Clara never knew he became a television star; Australia is very isolated, or at least it certainly was back then. What happened to Jimmy Mack?'

'He died after a heart attack in 2004, according to what I could find online, but we don't know a lot about him for sure,' Zach replied.

'And we're not sure he didn't know about you,' Bernice said quietly.

'How do you mean?'

Meredith was glad her mother had taken up this difficult subject.

'If you read the letters you'll understand.'

Dennis traced his fingers over the lid of the biscuit tin before standing up and handing the locket back to Meredith.

'Well,' he said. 'I'm not reading them tonight. Shall we pause things here and go for some food? If I have another drink on an empty stomach I'm liable to get maudlin.'

As they stood up to get ready to leave, Meredith touched her father's arm.

'Dad?' she asked.

'Yes, love?'

'Was Clara happy? I feel as though she left so much behind when she went to Australia – you, James. I'd hate to think that she lived her life regretting leaving.' She shrugged, unable to explain why it meant so much to her, why she wanted that happy smiling woman in the photograph inside the locket to have kept smiling throughout her life.

'There's more than one way to find your happy ever after, love, and I think you've probably worked out now that Clara Samuels was far from conventional. But she was happy. Yes, she loved her life in Australia.'

* * *

They went for dinner at The Queen's Head, where Meredith introduced her father to Alf. The two men shook hands and as they walked away she heard Alf say to Zach, 'I thought he was missing or something?' She looked over at Dennis and realised, by the small smile on his face, that he had heard that too.

'Nobody as nosey as a pub landlord,' Dennis said.

As they ate Meredith filled her father in on everything that she had been doing since she last saw him fifteen years ago. Almost everything, anyway – she decided not to tell him about Joe and Jemma and the baby, or about the money that her mother and Lloyd had given her to pay Joe off, which she was going to pay back as soon as possible even though she knew they'd refuse it. If she was going to move on she needed a clean slate – no debt and no Joe seemed a good place to start. Before she had arrived in Carybrook, before Alexander Maddison had told her about Butterfly Cottage, she had thought about Joe all the time. He'd been the first thing she'd thought of when she woke up and the last thing she'd thought of before she went to sleep. But now, she realised, she barely thought about him at all. In fact, other than very briefly when Zach had first kissed her at Ickbury Manor, she hadn't thought about him since she'd left London.

She did tell her father about her hairdressing qualifications, the prize she had won, how she had felt she'd outgrown working in other people's salons and had thought the next logical step would be to open a salon of her own. She watched Dennis' face as she told him how that had gone, the muddle she had got in with the bills, how difficult she had found it all. She noticed that he listened to her calmly, that there was no judgement there. The only person who felt shame about what had happened to her was her.

'So, what happens next?' Dennis asked when she had finished.

'Well, I've got a lot to sort out,' she replied. 'There's a break clause in the lease or alternatively, another hairdresser might be interested in taking it over. I probably won't get the money I invested back out, but it will allow me to start again.'

'And what does starting again look like to you?' her father asked.

Meredith took a breath and looked over at Zach. When their eyes met she felt that shiver down her spine and they both broke into a grin.

'It looks like staying in Carybrook,' she said, feeling happy at the thought. 'It looks like simplifying my life. I've realised that, although setting up my own salon was the logical next step, it wasn't necessarily what I wanted. And now it's time to figure out what I want.'

'Well, I was chatting to a few women in the shop,' Bernice said. 'And they said the nearest hairdresser is Ickbury so I reckon you've got a ready-made clientele when you're ready.'

'And you'll live at Butterfly Cottage?' Dennis asked.

'We both will for now,' she replied, glancing at Zach again. 'And we'll see what happens.' She noticed her parents look at each other and waggle their eyebrows as if to say 'Well, it's completely obvious to us what will happen', but she chose to ignore it. 'After all,' she went on. 'We've got a lot of work to do if we are going to put it on the market any time soon.'

'And I won't be moving into the cottage until the autumn at least,' Zach said. 'So you are both welcome to stay as long as you need.'

'Well, I do need to get back to Spain in the next day or so,' Bernice said. 'Lloyd can only seem to look after himself for a few days at a time before going completely feral.' She rolled her eyes.

'What about you, Dad?' Meredith asked. 'Can you stay for a while?'

'I've got a couple of weeks before I have to be back

at work,' Dennis said. 'I can spend them here if you'd like me to.'

'I'd love that,' Meredith replied, and she realised that she really meant it. She may have only spent a few hours with her father over the course of the day but he was nothing like she remembered, nothing like the picture Bernice so often painted, and she wanted to get to know this version of her father – the man who had finally found out the truth about himself.

'We've got a lot to catch up on,' Dennis said. 'For which I am truly sorry.'

Meredith looked away. Fifteen years was a very long time to stay away, but he was back now. Staying angry wasn't an option. She wanted to be able to have a relationship with both her parents, she wanted to know about her father, about the last fifteen years of his life. She wanted to know about Australia, and about Clara.

They did have a lot to catch up on and she was going to grab this second chance with both hands because not everyone got that opportunity.

Clara and James hadn't, and Meredith felt so sad whenever she thought of them and how they had never been able to find one another again.

But tonight was not a night for feeling sad, so instead she raised her glass. 'A toast,' she said. 'To new beginnings and second chances!'

As they all clinked their glasses together Meredith felt Zach's fingers wrap around hers under the table and she realised that she felt happy for the first time in a long time. Perhaps this new idea of seeing what might happen was going to work out after all.

EPILOGUE

HOBART, TASMANIA, JUNE 2017

Clara laid the table carefully, knowing that this was the last time she would do so in this house. In just a few days she would be flying to England, returning for the first time in over fifty years, and she knew in her heart that she wouldn't be coming back to Australia. Tonight she was having one last meal with her son and telling him what her plans were. He would want to come with her, she knew that, but she also knew this was something she needed to do alone.

She'd asked him to come on his own, to not bring Nicola, and he had immediately known something was going on.

'It's bad news, isn't it?' he'd said.

And it was in a way, but Clara found it hard to see

it like that. It was inevitable news for an eighty-seven-year-old woman, and it was news that meant she had to face the thing she had been putting off for decades.

Dennis had agreed to come alone though, and now all Clara had to do was wait for him to arrive. She took a breath; everything was in order.

She was glad he had met Nicola, glad that he seemed so settled now. Tasmania suited him, just as it had suited her. He had lost that frightened look that he'd had when he first arrived, that sense that he could disappear at any moment. Finding out who he really was had helped, as had the job and the girlfriend and the gorgeous flat they had found together. She knew that she could leave him now, that he didn't need her any more. They had made up for lost time as much as they could.

When she had left England, Dennis had been just a baby. She had thought then that she was doing the right thing, that Esther and Richard could give him a much better life than she ever could. She wished she could have kept him with her, raised him on her own, but at the time that had been impossible. She knew that and so did Dennis. She was surprised by how little resentment he held towards her. She knew there were things he wasn't telling her and maybe she didn't need to know everything, but she wondered if she had done the right thing.

'You did what you thought was best,' he'd always said.

When he arrived she got him a beer out of the fridge – Cascade Blue, brewed here in Hobart, his favourite – and asked him to sit down as she dished up the meal.

She watched him tuck into the roast dinner she had cooked for him as she picked at hers. She hadn't been able to eat a proper meal for months; it was what had first made her go to the doctor.

'What's this about, Mum?' he asked.

She put down her fork, she wasn't even going to pretend to eat tonight.

'Can I get you any more?' she asked.

'I'll help myself in a minute. Please tell me.'

'I was at the hospital today.'

'About your stomach pains?' he asked. She'd told him the doctors thought it was an ulcer. She didn't want to worry him until she was sure.

'It's not an ulcer,' she said. 'It's cancer.'

'Mum, I—'

She held up her hand. 'Please listen to me, Dennis. I need you to listen.'

And she told him then about Butterfly Cottage,

the house she had bought with her father's money in 1963, the house she had been living in when she met the man who was Dennis' father, the house that had been in her dreams since she was a little girl.

She had been thinking about James a lot in the last few months. Thinking about him in a way that she had never let herself before. When she booked her passage to Australia and became one of the thousands of Ten Pound Poms who emigrated in the years after the war, she had promised herself that this was going to be a brand-new start, that she was not going to allow herself to dwell on what might have been, on what she had lost. And so she had never let herself think about James for more than a minute. If she caught herself day-dreaming about him, she shut it down immediately.

But now that she was an old woman, now that she knew she was dying, she allowed herself to indulge in her memories. They were clearer now, clearer than more recent events, in fact. It was funny, she thought, how the brain worked, the tricks it played on you.

She didn't tell Dennis any of this, she just told him about Butterfly Cottage.

'And it's been standing empty all these years?' he asked, surprised. 'Why didn't you tell me about it?'

'A lot of sad things happened to me in that house,'

she replied. 'Things I wanted to forget for a long time. But now I need to go back. I need to put the past to rest before I die.'

'Oh, Mum, you might have years left yet with the right treatment and—'

'I'm not going to have the treatment,' she said firmly.

'Mum, you have to.'

'Dennis, I'm eighty-seven years old and I've had a wonderful life in so many ways. The doctors say that the cancer is slow-moving, that I've got a few months before I'll need palliative care and in those few months I need to go home. I need to go back to Butterfly Cottage.'

'How can you talk like this?' Dennis asked. His face looked pale, stricken. Clara hated that she was hurting her son. 'How can you talk so flippantly about your own death?'

'Because I'm old, Dennis, and if you get to my age – and I really hope you do – you'll understand. Death stops being so terrifying eventually. It becomes something that is inevitable. None of us are immortal, my love.'

Dennis looked down at his empty plate for a moment as if considering his own mortality before looking back up at her. 'So, you want to go back to England then?'

Clara nodded.

'Then I'll come with you,' he said. 'You can show me Butterfly Cottage.'

'Dennis, this is something I have to do on my own.'

'You can't possibly fly to the other side of the world on your own at your age,' Dennis said. 'You've never flown further than Brisbane before now.'

'I'm sure I'll be alright – I got out here on a boat on my own, after all, and a flight is much faster.'

'Mum, you're not taking this seriously.'

'I'm taking this very seriously, my love. And I have to do this on my own. You'll see Butterfly Cottage soon enough. It will be yours when I die, just like this house.'

'I can't let you do this, Mum.'

'You have to,' she replied.

Clara knew there would be days of arguments, she'd known that from the moment she'd booked her flight to Heathrow. Tomorrow Nicola would come round and try to persuade her to take Dennis or even, heaven forbid, take both of them. She liked Nicola a lot and she was very good for Dennis but Clara wouldn't be able to stand a twenty-four-hour flight with her.

But she would stay strong and stand her ground, she would get through the arguments and the bickering and she would say goodbye to her son in her own way and in her own time, on Hobart ground.

After Dennis had left, Clara cleared the table, washed the dishes and made herself a cup of tea. She took it into the sitting room and placed it on a coaster on the table. She took a breath and pressed her hands together.

One last time, she thought.

She opened the drawer of the cabinet in the corner of the room and took out a videotape. It had no case or label and looked exactly as it had done when it had arrived at her door twenty-seven years before. She placed it carefully in her VCR. Dennis always said she must be the only person in Australia who still had a VCR, but Clara was fairly certain that she wasn't the only one still holding on to old things. Nicola had bought her a DVD player years ago and, more recently, tried to sign her up for Netflix, but Clara wasn't much of a television watcher. She still enjoyed the cinema from time to time but when she watched television it was for the news, or to watch a very specific videotape.

She pressed 'play' on the remote and sat back in her armchair to watch the recording from the 1990 Chelsea Flower Show.

The tape had arrived in a padded envelope one Tuesday morning when Clara was running late for school. She'd put the parcel to one side and it had been the weekend before she'd found time to open it. All that had been inside was the tape, no note or indication of who had sent it, no sender's address on the back of the envelope as there should be. All she could make out was the British postmark that said 'Hertfordshire'.

There was only one person that this could have come from. Only one person who knew where she was.

At first, she had been scared to watch the tape, anxious about what it might contain and what memories it might stir up, but eventually curiosity got the better of her.

She hadn't been able to understand why Esther had sent her a recording of the Chelsea Flower Show at first. Yes, Clara, had always liked gardens – but this seemed a little random.

Halfway through the tape she had understood and that was the section she watched tonight.

On her screen was a gardener named Jimmy

Mack. He had become quite famous over the previous decade and was known, amongst various things, for breeding roses. At the Flower Show of 1990, he unveiled a new variety.

She watched now as the face that had been so familiar to her, the face of James Mackenzie, smiled into the camera. He looked older of course, and careworn, but she would recognise him anywhere.

'This is a rose I'm very proud of,' Jimmy Mack was saying on screen. The camera panned into a white bloom edged with dark pink as he talked about how he had gone about breeding it.

As the camera panned out again the presenter asked Jimmy Mack what the rose was called.

He looked into the camera and smiled. 'Clara's Garden,' he said.

Clara paused the tape there and took a sip of her tea.

The existence of Clara's Garden had allowed everything to come full circle and she had always been grateful to her sister for sending the tape to her. She'd wondered for years what had brought about such an unusual show of empathy. She could only assume it was an apology, but she wasn't sure what for.

When she had first watched Jimmy Mack unveil a rose named after her she had understood that he had loved her as much as she had loved him and that sometimes, when you truly love someone, you have to let them be free to live the life they want to live.

Clara's life had been wonderful, she knew that now as she looked back on it. She had lived out her dreams on this small island at the end of the world in a way she never could have done if she'd stayed in Carybrook and got married.

Looking at James's face as he unveiled the rose, she knew that he too had lived the life he wanted, the life he needed, and that by walking away from each other they had opened up opportunities for themselves that would never have come otherwise.

'Better to have loved and lost...' Clara said to herself as she stood up and took the tape out of the VCR for the very last time.

Because she was leaving for England and she wasn't taking the tape with her. She wasn't intending to take much with her at all. She was being called back to Butterfly Cottage and she was heeding that call.

She'd always known she would go back in the end.

ACKNOWLEDGEMENTS

Writing a first draft is a lonely process that happens, for me, in a frenzy of 'don't wannas' and hair-tearing, alone in my office, typing like a crazy person on my nan's old desk (a version of which appears in nearly every book I write – you'll spot it!). A book appears from that first draft because of the team of amazing people around me for whom I am very grateful.

First and foremost my wonderful agent Lina Langlee and, over the last several months, Caro Clarke who has been holding my hand and dealing with my neuroses while Lina has been on maternity leave. Caro also thought up the ending of this book – praise the Lord as I thought it would never end.

Then there's my editor, Rachel Faulkner-Willcocks. Thank you for working with me again, and for taking a massive punt on a book that barely had an outline. Thank you also to everyone at Boldwood for welcoming me without a full manuscript (or even a full synopsis) – I am grateful to copy editor Gary

Jukes, proof-reader David Boxell, cover designer Jane Dixon-Smith, marketing geniuses Claire Fenby-Warren and Jenna Houston, and everyone else who helped bring this book to life.

Thank you to my dad, who tells anyone who'll listen about my books, and my brother who, although not a reader, often asks if he has read all my books and if there will be another one soon.

Thank you to my uncle, Tim Walpole, and his wife, Pauline Paton. Tim was born in Tasmania and after a lengthy trip around the world, returned there in the early seventies on a ship not too dissimilar from the one that Clara travelled on. Pauline was a Ten Pound Pom. I'm so grateful for your stories (which have made it into the book!).

Thank you to Sarah, always. To Lorna and Jenny for encouraging me to do this. To every reader, reviewer and book blogger.

And the biggest thanks will always go to my husband because if it wasn't for him, I'd have never found the time to write a word.

THE BUTTERFLY GARDEN
PLAYLIST

Getting to compile a sixties playlist was an absolute joy – my favourite period of music! Not all of these songs had been released in 1963 but I imagine Clara and James listening to them later in the decade thinking about what could have been.

'Twist and Shout' – The Beatles
'The Times They Are A-Changin'' – Bob Dylan
'He's So Fine' – The Chiffons
'Elenore' – The Turtles
'Be My Baby' – The Ronnettes
'Da Doo Ron Ron' – The Crystals
'The First Time Ever I Saw Your Face' – Roberta Flack

'I Saw Her Standing There' – The Beatles
'The Letter' – The Box Tops
'I Am A Rock' – Simon & Garfunkel
'Sunny Afternoon' – The Kinks
'I Only Want to be With You' – Dusty Springfield
'Blowin' in the Wind' – Peter Paul and Mary
'Alone Again Or' – Love
'Please Please Me' – The Beatles

FURTHER READING

Winds of Change: Britain in the Early Sixties – Peter Hennessy

One, Two, Three, Four: The Beatles in Time – Craig Brown

Ten Pound Poms: Australia's Invisible Migrants – A James Hammerton & Alistair Thomson

How Was It For You: Women, Sex, Love & Power in the 1960s – Virginia Nicholson

The Modern Cottage Garden – Greg Loades

The Millstone – Margaret Drabble

The Village School – Miss Read

The War on Our Doorstep – Harriet Salisbury and the Museum of London Group

ABOUT THE AUTHOR

Rachel Burton is the bestselling author of historical timeslip novels and romantic comedies. Rachel was born in Cambridge and studied Classics and English Literature before starting a career in law. She lives in Yorkshire with her husband, a variety of cats and far too many books.

Sign up to Rachel's mailing list for news, competitions and updates on future books.

Visit Rachel's website: www.rachelburtonwrites.com

Follow Rachel's on social media here:

f facebook.com/Rachelburton74

O instagram.com/rachelbwriter

Letters from
the past

Discover page-turning
historical novels from
your favourite authors
and be transported
back in time

*Join our book club
Facebook group*

https://bit.ly/SixpenceGroup

*Sign up to our
newsletter*

https://bit.ly/LettersFrom
PastNews

Boldwood

Boldwood Books is an award-winning fiction publishing company seeking out the best stories from around the world.

Find out more at www.boldwoodbooks.com

Join our reader community for brilliant books, competitions and offers!

Follow us
@BoldwoodBooks
@TheBoldBookClub

Sign up to our weekly deals newsletter

https://bit.ly/BoldwoodBNewsletter

www.ingramcontent.com/pod-product-compliance
Lightning Source LLC
Chambersburg PA
CBHW010657100726
47900CB00010B/2697